What Every
Woman Wants

Jimmy DaSaint

A Grown and Sexy Novel

Published By:

PO Box 97
Bala Cynwyd, PA 19004

Website: www.dasaintentertainment.com

Email: dasaintent@gmail.com

ISBN: 978-0-9823111-1-0

Acknowledgements

First I would like to give thanks to my Lord and savior Jesus Christ. Thanks to all the people that stood by my side while I was in my darkest moments: my mother Belinda Mathis, sisters, Dawn, Tammy, and Tanya, and my brother, Sean, my two sons, Marquise and Nigel, my ICH rap camp (SC, STONES, COLOSSUS, CHEESE, A-TOWN, YOUNG SAVAGE, BOSSMAN, SPORT, VAR, JEEKY, ELOHEMM, SHORTY RAW, T.P. DOLLAZ, SCARFO).

I want to give a special thanks to Tiona Brown (author of *Ain't No Sunshine*) for all the help and support you have given me since day one. Tiah "DC book diva," TLJ, Tiff and Zahir from The Firm Publications, and all my friends in the publishing industry. Sorry, but I have too many to name.

Last but not least I can't forget all my incarcerated brothers and sisters doing time in the fed and state prisons. Keep y'all heads up and never give up on your dreams!

This book is dedicated to all the women that chase after illusions, infatuations and false hopes. For the women that run after no-good men, and the ones that expose their bodies for money, sex and material items. To all the women that run away from love, and run towards lust. Please wake up ladies...Please wake up!

Sincerely,

Jimmy DaSaint

What Every Woman Wants

Chapter 1

Tuesday evening...

"Why are we still single?" Robin vented. She looked over at her best friend Tammy. She was sitting on the sofa, sipping on a Corona.

"Girl, please don't start with that again," Tammy responded.

Robin stopped pacing across the living room floor and walked over towards her girlfriend.

"Is it us, Tammy, or are all the good men really dead or are they in jail?"

"Maybe we're gonna have to change our golden man rule," Tammy suggested in a serious tone.

"Never!" Robin snapped back.

Tammy rolled her eyes and returned to nursing her Corona.

"I don't care how long it takes us Tammy. Remember the vow we made in college? D.˛.M. or nothing!" Robin said as she sat down next to Tammy. She nudged Tammy with her shoulder. "Dick, looks, and money! Girl one day our time is coming. Just like Dawn, Tanya, and Anissa, we're gonna find us our "Mr. Right" who possess all three."

Tammy smiled as she raised her bottle.

They touched their beers together in a toast and both started laughing.

Robin Davis was a tall, beautiful, thirty year old woman with gleaming light skin. She had a clean complexion, finely arched eyebrows, light brown eyes, and long silky hair. She had a bold, sassy attitude that gave people the impression that she was a cold-hearted bitch. The truth of the matter was that most times, she was. Tammy Washington was Robin's best friend since junior high school. However, as close as that were she was the total opposite. Tammy was 29-years-old, attractive, with almond brown skin that drove men wild. She was short and petite with an hourglass figure. In addition, she contained a bright welcoming smile. She had a positive aura about her that made people enjoy being around her. Her presence was magnetic.

They were two attractive, professional black women, with successful careers, homes, and cars. They also had one other thing in common; they were both miserably single. Finding a man was never a problem for either of them. But finding the right man? Now that was a major headache. It was like a broken record with them; close, but not quite right.

"So what's up with Trey?" Tammy asked.

Robin considered the question. "Cute, but way too young... Plus he is too broke."

"Okay then, Robin; what about Charles?"

Robin's mind did the tally. "Average looks," she said, then her tone lifted, "but wealthy very wealthy," she thought about the matter a little more. "But, he's got a little dick." She wiggled her little finger downwards. "I can't be with a guy with a little dick."

Tammy shook her head as they laughed.

"All right, then what about T.J.? You two have been seeing a lot of each other lately. What's up with that?" she grinned, waiting for Robin's laundry list of problems.

"I guess I'm just curious right now. We both know that me and T.J.'s little fling won't last. We have nothing to give each other but sex. And I don't care how good the sex is, I'm a woman who needs more. A lot more." Robin said; her tone very soft and honest.

"Does T.J. know this?"

"Yeah, we talk about it all the time. That's why we decided to just enjoy the moment. In fact, T.J. will be over at my house later tonight," Robin said as a sinister smile crossed her face.

Tammy took another sip, "Girl, you are something else." She stood up from the sofa and walked across the room to the entertainment system. After looking through a few CDs, Tammy finally came across the one she had been searching for. When she slid the disc into the player and pressed the 'play' button. The beautiful melodic sound of Floetry instantly flowed out of the speakers and filled the room. She turned with a satisfied smile on her face.

Tammy walked back over to the sofa and sat down. She grabbed for her black Prada purse and reached inside. She pulled out the two rolled-up marijuana sticks. Robin had a big smile on her face. After she lit both of them, Tammy passed one over to Robin.

"This will get you ready for T. J." Tammy said as she inhaled the weed into her body.

"Girl, be quiet, I can handle anything that comes my way. I still ain't met the person who can give me that earth-moving orgasm. You know, the kind of orgasm that will have me shaking all over while tears of bliss run down my face. I want to feel like I might explode because I'm so warm inside."

Robin took a pull from the stick. Slowly, she let a cloud of smoke gently leave her mouth. She sat and watched as the floating smoke traveled upwards and disappeared between them. Tammy looked confused.

"I thought you said that Trey and T.J. were both good in bed?" Tammy asked. The marijuana was starting to affect her. She could feel it pulsing through her body.

"They are, but I'm looking for 'great' in bed, not just okay. I am looking for the kind of sex turned Whitney's ass out!"

"That was a lot more than sex," Tammy replied. They both started laughing again.

"I'm fine, one day I'll find my Mr. D._.M. He can't keep running forever."

"Me too... But if you find yours first, ask him if he's got a brother, or at least an uncle or a cousin. Hell, I'm so desperate right now," Robin said, considering her idea of the perfect man. "I'm so desperate that I'd take his daddy."

They both busted out in laughter. The marijuana had them feeling good. Most nights this was how they found themselves. They spent their time drinking Coronas, smoking weed, and talking about the lost race of good black men. An hour later, the

Coronas bottles were empty and the weed was gone. They were left with their thoughts.

Robin was getting ready to go back home and prepare for a night with T.J. Tammy watched as she put on her Baby Phat jacket and picked up her cell phone from the coffee table. Like always, Robin was dressed to impress. After D.L.M. searching, shopping for clothes and shoes was their next favorite thing to do. Not a week went by without them getting into one of their expensive cars and driving out to one of the shopping malls. Neiman Marcus, Saks Fifth Avenue, and Macy's were just a few of their favorite stores. They shopped so much that most of the stores' employees knew them both by their first names.

Tammy stood up from the leather sofa and walked with Robin to the front door. After they hugged and kissed each other on the cheeks, Tammy opened the door for her friend. She watched as Robin walked towards her Mercedes Benz. It was a gold convertible, and *completely* Robin. It was parked right behind Tammy's sky blue Lexus coup.

"I'll call you when I get home," Robin said as she climbed into her car.

Robin started the car and made her way off down the dark street. Moments later, Tammy closed and locked the front door. The combination of the Coronas and weed had her feeling extremely good. She picked up her cell phone and pulled up a list of men's names. With a big smile on her face, she decided on who would be tonight's lucky man.

~

Forty minutes later, Robin was walking into her elegant, 2,500 square-foot, two-bedroom condominium, which was located on the 35th floor of a newly built high-rise building in downtown. Robin's condo was elegantly furnished. The walls were canvas cream-colored. The unit had soft wall-to-wall carpet, a large fireplace, built-in entertainment system, pearl-colored living room and matching dining room sets. To add a touch of class, she had special ordered gold chandeliers.

To the left of the living room were; a twenty-five gallon fish tank, glass coffee tables, and a large outside balcony where she could walk out and stare straight into the calm September sky. There were large glass vases, filled with the most brilliant flowers. Portraits were adorned with erotic Afro-American artwork. The place was warm and inviting. The people who visited as guest couldn't help but feel comfortable.

After Robin had taken a quick warm shower, she carefully rubbed lotion onto her entire body. She opened up her dresser and pulled out a large white D&G t-shirt. After examining it, she put it on. Taking out a small box of matches she made her way around the condo. She lit all of the scented candles that were situated throughout. The euphoric effects from the marijuana and light Mexican beer had her in a very sensual mood.

Robin walked over to the soft white leather sofa. Exhaling deeply, she sat down and leaned her head back to relax. Almost instantly, the intercom started to buzz and blink. She stood and made her way over to the small intercom box that was built into the wall near her kitchen. She pressed a large gray button.

"Hello?"

"It's me,T.J.," a voice answered.

Robin buzzed the person up and quickly walked across the carpet to the front door. After unlocking it, she made her way back across the soft carpet. She stood in front of the entertainment system and inserted a Mary J. Blige CD. Within seconds, the surround-sound speakers were saturating the room with Mary's soulful voice. She adjusted the volume just right to create the desired ambiance. She then headed over to the light dimmer switch to make the mood perfect. When she heard the doorknob gently turning, she stood there smiling with her arms crossed over her chest. T.J. walked in carrying a small leather bag.

"What's in the bag?" Robin asked coyly.

"Oh, just some little toys to get us through the night," T.J. answered with a grin.

Robin stared into the attractive dark-skinned woman's eyes.

"I have to be at work early tomorrow morning, so don't try to pull that shit you did last time." said Robin.

"Don't worry," T.J. promised, "I won't."

She took off her white jacket and hung it on a thin black coat rack. After she sat the bag down, she walked over to Robin and the two looked at each other. Slowly, T.J. kissed her finger and then pressed it to Robin's lips. Within seconds, they both closed in on each other, kissing very passionately. Their tongues locked deep inside each other's mouths. They allowed their tongues to roll and slither around each other like two lost snakes.

Tamara James, a.k.a. T.J., was a beautiful, tall, dark-skinned woman whose body demanded attention. She was a 27-year-old flight attendant for American Airlines. Robin and Tamara had met on a plane ride coming back from the Bahamas. Robin had been returning home to Philadelphia from a weeklong vacation she had taken with Tammy. That meeting took place six months ago. Since that first meeting, Robin and T.J. had been intimately involved with each other. They enjoyed every moment that they shared together. Tamara was the first and only woman that Robin had ever been sexually united with. Her curiosity had turned into a secret sexual affair. She never thought she would actually be involved with another woman. The thought of it drove her wild. The only person who knew about their relationship was Tammy. Robin wanted to keep it that way.

After their long, passionate kiss, T.J. backed away and picked up the black leather bag. Without saying a word, Robin stood up and led T.J. back to the elegant master bedroom. Robin walked over to the oval shaped queen sized bed and climbed on top. She got on all fours and moved in closer making all of her motions slow and exaggerated. She tossed the four large pillows to the floor. Robin pulled the white t-shirt up over her head and tossed it over her shoulder. She laid her 5'8" model shaped body out across the bed.

What Every Woman Wants

The satin comforter seemed to be giving her body an exotic glow. The nipples on her 36-B breasts were already erect. Other than the silky hair she had on her head, her entire body was shaved. She was moist with anticipation. It was the combination of everything that made her so excited. The smoke, the drink, the vanilla aroma of the scented candles, and the delicate fabric beneath her naked body all created a very sexually stimulated mood. She didn't just want to be touched, she wanted to be fucked!

Robin laid there with the two fingers on her right hand playing inside of her legs. Slowly she moved in and out of her body. Her entire body was throbbing. Her other hand was gently rubbing one of her dark brown nipples. She tried to stifle it, but a moan escaped her lips. Her tongue moved back and forth across her top lip. She watched T.J. who was just a few feet away, undressing slowly. She moved as if she was performing a striptease.

T.J. slid out of her black floral dress. Quickly, she kicked free her black Gucci sandals. With a practiced motion, she took off her bra and panties and laid them both on top of a large dresser. Robin looked at T.J.'s gorgeous naked black body and just shook her head as she smiled. T.J. had a body to die for: thirty-eight, twenty-four, thirty-eight. The perfect curved of her body looked like something an artist had rendered. Her dark brown hair was cut in a short new style, and it made her look very chic. She looked as if she had just stepped out of the cover of Vogue Magazine.

T.J. gave Robin a seductive look, and then reached down into the bag and pulled out a black 8-inch strap-around dildo. Robin watched T.J. put it around her body, securing it in just the right way. T.J. made her way over to the bed and began kissing her on the inside of her right calf. Slowly, she worked her way up her body, kissing Robin's knees, her inner thighs, and up to her navel, leaving Robin quivering for more. As their eyes met, they began to kiss again, more passionately than before. T.J. backed away and began kissing every part of Robin's body. She licked and sucked her neck, her shoulders, her stomach, and her breasts. Then, she worked her way back down to Robin's throbbing wetness, and her magical tongue went to work. Of all of the things that T.J. did, her wonderful oral pleasures were what Robin always enjoyed the most. In fact, T.J. was the best she had ever had. She could do things that Robin never knew were possible.

After separating Robin's legs, T.J. dove into Robin's wetness with her tongue. Slowly, she rubbed her tongue across Robin's very sensitive clitoris. T.J.'s tongue went from bottom to top, then from side to side like a runaway roller coaster. Robin's soft moans grew louder until they filled the bedroom. Her mind was somewhere lost between cloud-nine and deep space. T.J. licked and sucked Robin's pussy as if it was the last meal she would ever eat. Robin's manicured nails dug deeply into the soft satin comforter, folding it beneath her body. Without warning, her body began to tremble uncontrollably. She could feel the strong orgasm fast approaching.

"Oh my God!" Robin yelled out, as the orgasm swept all throughout her body.

Robin love juices spilled out of her paradise and into T.J.'s wanting mouth. T.J. turned Robin around onto her stomach and started licking around her lower back. She slowly made it towards her toned ass. Then T.J. sat up behind her and pressed her hands into the small of Robin's back.

"You ready?" T.J. asked in a low, sexy voice.

After a long sigh, Robin pushed her ass up into the air and answered, "Yeah, but take your time and go slow."

"Okay, Baby. Just remember, I want you to do it the same way," T.J. said, as she smiled.

Then, in one smooth motion, T.J. slid the black dildo into Robin's inviting love cave. With each stroke, Robin moaned out in pleasure. T.J. made long slow love to Robin. They both shared the intimate moment, bringing her multiple orgasms. It made Robin shiver out of control, her heart racing, and her mind spinning.

An hour later, it was Robin's turn to return the wonderful favor.

8

What Every Woman Wants

Chapter 2

Wednesday morning...

Roxborough, Philadelphia

After an amazing night of kinky sex with T.J., Robin still managed to get up, take a quick shower. After eating a bowl of Fruity Pebbles cereal she makes it to work by 8 o'clock in the morning. She parked her car and made her way into the building where she worked. Without a detour, Robin headed straight to her office. Normally, she might have stopped off to say 'hi' to some of her friends, but she had little sleep last night and was in no mood for gossip.

Robin was the Assistant Program Director at the Power 99 FM radio station in Philadelphia. Power 99 was one of Philly's top-rated stations, playing to the young urban music listeners. The popular station had one of the largest fan bases on the entire East Coast. It could be heard on the Internet worldwide. With listeners in Delaware, New Jersey, and all throughout Pennsylvania; it brought in a great deal of advertising revenue. Rap and R&B music was the sound that stayed on Power 99's continuous play-list, 24 hours a day.

Robin walked into her office and was greeted by a large stack of brown folders on her cluttered desk. After handing up her Versace jacket, she walked over and sat back into her brown recliner leather chair. She wiggled the mouse and watched as her computer awoke from its slumber. It quietly hummed as things came to life. Robin was in charge of a host of things at the station. Her duties included but were not limited to promotions, local media, scheduling guest DJ's, payroll and accounting, ticket giveaways for concerts, and almost every medial thing you could imagine it takes to run a successful radio station. She typed a few things into her computer, then stood up from her chair and walked out of her office as she yawned. When she entered the small staff kitchen, a few people were standing around talking and drinking hot cups of coffee.

As her eyes glanced around the room, the first person that she noticed was DJ Love-Daddy. He was an old-school disc jockey who had the late-night spot, from midnight to four in the morning. He played the very best of slow R&B songs and he had a large following. He was 42 years old with a dark complexion, and looked nothing like his listeners would have imagined after hearing his voice. He had a deep, sensual tone that drove his late night female listeners wild. His sexy appeal stopped at his voice. In reality, he was quite unattractive. Although he had been blessed with a deeply hypnotic voice, he had been cursed in the 'looks' department.

Ugly was not the correct adjective to use in describing his features. A while back, an intern who got angry at him said that he looked like somebody set his face on fire and then put it out with a pair of stilettos. He had funny shaped head, shaped like a potato. Around the office, the employees nicknamed him Mr. Potato. To be frank, he was just not a handsome guy.

Her eyes moved past his bulbous head and on to DJ Trey. He was a 20-year-old mix-tape DJ who stood tall, slim, with light brown skin, designer braids, and a cute face. He was always wearing something quite fashionable, He was known around the studio as a ladies' man. Trey stood there, slowly sipping on a hot cup of coffee. He had on a pair of black Rocawear jeans, a white Sean Jean sweatshirt, and brown Timberland boots. A large diamond was embedded in his left ear .To set it off just right, he wore an iced-out gold necklace with a matching bracelet on his wrist.

Standing behind him was Jennifer Douglas. She seemed self indulged in her own world of adding cream to her coffee that looked strong enough to pull paint. She was a 43-year-old Program Director. She was short, with a caramel complexion, and had thin, pretty face. She was in very good shape for her age. At least three days a week, Jennifer would be found at Bally's Gym working out every muscle in her 5'4" frame.

Scanning around the room Robin noticed Penny Smith. She was rummaging through the refrigerator. Penny was one of the radio station's secretaries. She always knew the latest gossip. She was a twenty-five year old white woman who could easily pass for Paris Hilton's twin sister. She was tall, blond, and hungry for attention. After Robin had grabbed a hot cup of coffee, she stood around talking for just long enough to be polite. She then headed back to her office. Hopefully the caffeine would hit her bloodstream soon and give her a boost of energy. She had a lot of work to do, and she wanted to get it finished as quickly as possible. She closed the door behind her and sighed as she looked at endless pile of paperwork on her desk.

A half-hour later, Robin was seated at her desk, busily typing on her computer. Several knocks on her door interrupted her concentration.

"Damn!" she said, under her breath, "Come in and make it fast."

When the door opened, Trey strolled in with a smile on his face. He closed the door behind him, and strutted towards her desk. Robin turned from her computer and smiled at her 20-year-old sex toy. Trey approached her desk and said,

"I left a few messages on your Blackberry last night. Why ain't you called me back, Sexy?"

"I was busy last night," Robin said bluntly.

"Too busy for Trey?" he asked in a soft voice.

"Yup," she replied, "Too busy for pretty-boy Trey." Robin folded her arms across her chest.

"So it was like that, huh?"

The big smile on her face answered his question. "Trey, I just saw you Sunday night. Don't you ever get tired?"

"No," he shot back, "Not when it comes to being with you."

"Oh, I keep forgetting that you are a 20-year-old human Duracell battery," Robin said, grinning, "You just a baby with a whole lot of energy."

"I wasn't a baby Sunday night," Trey teased. He edged closer to her desk, leaning forward. "So what's up? When can I see you again?"

"Not tonight, Mr. Duracell. I have a date with Charles."

He backed away, pretending to be offended. "Oh, yeah? Is that your super-rich boyfriend? Is that who you was with last night?"

"No, and who I was with is none of your business," Robin said, in a serious tone.

"My bad, sweetie, our thing is our business. Just sex and nothing more," Trey said flatly. A devilish grin started to form on his face. "So you still didn't answer my question. When can Trey have his turn with the beautiful, sexy Miss Robin Davis?"

Robin stared into Trey's handsome young face, smiling as she shook her head and thought: 'Boys ' Trey had been her secret young sex toy for almost four months. There was something about Trey that brought the youthful wildness out of Robin. She felt more vibrant, more alive. However, there were still issues to deal with. The problem with Trey was that he lacked experience. Robin was nearly ten years older than Trey. Most of the time when they were together she felt like a horny old teacher schooling her favorite young student. It was wrong, but it was so right.

Robin glanced down at her gold watch and then back up at Trey, "You got condoms?"

His eyes grew about three times larger, "Yeah, a fresh new pack of three." His smile was ear to ear.

"Right now, I still have a lot of work to take care of. My lunch break is at twelve. I'll meet you at your truck," Robin said. She turned back to her computer.

"Bet. I'll see you at twelve, sexy," Trey said. He turned around and headed out of the office. The grin on his face could convince anyone that he had just won the lottery.

She dove back into her work, but a ring of the telephone interrupted her again.

"Damn, damn!" She stared at the phone, sighed, and then picked up the receiver. "Hello?"

"What's up, girl? It's me," Tammy said cheerfully.

"Girl," Robin said, pleasantly relieved, "Where are you?"

"I'm home, I didn't go to work this morning. I called in and took me an emergency dick day," Tammy said as they both started laughing.

Robin looked around the office, lowering her voice as if somebody might be listening. "Who was the lucky fella?"

"Nathan. He's still in my bedroom, snoring up a storm."

"You must have put it on his ass," Robin joked.

"No. I made him take Viagra. That's why I ain't make it to work this morning," Tammy said between laughter, "That little blue pill "

"Girl, you is a cold freak!"

"I know that Ms. Freak Almighty ain't calling me a freak! How was your night with T.J.?"

Robin bit her bottom lip as she sighed, "Very enjoyable, I must say. She came over last night. You know how that goes. She did her thing and I did my thing. She left at about four o'clock to catch a flight to Chicago. I'll see her again next week."

"So she didn't drain you out this time?" Tammy teased.

"No," Robin laughed, "If she did, I wouldn't be seeing my boy toy on my lunch break." Robin leaned back in her chair, her mind picturing lunch.

"Damn, girl, you a nympho! Is there a person alive that can slow your ass down?" Tammy joked.

"If there is, I damn sure ain't find him yet! My D.L.M. is still hiding from me. Maybe I'll get lucky before my birthday next Friday."

"So what's up? What are we gonna do later?"

"I have a dinner date with Charles later. Sorry."

"Oh yeah," Tammy remembered. "Nathan told me that they canceled a few meetings at their office because Charles had some other plans. I guess those plans were with you."

"Lucky me, I wonder what he got me this time?" Robin said, twirling her fingers around the phone card.

"That man spoils you like a child. Hell, I get nothing but dick and a sore lower back from his partner Nathan. I knew I should have snatched up Charles before you did."

"That's what you get for always wanting the cute ones," Robin teased back.

"Plus, I made him wait. I tortured him."

"A week!" Tammy laughed. "A week is not torture."

"Stop hating. At least he ain't get it on the first night like Nathan did," Robin retorted.

"Whatever," Tammy said. "Hey, is he still sweating you about being his wife?"

Robin considered the question. "Not really. I know he is thinking about it, but I made it clear that it's the best if we just remain friends for a while longer. I'm not ready to be locked down to one man. Plus "

"Robin," Tammy said interrupted, "Please tell me you didn't tell him that he has a small dick. Girl, tell me you didn't?"

"Hell no. Girl, stop!" Robin laughed, "I got that man thinking he's got the biggest dick in the world. Why do you think he spoils me so much?"

They both busted out laughing again.

"The thing is; Charles is just too damn busy for me. He's all over the country with Nathan. All he does is travel the world in search of new projects. Every time I look around he is buying a new commercial property. They want everything they can get their rich hands on. Tonight will be our first dinner date in two weeks. You know me, Tammy. I'll play my part to perfection. I'll get my gift, blow his mind, and send him back home with another big smile on his face."

"Sometimes I wish it could be that simple for me. Nathan's tight ass don't even want to pay for the pizza half of the time," Tammy bitched.

"Maybe you need to cut him loose for a while."

"But he's my best lover. Plus, he's so damn fine."

What Every Woman Wants

"Don't forget he is tight! And married!" Robin reminded her, "We must not forget that your handsome, good loving friend is married with two children. The reality is that you will always be second."

"Please don't remind me."

"If he was single," Robin said, "He would be your perfect D.L.M., but he's not."

"You're right, girl," Tammy replied somberly.

Robin could sense that her friend was down. "Don't be upset. My world ain't all cherries either. I'm thirty, about to be thirty-one. I'm in sexual relationships with a rich man with a little dick. I am fucking a gorgeous woman whose body is better than mine. Top that off with the fact I am sexing baby who still has milk on his breath! If I could only combine them all together: Charles' money, T.J.'s skills in the bedroom, and Trey's handsome looks that would be the perfect man."

That seemed to raise Tammy's spirits as they laughed.

"I'll talk to you later. I'm about to go wake Nathan's tight-wad ass up and send him back home to his wife and kids."

"You go, girl. Love you. Bye," Robin said, as she turned back to her computer.

"Bye," Tammy said, as they both hung up the phone.

For a few moments, Robin sat at her desk suspended in deep thought. "I'm gonna find you one day, D.L.M. man," she whispered to herself, then touched the keyboard, bringing the screen back to life. She took a long, slow breath and then scooted forward. Seconds later, her fingers were clicking away at the keyboard.

~

Bryn Mawr, Pennsylvania…

Charles Mitchell examined himself in front of the full-length mirror. He was proud of what he saw. He stood there, admiring his tall, naked, black body. He then walked over to the bedroom window and looked out at the beautiful scenery. Charles lived in a large, all white, newly built home that had eight bedrooms, six baths, equipped with a playroom, a spa with a steam shower, a massage table, twenty-two foot high living room and dining room ceilings. The suite also had a penthouse master-bedroom suite that was to die for. In addition to all the luxuries,: the house also had a four-car garage and a C-shaped swimming pool out back. The four point three million-dollar home was surrounded by tall trees and a large manicured lawn. He had all of the things that money can buy you.

Charles Mitchell was thirty-nine years old. He was tall, with dark skin, and not unattractive. Of course, his money made his average looks seem greater. He was a self-made millionaire. He was one of the most successful real estate investors on the entire East Coast. At just twenty-four, Charles had made his first million from the buying and selling of commercial properties. He and his partner, Nathan Richards, were the two co-owners of the Mitchell & Richards Real-Estate Investment Company. Their company specialized in commercial properties all along the East Coast. Life was going his way.

After taking a quick hot shower and getting himself dressed, Charles walked downstairs and out into his lavish garage. Parked inside the four-car garage were a blue Bentley, a white Mercedes Benz wagon, a green Cadillac truck, and a cherry-red BMW. He walked casually over to the Bentley Azure. He pressed a button to disarm the alarm system. At the click of a button the door opened. As he started it up, the quiet purr of the engine sounded clean and expensive. He took a moment to think about the fact that he was surrounded by more than three hundred and fifty thousand dollars worth of European-made luxury. None of it really mattered. All he could think about was being with Robin. He and Nathan had been in Atlanta for five days, and he still had not seen her. Suddenly, he couldn't resist the urge. He just wanted to see her face. She was the only woman that Charles lusted after. Deep down, he could feel that he was in love with her. He didn't mind spoiling Robin with the best gifts that his money could buy. In fact, one of his gifts was a one hundred thousand dollar Mercedes Benz, that Robin currently drove. He liked to think that every time she got into the car, she would think of him. To Charles, it didn't matter what he spent on her because he was determined to make her happy. He wanted her to be his wife K the future mother of his children. Robin was everything he had ever wanted in a woman.

To Charles, Robin was something rare and perfect. She was beautiful, intelligent, bold, persistent, and spontaneous. Her body was incredible, and the intimacy they shared in bed was mind blowing. It was the best sex he ever had with any woman. The only stumbling block was that she was sexually involved with other people. Although he respected her wish that they only remain friends, he still wanted her more than anything. His money was long and his patience was even longer. One day, God willing, she would be his. Well, that is what he kept telling himself. Charles knew that Robin enjoyed the finer things in life. He could provide her with her every dream, desire, and fantasy that she could possibly imagine. Still, with all of the success and money that Charles had, he possessed a deep, hidden secret that only one other person had known about. This was a secret that Charles never wanted to be exposed. He especially did not want Robin, the woman that he was falling in love with, to find out. If she ever found out about his dark secret, she would leave him and never return. He was sure of it.

After hanging up his car phone, Charles slowly pulled the Bentley out of the garage. He had just finished a call with his personal jeweler. As he drove off his pristine piece of property, he headed towards downtown Philadelphia. He was on his way to Jeweler's Row. There he would pick up the newly crafted, designer piece that he had purchased for Robin. If the jeweler had gotten it right, it would take Robin's breath away.

What Every Woman Wants
Chapter 3

Not too far away from the Power 99 radio station, Trey had his dark tinted black Lincoln Navigator parked in the back of a Burger King parking lot. The music was turned up just enough to cover the heated moans that Trey and Robin were making inside. Trey was lying down on the back seat, while Robin was positioned on top of him. She was riding the shit out of her young, handsome toy, her hips thrusting back and forth.

"Yes, Baby! Yes, ooh yes! Work that young dick!" Robin said, as she raised and lowered herself with the support of the truck around her.

Robin was like an elevator out of control as she lifted quickly and then fell onto him. Straddling him, she pushed him deep inside of her. Trey's hands were wrapped around her hips, trying to keep up with the older and much more experienced sexual veteran. The sweat was pouring down both of their faces. Trey had already come twice, and Robin had yet to come once.

"You love this pussy, don't you? Don't you?!" she said, staring deep into his satisfied eyes. When Trey didn't answer her, Robin started riding him faster. "I said, you love this pussy, don't you?!" Still, he didn't answer. He was lost in the moment, the pleasure too great to speak. "Tell me you love it or I'm gonna fuck your young ass to death!" she said. She sped up her motions, pumping up and down on him like a machine that's gone out of control.

Trey laid there on the seat, feeling his body about to explode with its third orgasm in less than an hour. Finally, he gathered the strength to speak.

"Yes! I love this pussy!" They both began to climax at the same time. His breathing became more rapid. He yelled, "I love this pussy!" With an explosion that passed through both of them. They shared their orgasm.

Slowly, he slumped back as Robin laid down on his chest. Her face was inches from his. She turned her head and used his chest for a pillow as they both calmed their breathing. Both of them were sexually exhausted. Trey had sweated out his designer braids. Robin could feel his body trembling beneath hers. She knew that she was slowly turning Trey's ass out. She loved every moment of it.

She looked up, peering into his eyes and said, "That was to let you know that Sunday night I let you get your shit off. So, next time cutie, don't get it confused." She kissed him on top of his nose, sat up, and started getting dressed.

After Trey had dropped Robin back off at work, she went into her office and grabbed the white Coach bag that was sitting on the floor. Inside the bag were a wash rag, a towel, and extra pairs of underwear that she kept inside her office in case of a quickie-sex-emergency.

Robin exited the employee bathroom. She cleaned herself off and changed her underwear. With a contented smile on her face, she headed back to her office and got back into doing her work. By four o'clock, she had finished all of her work and walked out of the building. In just eight short hours, she had a staff meeting, a long interview with a local hip-hop magazine, her daily conversation with Tammy, and one hell of an orgasm!

So far, today was going perfect, she thought, as she walked over and climbed into her gold Mercedes. Robin was in a rush to get back to her condo and get herself ready for her date with Charles. As she was driving down Domino Lane, she stopped at a red light. She let the top of her convertible down. She took in the cool breeze enjoying every minute of it. The music was turned up with Jill Scott's new song playing out of the speakers. She had on a pair of black tinted Dolce & Gabbana frames. When the light changed, she pulled off down the street. However, at the next corner, she was once again stopped at a red light.

Glancing in her rear view mirror, she saw a large SEPTA bus holding up traffic. She also noticed idling cars behind her. Her eyes darted past the bus stop. She noticed a man that made her remove her glasses to get a better look.

"Damn," she said. *"He is fine!"*

He was standing at the bus stop beside two older white women. He stood about five foot nine inches tall, light brown complexion, dark wavy hair, slanted brown eyes, and shaped-up goatee. He stood slightly bowlegged. The handsome stranger was dressed in a pair of dark blue jeans, a gray T-shirt, and a pair of black ankle-high boots. Robin noticed his muscular arms covered with tattoos. The sound of a honking horn snapped her out of her lustful trance. When she looked up, she noticed that the light was now green. She also realized that the man had noticed her staring at him. He smiled at her, showing his pearly-white teeth. The cars behind Robin's Mercedes were still blowing their horns, but she didn't move.

A voice deep inside of her soul was now talking to her. After a long pause, she sighed and said, "What the hell, why not?" She pulled her car over to the side of the road. "Hey, you need a ride?" she asked, looking at the man with the dumbfounded expression on his face. The man pointed to himself, not sure whom she was talking to.

"Who? Me?" he said curiously. He looked behind him to make sure she wasn't talking to somebody else.

"Yeah," she said, as she unlocked the passenger door. "You." She pushed the door open.

The man shrugged and then quickly walked over to the car and got inside. After he shut the door and gave her an awkward smile, Robin pulled out into traffic, easing her way into the line of cars. When she had gotten a closer look at the stranger, she realized that he was even finer than she had originally thought. His face was flawless, and he had a set of red, juicy lips that would put LL Cool-J to shame.

"Where are you going?" she inquired.

His eyes met hers momentarily, "West Philly, Forty-Second and Westminster Avenue," he said.

His eyes scanned her quickly, noticing just how attractive this woman actually was.

"Damn! The ghetto!" Robin said.

He looked down. "You can drop me off at the next bus stop. I understand," he said honestly. Even his voice was sexy, she thought.

"No, I'm cool. I have to go that way anyway," she lied.

"So, what's your name?"

"Kevin," he said, a gentle smile on his face. "Kevin Taylor."

"My name is Robin," she said, extending her manicured hand. When Robin felt the stranger's hand touch hers, a strange chill coursed through her body. 'Please, God,' she thought to herself 'Let this man be the one.' She returned his smile. "So, do you mind me asking you a few questions, Kevin?" she said, as they got on the expressway.

"No, not at all, but can you handle the truth?"

She smiled. "I can handle anything! Why do you ask?"

He turned his head, looking out of the windshield, "Because I like to be straight up with everyone that I meet. If a person accepts me, I want it to be because of who I am, and not some made-up fictional person that I created. Sometimes, when people ask questions, they aren't prepared for the answers. You know how it is."

"Is that right?"

"One hundred percent," he said with a serious look crossing his face.

"So," she started, "are you married, Kevin?"

"No."

"Children, baby mamas, step-kids?"

"No," he laughed.

"Undercover brother, homo, Satan worshiper, rapist?" she asked.

"No!" Kevin said, laughing even harder.

"Well," she said, as she thought of her next question, "How old are you? I mean, if you don't mind me asking."

"No, I don't mind. I'm thirty-seven."

That threw her for a spin.

"Hold up! Hold up! Ain't no way in the world a man as handsome as you ain't got no children, no baby mama, and ain't creeping around with other men on the D.L."

He shrugged.

"You must be the perfect man," Robin said, looking at Kevin with a big smile on her face.

"No," he warned, "I'm nowhere close to perfect. Everyone has their flaws, even me." His tone was very serious.

"So, where were you coming from when I picked you up? Robin inquired, changing the subject.

"A job interview."

"Did you get it?

He looked up, frustrated. "No, I don't think my resume impressed them enough. It's cool. I have a few more lined up for tomorrow. You know, you just keep throwing darts, hope that something hits."

"So, what is it that you do?" she asked.

"Almost everything with my hands: I can lay carpet, drop ceiling, plumbing work, electrical work, fix cars, paint, and just about anything else you can imagine."

"Wow, you're quite a handy man. So, why didn't they hire you?" Robin said, as she maneuvered her Mercedes through the evening expressway traffic.

"Because I just got out of prison," Kevin said; his eyes unsure of how she would take the news.

Robin looked over at him and said, "Prison?"

"Yes. I just got out four days ago."

"How long did you serve?" she said, trying to use the right lingo.

He smiled briefly.

"Eight years and six months," he muttered softly, "Eight and a half." He sighed.

"For what?"

"Drugs. I was once a drug dealer. That was before the feds indicted me and I was arrested and sentenced to serve one-hundred and twenty months " He looked up. "Ten years in federal prison."

"So you've only been home for four days after serving all that time in prison?" Robin asked hesitantly. Her mind was racing in every direction.

"Yup."

"So, who is the lucky lady who did your time with you?" Robin asked, with an understanding smile on her face.

"My mother. My ex-girlfriend left me after the first six months."

"Couldn't wait, huh?"

"Nope. But I ain't expect her to, either. I had too much time and she was young with her whole life ahead of her. She didn't need me hangin' around in the shadows, bringing her down."

"That's no excuse. All that was phony love. Maybe God wanted y'all to be apart. He knows what's best for all of us," she said, philosophically.

"I thought she was my soul mate," Kevin said, turning his head away.

"Some people are placed in our lives to guide us towards our true soul mate."

"You ever heard of this author, Jimmy DaSaint?" he asked her.

"Yes," she said excitedly, "He's one of my favorites. I have all of his novels. I also have Carl Weber, Eric Jerome Dickey, Omar Tyree, Mary B. Morrison, and my favorite Zane."

"Well," he continued, "In one of Jimmy DaSaint's books, he wrote, 'everyone has a soul mate. Some keep running. Some keep hiding. Others are waiting to be discovered.' I used to think about that all the time. Inside, you have plenty of time to just think. I always like that because it gives you hope that at any moment it could happen. Lightening could strike."

Robin pulled off of the expressway without saying a word. Then she drove down Girard Avenue, heading towards 42nd Street. The whole time her mind was racing with thoughts; being in this stranger's presence made her feel something that she had never felt before. Her intuition was telling her that this man was the one she had been searching for her entire life. When she glanced over at Kevin, he was staring back. In her sight was the most handsome man she had ever laid eyes on.

She pulled her car up in front of a small brick row house. A beautiful elderly lady was outside sweeping the leaved away from her house.

"That's my mother," Kevin smiled.

"Mom," he motioned to her, "come here." The elderly woman walked over to the car, holding the broom in her hand.

"Mom, this is Robin. She gave me a ride home." He smiled the most beautiful smile that Robin had ever seen.

"Hi, Robin," the elderly woman said.

"Hello, Ma'am," Robin replied.

"You can just call me Mrs. Silvia."

"Okay, I'll remember that," Robin said, staring at the beautiful brown-skinned older woman. "Nice man, nice mother," she thought to herself. She felt strangely comfortable around them.

"Alright then, y'all take care. I'll see you when you get inside, Kevin," Mrs. Silvia said, as she turned away. They watched her as she walked inside the house and closed the door.

"She seems like a very nice woman," said Robin.

Kevin smiled affectionately, "She's the best."

"You look just like your mother," Robin said softly.

"Thank you," Kevin blushed.

"So, you live here with your mom, huh?"

"Yeah, only until I find a job and get back on my feet. She likes me being around 'cause I'm her only child and she missed me while I did all that time. But she also knows that I need my own space. You know, be me. Feel me?" Kevin noticed Robin looking down at her expensive-looking gold watch and said, "Do you have to be somewhere important right now? I don't mean to hold you."

"No, no," she lied, "I'm fine." Even though she knew that she only had an hour and a half to get ready for her dinner date with Charles, she wanted more time near this man-near Kevin.

"Okay," Kevin said with a newfound confidence, "Since you have time, I would like to ask you a few questions."

Robin turned off her car, then crossed her arms and said, "Okay, shoot."

"How old are you, if you don't mind me asking?"

"I'm thirty, well, I'll be thirty-one next Friday."

"Any children?"

"None. Not yet, anyway," she smiled.

"Do you have a special someone in your life?" he asked.

Robin thought about it. "Friends, but no special someone."

"Brothers? Sisters?" he questioned.

"I have an older brother named Billie. He's a lawyer. Our parents died in a terrible plane crash a long time ago," Robin said sadly.

"I'm sorry to hear that," Kevin said, very sincerely. His face brightened.

"Let's change the subject. Why did you stop the car and offer me a ride?" He was genuinely curious.

"I don't know," she answered, "Just being spontaneous, I guess. Right now, I'm glad I did." she looked deep into his sexy brown eyes.

Before Kevin asked another question, Robin's cell-phone started ringing. She reached inside her Gucci purse and took it out. When she looked at the screen to see who was calling, she quickly answered.

"Tammy, I'll call you back." Click! She hung up.

"Is everything okay?" he asked.

"Everything is fine. That was my best friend calling to check on me."

For the next hour, Robin and Kevin sat inside her car, talking and laughing. Before he got out, Robin reached into her purse and pulled out one of her personal cards. When she reached to give it to him, Kevin said, "No, Pretty, you keep that. You know where I live, and now, I know where you work. If it's meant for us to see each other again, let it be in person and not on the phone."

"Are you sure?" Robin asked, confused. She had thought everything was going well.

"I'm positive. Like I said, you know where I live, right here with my mother." Kevin said, as he opened the car door slowly.

Robin grabbed Kevin's hand and leaned over, giving him a kiss on his check.

"What was that for?" he asked, with a surprised look on his face.

"I don't know, maybe the same reason why I picked you up off a bus stop. It just felt right."

She was blushing. Robin watched as Kevin got out and walked around to her side of the car.

"You be safe, Robin, and don't stop for no more strangers. The next person might be some lunatic who just got out of prison a few days ago," Kevin joked.

"If he's like you, then I'll take my chances," she smiled.

Kevin leaned down and put his mouth close to Robin's ear, whispering, "There's nobody else like me, and I can promise you that."

Robin sat there feeling herself becoming moist and wet. She watched as Kevin turned and walked away. When she glanced down at her watch, she saw that a whole hour had passed. But at that moment, Charles was the last person on her confused mind. Kevin waved goodbye as Robin started her car and drove down the street. When she had disappeared from his view, he walked into the house.

As Robin drove on her way to her luxurious downtown condominium, she couldn't get Kevin out of her mind. He was all she could think about.

"Damn, he's fine," she said to herself. "But, he's broke and he lives with his mother! God, please help me with this one."

She maneuvered her Mercedes through the slowly moving traffic. Robin had never felt so overwhelmed by a man that she had just met. She had met all sorts of men from all walks of life... but this was different. When she heard her cell-phone ringing again,

26

she didn't answer it. A part of her soul was still down on 42nd Street with Kevin - in the ghetto.

Twenty minutes later, Robin pulled her car into the underground car garage, beneath the condominium high-rise. The first car she noticed was Charles' brand new Bentley Azure, parked in her guest parking space. She tried to get herself together, but it was too late. Charles walked up to her car and looked at her face. He could tell that Robin had been crying. Although he didn't know it, those tears were made not just from confusion, but fear. She faced fear of the unknown man that had now entered her life. One minute she had just been minding her own business, driving down the road. Moments later, Kevin was there.

Her tears were much more pure and deep than anyone could ever imagine. She didn't even realize how deep it was, this situation had her puzzled.

A few hours later...

Kevin was lying across his bed when his mother tapped on the bedroom door and entered the room.

"Are you okay, Kevin?" she asked, seeing the different look in his eyes.

"Yes, Mom, I'm fine," he said, as he sat up on his bed.

"Thinking about that pretty girl, aren't you?"

Kevin looked at his mom and smiled. She knew her only child better than anybody.

"Yeah," he answered, "It's just, there's something about her."

"She's very pretty. To be honest, you two look good together. I was watching both of you from the window," she said, with a sparkle in her eye.

"Mom," he said, pretending to scold her, "Don't tell me you were snooping around." He was feeling a bit embarrassed.

"No, I just looked out the window a few times to make sure that you were okay." Her eyes stared towards the window in his bedroom.

"This neighborhood has gotten a lot worse since you left."

"I'll be fine, Mom," Kevin assured her.

"Okay, Kevin, I'll let you get back to thinking about that pretty girl. Maybe you could invite her to dinner one day?"

"Naw, I don't think that'll ever happen, Mom. Me and Robin are from two different worlds. She's rich, and I'm-" his voice trailed.

"Rich with honesty, God, and love; no woman alive can resist that combination. Mark my words," his mother said.

"But Mom," Kevin said, cutting her off.

"No buts. You're a good man, Kevin. You might not have all the fancy cars, clothes, and jewelry that these drug dealers and rich people out there have, but you got something more valuable, a genuine loving soul. If you have to win a person over with money or fame, then that person is not meant for you. Remember Kevin, you lost one girl over that, don't make the same mistake twice," she said, as she left the bedroom.

After a long sigh, Kevin lay back across his bed, letting his thoughts swim around.

"God," he whispered, "You have brought me this far, so I'm going to keep following your lead."

He placed his hand behind his head and stared up at the ceiling.

~

Ritten House Square...

Inside a fancy 5-star restaurant, Robin and Charles were seated at a private table, near the back. Robin was dressed in a long black Roberto Cavali dress, and black Prada heels. Her long, silky black hair was tied in a ponytail that accentuated the beauty of her gorgeous face. Charles was dressed in a blue tailor-made Italian suit, with a pair of matching crocodile shoes. He looked across the table at her.

"Would you please tell me why you were crying?"

"I told you it was nothing. Now, please, let's finish enjoying our meal."

Charles could sense that something or someone was on Robin's mind. Even a blind man could see that her head was somewhere else. Charles wondered if the time was right. Slowly, he reached into his pocket and pulled out a long, black velvet box. He lifted it up and set it in front of her, next to her plate.

"Here, this is for you, beautiful," he said as he leaned forward.

Her face lit up as she smiled for the first time that evening. When she opened the box, her eyes widened with shock. The five-carat platinum necklace was one of the most beautiful pieces of jewelry that Robin had ever laid her eyes on.

"Charles! It's beautiful, it's incredible," she said, as she took the necklace out of the box.

"Let me put it on for you," Charles said, as he stood up and walked around behind her. Gently, he moved her hair to the side as he placed the ornate necklace around Robin's neck.

"Perfect," he said, leaning down and softly kissing her on the check. He walked back around the table. The table was dimly lit. Standing between them were two candles.

"The perfect necklace for the perfect woman." He mused.

She ran her fingers slowly across the necklace. She took a breath, imagining what she looked like from across the table.

"Thank you so much, Charles. I don't know what to say, this is just--"

"Say nothing. Just smile," he told her.

"Why do you spoil me so much?"

He gazed into her eyes.

"Because, Robin, like I've told you so many times, I love you. Hopefully, one day you'll accept my marriage proposal. For you, beautiful, I'll wait a lifetime if I have to. The world is out there and I want to give it all to you." His voice was very serious and intense.

Robin sat there speechless. She knew that Charles had meant every word out of his mouth. She also knew that she could never love him the way that he loved her. She was a woman who needed to be totally satisfied. That was something that Charles could not do. Robin knew that if they ever got married, she would just end up cheating with another man, or woman. So, in her heart, she knew that it was best if they remained friends.

They sat for a few minutes without talking, just taking in the ambiance around them.

"What are you thinking about, beautiful?" he asked, breaking the silence.

"I'm ready to leave," Robin said with a wink.

After Charles had paid the bill with his Membership Only Black Card. They walked out of the restaurant hand-in-hand. His Bentley was waiting out front, and almost as quick as the valet had shut their doors, her hand was working its way down his pants. The drive back to the underground garage was both heated and torturous as she stroked him. After parking, they rushed over to the empty elevator. As soon as Robin pressed the button to the thirty-fifth floor, the doors closed. They attacked each other like two wild animals. When the elevator reached its destination, they quickly stepped off, both of them half-undressed, and filled with sexual desire.

Inside her cozy condominium, Robin slid off her dress, shoes, and underwear. Charles took off his pants and underwear and then took Robin into his arms. They locked in a long, passionate kiss barely stopping to breathe. Robin grabbed Charles' hand and led him over to the sofa. Her eyes narrowed.

"I want you to fuck the shit out of me with that big, fat dick!" Her voice was deep and sultry. She turned around and bent over the sofa, looking back over her shoulder at him. Charles stood behind her and placed his hand on her hips. After slowly spreading her legs and preparing to enter her, she stopped him. "Hold up!" She slid free and ran into her bedroom. Fifteen seconds later, she came back with a condom in her hand. "Better safe than sorry," she said, rolling the condom onto Charles' small, hard dick. Robin got back into her favorite position and said, "Okay, I'm ready." she closed her eyes and imagined that Kevin was the man behind her.

She secretly wished he was the man entering into her body, becoming one with her. While Charles was smacking his thighs against her ass, Robin was moaning and grunting. "Yes! Daddy! Fuck me with that big dick, Daddy! Yes! Yes!" Robin yelled out. Under her breath she started saying, "Kevin, yes! Kevin, yes! Yes! Oh my God, yes, Kevin, yes!" Charles was too caught up in his own performance to understand what Robin had been mumbling. But then she exploded, yelling, "Yes, Kevin!!!" Charles stopped in mid-stroke. Robin turned around and looked over her shoulder. Think fast, she thought. "Yes, Heaven! Oh, yes, Heaven! Thank you God!!" she yelled even louder.

Charles smiled and went right back to thrusting in and out of her. Close call, Robin thought. She realized that she had just experienced her first orgasm from Charles. That only occurred because she had imagined him being somebody else, the mystery man. Robin turned around and stood up. Charles could see her body trembling all over. This was something totally new for him. In her eyes, he had seen a look of pure passion and bliss-satisfaction. Robin pushed Charles down on the sofa, then spread open his legs and knelt down in front of him. Robin grabbed his still-hard dick and slowly took it into her mouth. He felt nothing but soft, wet heat. Even with the condom still on, Charles could feel her mouth tightening around him. Her performance was epic. Robin was like a woman possessed. With one hand, she managed Charles' testicles, her mouth squeezing and relaxing as she took him in and out. Charles had his head back and his eyes closed in total darkness. This was more than just a blow job; it was the most incredible thing he had ever experienced in his life. No hands, all mouth, tongue, and lots of warm saliva.

Robin was still imagining Charles to be Kevin. This had only made her put more emotion into it. She swallowed Charles' entire dick into the depths of her mouth; slowly sliding back out, and then doing it again. With her free hand, Robin moved her fingers slowly underneath his ass. She eased her finger easily into his asshole. The sensational feeling sent Charles straight into orbit. "Ahhhh! Yes, Robin! Yes!" he yelled, as he finally exploded into the condom. Both of their bodies were dripping wet with sexual sweat.

When Robin stood up and looked into Charles dazed eyes, they were watery, and a tear was falling down the side of his face. She looked down at her sexual prey and smiled. If only he knew, she thought to herself.

Early the next morning, Charles was rushing out the door to meet up with his partner, Nathan. They had an early morning meeting with some Japanese investors. As he raced to get dressed, he commented that the Japanese bought anything American. One day, he said, they would own America.

What Every Woman Wants

Throughout the night, Robin had made continuous love to Charles. Each time, she had imagined Kevin in his place. Every time that Charles thought that he could go no longer; she had somehow made him cum once again. Charles was her sexual slave-a victim. The sad part was that he didn't even know it. What she was giving him was like no drug he had ever tried. The all-night affair had drained Robin. She picked up the phone to call the radio station, requesting to take one of her paid vacation days. Her boss, Jennifer, didn't protest. After taking a long, hot shower, she put on a pink Nike sweat-suit and a pair of matching Nike Air sneakers. Then she sat on the edge of her bed and called Tammy.

"Hello," Tammy answered the phone, noticing that the time was seven o' five in the morning. Robin knew that Thursdays was Tammy's day off from the bank where she worked.

"Tammy," Robin stated emphatically, "I think I found him!"

"Found who?"

"My soul mate!" Robin said.

Tammy jumped up in bed. A handsome brown-skinned man was lying under the covers, sleeping next to her.

"What?"

"You got company?"

"Yeah. It's only Chuck," Tammy explained, "What's up, girl? Talk to me!"

"Tammy, I met this guy yesterday and I'm telling you, girl, I honestly feel it in my heart."

"Feel what in your heart?"

"You know," Robin pleaded, "That he's the one!"

Tammy thought she couldn't be hearing her correctly. "Girl, are you serious?"

"I'm serious, Tammy. The man is so damn fine that it hurts to look at him too long. And he's bowlegged, so you know he's packing," Robin said, as they both burst out laughing.

"Remember," Tammy warned, "Looks can be deceiving."

"No girl, not this time! I know he's the one. I fucked Charles all night long imagining him to be Kevin."

"Who the hell is Kevin?"

"The person I'm talking about, Tammy. Now, listen. I met him yesterday at the bus stop and-"

"The bus stop!" Tammy said, cutting Robin off.

"Yeah, whore, the bus stop. Damn, will you just listen and stop interrupting me for a second," Robin said back, in an angry voice.

"Proceed," Tammy replied softly.

"Anyway, like I was saying, I met him at the bus stop, by my job. I offered him a ride and drove him home to his mother's house, down on Forty-second Street."

"Mother's house? On Forty-second Street?" Tammy interrupted again, "Hell no!"

"Girl, you're gonna make me hang up this damn phone on your ass," Robin said, sounding frustrated.

"Kevin is so sweet and he's really trying to do something with his life, now that he's out of prison and-"

"Prison!" Tammy blurted out, before she could think.

Click. Robin slammed the phone down. Just as she finished taking a calming breath, her phone started to ring. She picked it up after a few rings, letting her frustration subside.

"You're gonna make me drive over there and kick that little ass. And Chuck will get a beat-down too if he tried to pull me off your black ass!" Robin chastised her.

"Okay, finish telling me about this ex-felon, bus stop waiting, mama's boy, that got you all screwed up in the brain," Tammy said sarcastically.

"Like I was trying to say, smart-ass, Kevin is different and I know what my mind, body, and soul, are telling me."

"Girl, I'm going to call you a doctor because you are scaring the hell out of me! This guy does not have our D.L.M. requirements. He's an ex-felon who lives with his mother, Robin! Factor in the fact that he's broke. Are you serious must I remind you that you are the one who made up the rules? Didn't you just tell me, yesterday, that it's D.L.M. or nothing?"

Robin was speechless at Tammy's response.

34

What Every Woman Wants

"Robin, you make over eighty grand a year. You have everything you have ever wanted. You have a Mercedes, a condo, money, and all the sex you can handle for a lifetime from anyone you choose to sleep with. This man, Kevin- he can't offer you shit! You'll end up regretting you ever met him. He will probably get you for everything you got! Don't trust him. He will tell you anything to get close to you and I bet."

"I cried," Robin said, cutting Tammy off.

"What?"

"Tammy, I cried. I cried after I dropped Kevin off at home and drove away," Robin explained, as tears started to roll down her cheeks.

Tammy stayed quiet. She knew that this was real serious. Robin never cried—ever. She didn't even cry at her own parents' funeral. She just accepted it and moved on. She did that with everything.

"Tammy," Robin said, "I can't even explain it. I don't know what it is about this guy, but he's not like anyone that I've ever met before. He didn't even take my personal card with all my numbers on it."

"He didn't? Why not?"

"No, he didn't. He said that if I want to see him, I know where he lives, and he left it at that," Robin said, as tears continued to fall down her face.

"Robin," Tammy asked carefully, "Are you crying?"

"Yes, Tammy. I'm sitting on the edge of my bed fucking crying I'm crying about some man that I don't even know anything about, and ain't even fucked, for God's sake! They both started laughing, even through the tears.

"Damn, girl. This is serious. What are you gonna do?"

After a long sigh, Robin wiped away the tears on her face and said, "I honestly don't know. This shit is really freaking me out! Why would God do this to me?"

"Maybe because it's all you ever ask for. You know what the wise people say; only He knows the desires of our hearts," Tammy offered.

"So, are you gonna see this guy again?"

"I want to, but I don't want to seem all desperate. It might turn him off," Robin said, in a serious tone.

"If he's your soul mate, then it's inevitable for y'all two to be together. Plus, I know you, girl, you won't rest until you find out if all of this is just a dream, or some fantasy, or..."

"Reality," Robin said.

"Yeah, reality."

"Girl, you know me too good," Robin said, a smile softening her face.

"I'm gonna kick Chuck out of my house. I'll be over there in about an hour. Love you," Tammy said quickly.

"Love you, bye," Robin said, hanging up her receiver.

Robin set the phone down on the floor and fell back onto her bed. She began staring up at the ceiling. She couldn't get Kevin out of her mind. And a big part of her didn't want to. Robin felt something warm in her chest. She knew that she would see Kevin again. Her spirit was yearning for him. He had a peculiar quality that she couldn't put into words. He was a human enigma that she had to solve on her own. They were connected in a way she couldn't understand. As crazy as the idea was, Kevin was her long-lost soul mate. Her intuition, her heart, her soul, and the tears that fell to her bed all told her so. He was that perfect something that she could never fully describe to someone else. Kevin was the one.

Chapter 5

After Tammy came over to Robin's condo, the two women sat in the living room, talking and laughing. Robin told Tammy everything she knew about Kevin. She also told her about the 'quickie' with Trey, and the night out on the town with Charles. She elaborated about the dinner, diamond necklace, and the night full of blissful lovemaking - all courtesy of her imaginative mind.

"It wasn't Charles that I was making love to, it was Kevin. That's why I came so much. That's why I put it on Charles' ass and sent him back home drained and crying like a baby," Robin said, as they both started laughing.

"Girl, how can you do that?"

"It's easy, just close your eyes and concentrate real hard. I do it all the time with Charles. The last time we were together, I imagined him being Denzel's fine ass."

"But you said that you didn't come the last time you was with Charles."

"I didn't! Only because he broke my concentration when he started smacking my ass and asking me, 'who's pussy is this?!'" Robin said, as they both busted out in laughter once again.

"Well, at least you be getting something out of the deal. That necklace he gave you has to be worth your yearly salary at the radio station. You must be one hell of an actress."

"Halle Berry's Monster's Ball, Jennifer Hudson's Dreamgirls; what, you ain't know?" Robin said, with a smile.

The doorbell interrupted their conversation. Robin stood up and walked over to the door. She looked out the small peephole and said, "Damn, I almost forgot," she said.

When she opened the door, two short Spanish women were standing there, waiting.

"Maria, I'm sorry, I almost forgot that today was your day to come through and clean up around here," she said apologetically.

"No problem, Miss Davis. If you are busy, we will come back later," Maria said.

"Who is your friend?" Robin asked, looking at the pretty young Spanish girl that was with her.

"This is my niece, Carla, she's gonna be helping me from now on She will be working every Tuesday, Thursday, and Saturday," Maria said.

"Why don't y'all just come back in about a half-hour? I have a few things to do and then me and my girlfriend, Tammy, will be out of y'all way."

"Okay, Miss Davis, I'll get the extra key from the manager," Maria said. She and her niece turned and walked away.

After Robin closed the door, she walked over to the entertainment wall-unit and said, "That was Maria, my maid. She and her niece will be back here in a half-hour to clean the place up," she said. Quickly, she sat down and turned on her computer. "What's up now? What do you want to get into for today?" Tammy said, already knowing what Robin's answer was going to be.

"What else? Shopping!" Robin said, facing the computer while looking at her email.

After both women had finished checking their email, Robin grabbed her purse and car keys. They walked out the front door. They climbed inside of Robin's Mercedes. She dropped the convertible top down, slid in India Aries' latest CD and drove out of the underground garage.

As the car cruised through the afternoon traffic, the warm breeze brushed up against their faces. While the wind blew back their hair, both women were singing and smiling. Thirty-five minutes later, Robin's Mercedes pulled into the parking lot of Lord & Taylor's high-fashion department store on City Line Avenue.

After finding an empty parking space not far from the entrance, both women got out of the car and walked into the large store.

With their platinum credit cards in hand, they headed straight for their three favorite departments: Prada, Gucci, and Dolce & Gabbana. They walked around picking out blouses, hats, jeans, dresses, sandals, and new perfumes.

Before walking over to the cash register to pay for all of their expensive new items, Robin said, "Tammy, hold up. Walk with me over to the men's section."

"What for?" Tammy asked, a look of bewilderment on her face, "I know you ain't about to spend no money on a man!"

"Girl, just come on," Robin said, as she rolled her small shopping cart through the aisles. Tammy stood there watching as Robin picked out a nice blue and white Gucci shirt, and a pair of dark Polo denim jeans.

"Yeah, I sized him up pretty good. This will fit," Robin said, as she tossed the clothes into the shopping cart.

"Girl, this guy better be all that. The dick better be the bomb or else I'm cutting you off."

Robin looked into her girlfriend's eyes and said, "The man just got out of prison after eight and a half years without a woman. Hello?!"

"Do you think that myth is true? You know the one about guys coming home from doing time and giving women the best sex they ever had?" Tammy asked, as she followed Robin over to the cash register line.

"When I find out, you'll be the first to know," Robin smiled and blinked.

"So then you're expecting the earth to move?"

"No, I wouldn't go that far. A small hurricane or tornado will do me just fine," Robin said, as they both started laughing.

After they paid for all of their new clothes and accessories, they went back to the car and put the shopping bags in the trunk. Their next trip was to the King of Prussia shopping mall. While there, they bought a few items from Bed, Bath, and Beyond, the Gap, and Armani Exchange.

After leaving the mall, they drove back downtown to get fresh manicures and pedicures. Afterward, they stopped at a popular downtown eatery. They both ordered chicken Caesar salads, and fresh ice-cold lemonades.

"Where to next?" Tammy asked, sitting back in her seat, enjoying the smooth voice of Vivian Green flowing out of the speakers.

Robin stopped her car at the intersection on twelfth and Chestnut St. and said, "We're going to West Philly," she said, I'm dropping off the clothes I bought for Kevin. Plus I'm dying to see him again."

A half-hour later, Robin pulled up and parked her car in an empty space. A group of thugged-out looking men were standing around, just hanging out on the corner. The men were all eyeing the luxurious set of wheels, and checking out the two fine sisters who had just entered their ghetto domain. While Robin was grabbing a shopping bag from out of the trunk, Tammy's roaming eyes scanned through the crowd of men.

With a big smile on her face, she had already spotted her next male prey. 'Damn, he fine,' she thought to herself. She stared at the stocky, brown-skinned man with the handsome face and short, black, curly hair.

"You coming?" Robin said, interrupting Tammy's lustful stare.

"No, go ahead, I'll wait in the car. You can bring him out to meet me," she said, going into her purse and taking out her cherry lip-gloss. Robin looked over at the men, then looked at Tammy.

"I thought you ain't like thugs? Miss goody-two-shoes, Vice President bank manager," said Robin.

Tammy smiled, looked into Robin's face, and said, "You got one, you think I'm gonna keep letting you have all the fun? Maybe I need a change from all the tight-suit corporate assholes who can't even pay for half of the damn pizza!"

"Okay, Miss Hot ass, do you; but you better be careful. Those guys all looked like they just got out of jail," Robin said. She grinned and walked away, holding the shopping bags in her hand.

"Yeah, maybe the same one your Kevin just got out of," Tammy joked.

Robin put up her middle finger and kept on walking. When she approached Kevin's house, she walked up the small concrete steps and knocked on the door. Nervously, she stood there waiting for someone to answer. 'Damn, maybe I'm being too persistent,' she thought. Running after a man was something that Robin had never done in her life. She was so beautiful that she didn't have to. Men constantly broke their necks trying to get with her. So did a lot of women for that matter.

'Maybe nobody's home,' Robin thought, as she turned to walk away. Suddenly the front door opened and Mrs. Silvia stood there with a big smile on her face.

"Hi Mrs. Silvia, is Kevin home?" Robin asked, as she looked at the lovely older woman with salt-and-pepper silky hair.

"I'm sorry, Robin, but Kevin got up early this morning and went out job searching."

"Damn!" Robin mumbled under her breath.

"Would you like to come in for a moment?"

"Yeah, sure," Robin said, following her into the house. When Robin walked in, she was surprised to see how cozy and well decorated it was.

"You have a lovely home, Mrs. Silvia," she said, as she walked over to the wall mantle and looked up at a row of trophies and pictures.

"That's my Kevin when he was younger, before being sent to prison," she said, as she walked up beside Robin.

"Wow, is that you?" Robin said, pointing to a picture with a gorgeous young woman and child.

"Yes, that's me and Kevin on the beach in Atlantic City." Mrs. Silvia smiled.

"You were beautiful. I mean you're still very pretty."

"I understand," Mrs. Silvia said.

Robin had noticed that there were no pictures of any men around.

41

"Where's Kevin's father, if you don't mind me asking?"

Mrs. Silvia hunched up her shoulders and said, "Who knows? He was gone three months after Kevin was born."

Robin shook her head.

"I see the wedding ring. Are you married, Mrs. Silvia?"

"Twice, and twice divorced. My life has been a very eventful one," she said, with a smile.

"A woman as beautiful as you are, I know you had men falling all after you."

"That was my biggest problem," she said, in a sad tone.

Robin looked straight into her eyes and asked, "What was?"

"Having so many men around me that I missed the only one that really mattered; my soul mate."

The words hit Robin like a ton of bricks.

"What do you mean?"

Mrs. Silvia looked at Robin and said, "Sometimes being very pretty or having a nice body can be a woman's downfall. We get so much attention from men that we get too caught up in ourselves. I lost the man who truly loved me for a man that spoiled me and who was more infatuated because of my looks, than who I really was on the inside. The biggest mistake of my life was choosing a man's fame and money over another man's genuine love. I guess that's why I'm 54 years old and all alone."

Robin stood there staring at the beautiful older woman holding back her tears. Her poignant words touched Robin deep in her soul.

"Would you like something to drink?" Mrs. Silvia asked.

"Please. Do you have some orange juice?"

"Coming right up. That's Kevin's favorite, too," she said, walking toward the kitchen.

Robin stood there looking at all of Kevin's sport trophies. Most of them were for baseball and football. There were also a few for boxing, swimming, and track and field.

"Kevin is a very good athlete," Mrs. Silvia said, walking back into the living room, holding two glasses of fresh orange juice.

"I see," Robin said, as Mrs. Silvia passed her one of the glasses. They walked over and sat down on the sofa. "I don't understand how a man like Kevin could've ended up in prison. It seems like he had so much talent," Robin said, in a serious voice.

"He still does. Kevin can draw, cook, write poetry, and even play music; but once the street called his name, he never looked back. Drugs, fast money, and street fame were his biggest downfall. The ghetto-life hurts so many of our good black men. Most of the fathers are gone, so the young boys grow up looking for guidance, role models, and leadership. Ninety- Five percent of them end up dead, strung out on the white man's drugs, or locked up in prison; just like my Kevin did."

Robin sat there listening as the wise older woman spoke the truths about life. She could feel herself growing closer to the older woman. As Mrs. Silvia continued to talk, Robin felt a strange warm feeling running around inside of her. She felt a feeling of comfort and motherly love.

"So where did you grow up?"

"The suburbs, Springfield, Pennsylvania. My parents were both lawyers. My older brother is also a lawyer."

"You seem like a fine young woman, Robin. I really hope you and Kevin get along."

"Me, too. I really like your son, Mrs. Silvia."

Mrs. Silvia looked into Robin's beaming eyes and said, "I already know, it's written all over your face."

When it was time to leave, Robin gave Mrs. Silvia a warm hug and they walked to the door.

"I'll be sure to tell Kevin you stopped by and I'll give him the new stuff you bought him. It's some nice stuff, I'm sure he's gonna like it," she smiled.

"Thank you so much, Mrs. Silvia, I'll see you soon," Robin said, as they both stepped out on the porch.

When Robin looked over at her car, she saw Tammy leaning up against it, talking to a handsome young man. She had forgotten that Tammy was outside in her car, waiting.

Mrs. Silvia watched as Robin waved goodbye and walked away. Then she turned around and went back into her house. When Robin approached her car, Tammy was smiling from ear to ear.

"Come on girl, he wasn't home," Robin said, as she got inside her car.

Tammy turned to the handsome, stocky young man and said, "Okay, Hakeem, you got all my numbers, call me."

"Don't worry, you'll be hearing from me Shorty, you can bet that," he said, as he smiled and walked away.

Tammy stood there watching Hakeem stroll down the street. When she got back into the car, she said, "Damn, girl, did you see the muscles and ass on him? Whoa!"

Robin looked through the rear-view mirror. "He's cute, but he ain't got nothing on Kevin." She then started the car and pulled off down the street.

"What happened?"

"Kevin wasn't home; his mother said he left out this morning to find a job," Robin said, turning on Mantua Avenue.

"So, what took you so long?"

"Me and his mom sat around talking. She's a sweetheart, and she is so pretty and so wise," Robin said, as she turned her car down Girard Avenue.

"I thought you forgot about me," Tammy said, as she sat there programming Hakeem's number into her cell phone.

"Never that," Robin lied.

"Anyway, you was too busy smiling and blushing with Braheem all in your face."

"Hakeem! Get it right," Tammy grinned.

Robin looked over at her blushing girlfriend and said, "Just make sure he wears a condom!"

"If they wanna play, ain't no other way to lay!" she said, as they gave each other a high-five.

A half-hour later, Robin pulled into the garage and parked next to Tammy's blue Lexus coup. They got out of the car and grabbed all their shopping bags from out the trunk. Robin watched as

44

What Every Woman Wants

Tammy put her bags on the backseat and got into the car. Then she walked over and said, "What are you about to go do, now?"

"I'm going to get my car washed. Then I'm going home to try on my new clothes and shoes. Why, what's up?"

"Let's go check out a movie down on Delaware Ave.?"

"Why? No date tonight?" Tammy teased her, knowing that the only time Robin wanted to go to the movie theater is when she was bored.

"Nope. T.J.'s in Chicago, Charles is running around with Nathan. I did Trey yesterday afternoon. I'm sure he's somewhere still recuperating," Robin said, as they watched Tammy back out of the parking space and drive out of the garage.

~

When Robin entered her condo, the first thing she noticed was the sweet vanilla scent of burning scented candles, and the vacuumed carpet. She walked into her bedroom and saw that everything was well organized, and the bed was beautifully made up. Robin sat the shopping bags on the bed and walked around, checking the place out. Like always, Maria had done a wonderful job. All of the plants had been watered, the dished were all washed and put up, the laundry was done, all the glass and appliances were sparkling clean. Maria and her niece, Carla, had done an excellent job. The best part about it was that they would be back on Saturday.

After checking her email and a few websites on her computer, Robin used her cell phone to check her voicemail messages. There was one from her older brother, Billy; one from T.J. and Trey; another from her boss, Jennifer; and two from Charles. Robin pressed a few buttons on her cell phone and listened to one of Charles's messages.

"Baby, I'm missing you already. Last night was truly a night that I'll never forget. To be honest, I felt like a victim inside of your love prison. Wow! You were on fire last night. I'm shivering right now just thinking about it. I'm glad you enjoyed my gift to you. Just wait until you see what I got you for your birthday! I'll see you in a few days. Nathan and I have some very important business to take care of in New York. Take care, I love you!"

Robin pressed the 'end' button on her cell phone, and tossed it on the sofa. "If only Charles knew that it wasn't him that I was making love to last night," Robin thought as she walked back into her bedroom. Robin fell back on top of her bed and stretched out her arms. She stared up at the high bedroom ceiling, and then looked over to her right. Her urban novels stacked neatly in the corner: Eric, Omar, Teri, Sister Souljah, Zane, Jimmy DaSaint, Nikki, and a few others were a part of her treasured collection.

Working at the radio station and reading urban novels were the closest she had ever been to the ghetto-life experience. Robin looked back up to the ceiling and smiled. A vivid picture of Kevin entered into her mind. She imagined it was pouring rain. They were outside, wrapped in each other's arms.

What Every Woman Wants

Chapter 6

A few hours later...

Robin stood in front of the dresser mirror, checking herself out. From head to toe, she was dressed in some of the top fashions in the world. She wore a Vera Wang frock, Manolo Blahnik shoes, with Chanel earrings and fragrance. Robin walked off of the elevator and into the underground garage where Tammy was sitting behind the wheel of her sky-blue Lexus coup, waiting on her. Just like Robin, Tammy was also dressed to impress. She was rocking her Manolo halter top, Baby Phat jeans, and Chloe perfume. When Robin walked over and got into the car, Tammy turned up the music on the CD player. As Patti LaBelle's soulful voice flowed out of the speakers, she put her car in drive and drove out of the garage. Thirty minutes later, they pulled into the AMC movie theater on Delaware Avenue. A new Will Smith movie was showing, so the parking lot was filled up with lots of cars. After finally finding a place to park, the two black beauties stepped out of the car and headed towards the crowded entrance.

After getting their movie ticket, they walked inside. The huge theater was crowded with all races of people. Blacks, whites, Spanish, and Asians were all coming and going.

"Come on, girl, we still got five minutes till the movie starts, let's grab some popcorn," Tammy suggested.

They walked over and joined the long popcorn line. As they stood there waiting for their turn, two attractive looking white men came up behind them. The two white men were smiling and checking the two black beauties out. Robin and Tammy had both noticed them staring, but neither said a word.

"Excuse me," one of the men said. Both women turned around and looked up at the tall, blond-haired Brad Pitt look-alike.

"Yeah," Robin said nonchalantly.

"Hi, my name is Tommy and this is my friend, Mike. We were just wondering if—"

Robin put up her right hand, stopping the man in mid-speech. With a serious look on her face, she stared into the man's piercing blue eyes and said, "Sorry, but we don't do white boys!" Then she turned back around without saying another word.

While Tammy stood there trying her best not to bust out in laughter, the two white men looked dumbfounded. After Robin and Tammy had gotten their popcorn, they turned around and noticed that the white men were gone.

"Damn, girl, that was cold," Tammy said, as they walked through the boisterous crowd of movie goers.

"Well, it's the truth, ain't it?"

Tammy nodded her head in agreement.

"There are too many fine-ass black brothers in the world for a sister to have to be with a white man," Robin stated.

"Preach girl!" Tammy cheered, as they found two empty seats and sat down.

"Maybe that's why they lock up all of our good, strong black men, so a sister will be out here running after a pink dick. Not me!" Robin said, as they both started laughing.

Two hours later, the movie had ended and they were back inside Tammy's car. They drove through the parking lot; they saw the same two white men from earlier standing in the lot and talking with two Asian women.

"Now that's more they type," Robin said, as she sat back checking the emails on her cell phone.

Tammy pulled into the condominium's garage and parked. Robin leaned over and gave her girlfriend a hug.

"I'll call you when I get in," Tammy said.

Robin stepped out of the car and walked over to the empty elevator. Before the elevator doors closed, Tammy was already out of the parking lot.

What Every Woman Wants

Thursday Night; West Philadelphia...

Kevin sat down on his bed and once again started looking at the new clothes that Robin had bought him. It was the first time that a woman, besides his mother, had bought him anything. His mother had told him all about Robin's surprised visit, and how she had really enjoyed Robin's company.

"She really likes you," she told Kevin.

After Kevin had eaten a delicious homemade chicken dinner, he took a long, hot shower and retreated back into his bedroom. When he returned to his room tried on the clothes, they fit him perfectly. From the first moment that Kevin had gotten into Robin's car, he felt an unusual attraction to her. Robin was actually one of the most gorgeous women he had ever laid eyes on. Even though Kevin had always dated attractive women, Robin Davis was in a league of her very own. However, what Kevin had also realized about the gorgeous Robin Davis was that she had been spoiled all her life. And that was one thing he would not let himself be a part of. Kevin was almost positive that Robin had men falling and running after her constantly, and he wouldn't have been surprised if there were a few women doing the same! Kevin knew that women like Robin were raised with platinum spoons in their mouths. He had nothing to offer her besides his honesty and love. These were the two things that most women would push to the side for lust and money. Kevin reached over to the dresser and grabbed a notepad and a pencil. Then he sat back comfortably on the bed and started writing a poem.

~

In the tranquility of her cozy bedroom, Robin had her slim, naked, brown body lying across her bed. Her eyes were somewhere lost in the back of her head. As soft moans escaped her mouth, and

49

she inhaled the exotic scent of the air, the smooth, soulful voice of Prince was flowing from out of the bedroom speakers.

Robin had her small black vibrator moving all around her moist clitoris. With a vivid picture of Kevin painted in her mind, she had already come once,. She was now working on her second orgasm. The combination of Prince's voice, tropical-scented candles, and her favorite sex toy, had Robin in a place of pure ecstasy.

"Ooh! Kevin Kevin! Oh yes, Kevin!! Yes, Daddy, yes!!!"

While at the movie with Tammy, she had been thinking about Kevin the whole time. The man already had a spell over her that no other man had before. Robin was determined to find out why. Kevin was a broke ex-felon who lived with his mother, but for some strange, unknown reason, Robin didn't care. There was a reason why Kevin Taylor was brought into her life; she was almost sure of it.

As the powerful second orgasm swept throughout her shivering naked body, Robin continued to mumble out his name.

"Kevin! Oh God, Kevin!! Yes!!!"

The sound of the telephone snapped Robin from out of her world of sexual bliss. She sat up on the bed, breathing heavily. After a deep sigh, Robin reached over and answered the ringing telephone.

"Hello?"

"Hey, my love, it's me, Charles. I was just lying here in bed, thinking about you," he said.

"Wow, what a strange coincidence; I was just in bed thinking about you, too," she lied.

Chapter 7

Friday Afternoon...

Robin's job at Power 99 FM radio station kept her busy. She was nestled inside of her office, finishing up a long, tiresome day. After turning off her computer without a moment's hesitation, she grabbed her cell phone and her brown Louis Vuitton tote bag, and walked out of her office. When she entered the parking lot, Trey and the white girl, Penny, were standing by his black Navigator, talking.

"Hold up Penny, I'll be right back," Trey said, as he strolled over to Robin's car.

"What's up, Pretty? I got my energy back; can I come over and see you tonight?" Trey flirted.

Robin just smiled as she got into her car and started it up. After rolling down the window, she said, "Come here, Trey, let me whisper something into your ear." Trey smiled and leaned down to give her his right ear.

"If you knew how to eat pussy, I would probably take your young, fine ass up on that offer. But since you don't, and all you got is a handsome face and a nice-sized dick, I think I am going to have to pass on your offer. I'll call you when I need another quickie," she said, with a smile on her face.

Trey stood up and watched as Robin rolled up the window and sped off out of the parking lot. After standing there with a dumbfounded expression on his face, he walked back over to the waiting Paris Hilton look alike.

The Philadelphia Federal Credit Union was located in the heart of Center City, Philadelphia. Tammy Washington was the bank's well-liked vice-president and had been working at there for almost five years. Tammy was a graduate of Temple University, with a Bachelor's Degree in finance and accounting. Her best friend,

Robin, had a received a Bachelor's in journalism and an Associate Degree in business management. They were the best of friends in college, and not a day had gone by without the two girls being seen together. All throughout college, they were two of the most popular students. Men from the basketball and football teams were all chasing after their attention. Hell. even a few of the professors were after them as well! While in college, they had created the "D.L.M. crew". There were three other pretty black women in the D.L.M. crew, and Robin was the crew's outspoken leader; the other three women's names were Dawn, Tanya, and Anissa. It was Robin who had made up the N1 rule, which later became their lifetime motto.

"No matter what, each girl in the crew had to one day marry a black man with a big dick, handsome face, and lots of money."

One night during one of their private dorm meetings, they had sworn on it. After college, they had all gone on to marry handsome, successful black men. Robin and Tammy were the last two members of the crew who were still single. They both had no children or serious, stable relationship. Since graduating, they had been two attractive women, running through lots of men, desperately searching for love.

Tammy was sitting inside her office, typing on her computer, when the soft tap on the door startled her. When she looked over to see who it was, Robin was standing there with a big smile on her face.

"Come in," Tammy gestured with her hand. Robin walked into the office holding a blue City blue shopping bag.

Tammy just shook her head and said, "So, what did you buy this time?"

"A blue Rocawear sweat-suit and a pair of white Air-Force Ones."

"Damn, girl, you really strung out on this man! I'm telling you, he better be worth it or I'm cutting you off," Tammy said, turning her computer off and standing up from her chair.

"Well, we're going back by his house, so you'll get to see him for yourself. So come on, you're off now, follow me over to my spot and get in my car," Robin said.

Twenty Minutes Later...

Cruising in Robin's car, the two women headed towards West Philly. Tammy looked over at her best friend and still couldn't believe that she had fallen for an ex-felon who lived at home with his mother and was broke! 'What is this world coming to?' she thought. First Bobby and Whitney break up, and now this! Just two days earlier, Robin was going over the D.L.M. golden rule, and now she was breaking her neck to go see a broke ex-con.

While Robin was driving, grinning from ear to ear, Tammy sat back with her arms crossed. As the car drove down 42nd and Girard Avenue, Tammy looked out the window and suddenly an image mesmerized her.

"Hold up, girl! Look at that fine-ass man! Pull over! Pull over, I gotta say something!" she said, excitedly.

"You sure? He might be a nut," Robin said, with a smile.

"Girl, just pull over, I'm not gonna get out of the car. Damn, he fine!" Tammy said, watching the man walk down the street.

"Okay, but make it fast," Robin said, as she pulled her car over to the side of the road. "Do your thing, girl."

Tammy pressed the button to lower the passenger-side window. "Excuse me, Handsome, but can I have a quick word with you?" Tammy said, with a grin on her face. The man stopped and stared at the two beautiful women inside the car. Tammy was lustfully eyeing him down from head to toe. Where have you been all my life, she thought.

"You promise not to bite?" he asked, walking over to the passenger window.

"Nope, I can't promise you that," Tammy flirted.

"How can I help you?" he said, showing his pearly white teeth. Robin sat there looking at the man, smiling.

"Hi, my name is Tammy, I was just telling my friend, Robin, here, how handsome you are. By any chance, are you single?" Tammy was definitely not shy.

"Yes, I am," he replied.

"Good. One for one." Tammy smiled; she couldn't take her eyes off of the man's gorgeous face.

"Well, I can give you my phone numbers and maybe you can give me a call. I'm always free, and very flexible," Tammy grinned, lustfully.

"Oh, I don't think I could do that, Tammy, but believe me, the offer is very tempting," he said.

"Do you mind telling me why?" Tammy said, with a perplexed look on her face.

The man looked deep into Tammy's lustful eyes and said, "Because I don't think your girlfriend would like that very much. Ain't that right, Robin?"

"Yes, Kevin," Robin said, in a soft, sexy voice. Tammy looked over at her blushing girlfriend and then back at Kevin, who was also blushing.

"Hell no! No the hell you didn't just play me like that!" Tammy said, embarrassed.

"I'm sorry, Tammy, but while you were talking, Robin was winking her eye at me and I just played along," Kevin said.

Tammy turned and said, "I'm going to get your ass back for this one!" Then they all busted out in laughter.

"Tammy, this is Kevin, the guy I told you about," Robin said, unable to take her eyes away from his face.

"Hi Kevin," she said, as they shook hands.

"Kevin, are you on your way home?" Robin asked.

"Yeah, I just got off the trolley."

"Hop in, I'll drop you off."

After Kevin got in the car, Robin pulled off down the street. Tammy still couldn't believe that this was the man that Robin had been talking about;. Everything she said about him had been true. The man was drop dead gorgeous, with a flawless smile that would

drive any woman wild. A few times, Tammy couldn't help herself
from turning around and looking at him, smiling and shaking her
head. Robin pulled up and got an empty parking space in front of
Kevin's house.

"Did you like the clothes?" she asked.

"Yes, thank you very much," he said.

"Good, cause that City blue bag on the backseat is yours also. I
saw something that I thought you might like," she said.

Kevin just sat there grinning and shaking his head. Damn, she's
persistent, he thought.

"Do you mind if I go in the house and put it up? Plus, I want to
go check on my mother."

"Sure, go ahead, and tell her I said hi," Robin said.

"I'll do that, I'll be right back," he said, grabbing the bag and
getting out of the car.

After Kevin had walked into the house, Tammy looked into
Robin's beaming eyes and said,

"Girl, let's do him together!"

"Nope! This ain't college no more," Robin teased.

"Damn, he's fine! Now I see why you been acting so crazy over
this man."

"I told you," Robin said, as she playfully pushed Tammy's
shoulder.

"You said he's been in prison for eight and a half years?"

"Yep!"

"No woman?"

"Nope!"

"You lucky bitch!" Tammy said, as she playfully returned the
push. "Robin, that man is gonna be a lot of trouble."

"Why do you say that?" Robin asked, in a serious tone.

"Girl, look at him, he's everything you ever wanted. If the sex is
as good as his fine face; you'll really be strung out. I ain't never
seen you act this way over a man before. Never! The only thing he
don't have is money, and you have enough for the both of y'all.
With all the money your parents left you, you never have to work a

day in your life. I just hope this guy is truly sincere about you, and he don't try to get you for every penny you own."

"Trust me, Tammy, Kevin's is a sweat-heart, I had a good talk with him and he's not deceitful. He ain't into some cash scam to play me for my money. I don't even think money fazes him. He's different, Tammy, I can feel it. Trust me, girl, I can feel it!" Robin assured her.

Tammy stared into Robin's eyes and saw a look she had never seen before.

"Okay, girl, I believe you," she smiled, breaking the eerie silence.

"So, what about Charles? That man bought you a Mercedes, clothes, jewels, and got you living inside one of his million-dollar condominiums for free. He don't even sweat you about the company you have over. We both know that Charles is deeply in love with you, Robin. He will feel played if you left him for another man! The man actually thinks you're gonna be his wife one day, and be the mother of his children." Tammy said, seriously.

"But Tammy, me and Charles are only friends, he knows this."

"That man loves you, Robin! He's only playing the friend game with you to give you your space. Plus, he's been busy getting his company off the ground with Nathan. But I can almost assure you that Charles is not concerned with anyone you're seeing, because he believes you're gonna marry him one day."

Both women got very quiet. Robin knew that everything Tammy had said was the truth.

"Well, I'm not in love with Charles.. Right now, I have to find out why I'm feeling Kevin so much. Who knows what will happen in the near future, I'll just play it by ear," Robin said.

"Just don't play yourself and end up with neither one of them. Remember, only one man can win." Tammy reached out and grabbed Robin's hand.

"Just be there for me," Robin said.

"Always." Tammy leaned over and gave her a warm hug. Just then, Kevin walked out the front door and over to the car.

"My mom was asleep, but I'll tell her you asked about her," he said.

"Are you busy tonight?" Robin asked.

"No, what's up?"

"How about me and Tammy treat you to a night out on the town? It's Friday, no work tomorrow," she said, blushing.

"I'm all ya'll's!" Kevin said, as he opened the door and got inside.

What Every Woman Wants

Chapter 8

An Hour Later...

Down on South Street, Robin, Tammy, and Kevin were all enjoying the calm September breeze and having a wonderful time out. South Street was crowded with lots of boisterous people. They were shopping and socializing. Music, laughter, and the smell of good food filled the air. Together, they sat outside at one of the small food tables and ate cheese-steaks and cheese-fries. After shopping at a few of the small boutiques that were still open. For Kevin, it was the most fun he had had in over eight and a half years. There was nothing like being a free man again, he thought.

The whole time, Robin held on to Kevin's hand, giving him all of her undivided attention. Every time she would catch another man staring at her, she would wrap her arms around Kevin's to show the man that she was happy and content with whom she was with. Kevin had spotted a few wandering eyes from men watching him and the two beautiful women, but he paid no mind. As long as he wasn't disrespected, they could stare all they wanted. Before they had left South Street, Robin bought a few new CDs to add to her already large music collection. Most of the CDs she had were given to her for free, a perk from working at the radio station. Still, once in a while, Robin would but some new CDs to support her favorite artists. With bags in hand, they all climbed back into the car and headed towards Delaware Avenue.

Fifteen minutes later, Robin pulled up and parked inside the crowded Dave & Buster's parking lot. Just like South Street, the place was packed with more boisterous people coming and going. While inside, they walked around talking, and playing some of the arcade games. After Kevin had tired both women out on the miniature basketball court, they all went over to the bar and ordered Heinekens and Coronas with lemon.

"Enjoying yourself, Kevin?" Robin asked, as they sat next to each other holding hands.

"Yes, I am!" I needed to get out," he said, showing his all thirty-two of his pearly whites.

Throughout the night, Tammy had been keeping her eyes on Kevin. She had finally come to the conclusion that Kevin was a genuinely nice person. He had a beautiful spirit about himself. Secretly, she wished that she could've met him first.

While they sat at the bar talking, Kevin had spotted a few familiar faces in the crowd. For a moment, he thought that he was seeing things, but when the people spotted Kevin staring, he knew that it was all too real. Kevin watched as the man and woman started walking towards the door.

"Come on, y'all, I see a few people I know," he said, getting up from his stool. Robin passed the bartender a twenty-dollar bill, and the two women followed behind Kevin.

Before the man and woman could make it out the exit, Kevin had caught up to them. "Vera, Gee, what's up?" he asked.

The two people turned around and faced him; both had shocked looks on their faces. Robin and Tammy stood on Kevin's side, not saying a word, but each was eyeing down the short, attractive woman.

"Kevin, what's up? I heard you just got home," Gee said, extending out his hand. Kevin was very hesitant, but he decided to shake Gee's hand.

Gee was a tall, slim, dark-skinned man, with handsome features. He was also Kevin's first cousin. The woman's name was Vera. Before Kevin had gone off to serve his time in federal prison, she was the love of his life K until she had abandoned him and eventually married his own cousin.

"What's up, Vera?" Kevin said.

"Nothing, just hanging out," she said, staring at the man whom she had left many years ago. Still, deep down inside, Vera had never stopped loving Kevin.

"Robin, Tammy, this is my cousin, Gee, and this is Vera, Gee's wife. "She was once my ex-fiancée"

Kevin said, with a serious look in his eyes.

"Damn!" Robin blurted out. Tammy stood there, tightening her lips and shaking her head.

"Kevin, I know " Vera began.

"It's cool, Vera, things happen and people move on with their lives," he said, cutting her off.

Robin stood there, staring in Vera's face, waiting for her to say one wrong word so she could be all over her ass like white on rice. "Well, it's good to see you, Kevin, but me and my wife have to go," Gee said, knowing that his words would pierce Kevin right through the heart.

"Y'all take care," Kevin said, as he watched his cousin and ex-fiancée hurry away.

Before Vera had walked out the door, she turned around and looked at Kevin for one last time. Even from a distance, Kevin could see the tears welling up in her eyes.

"You okay?" Robin asked.

"Yeah, I'm fine," Kevin said, as he put his arms around the two beautiful women.

"Let's finish enjoying ourselves, tonight is still young."

An hour later, they walked out of Dave & Busters and got back into Robin's car. Tammy's cell phone had been ringing like crazy. While Kevin sat up front, talking to Robin, Tammy was in the back whispering into her cell phone. Every now and then she would let out a low giggle.

After closing her cell phone, Tammy said, "Robin, I need you to drop me off at my car."

"Damn, it's only eleven o'clock!" Robin said.

"Y'all two can enjoy the rest of the night without me, I have something to do," Tammy grinned.

"Whatever!" Robin said, making a u-turn and heading towards her condominium building.

Twenty minutes later, Robin entered the underground parking garage and pulled next to Tammy's Lexus. After saying their goodbyes, Tammy rushed over to her car and got inside. Seconds later, she was speeding out of the garage.

"My place is on the thirty-fifth floor, you feel like coming up for a few?" Robin asked.

Kevin looked into Robin's beautiful eyes, he couldn't resist her.

"Yeah, why not, but only for a few.," he said.

"Don't worry, Handsome, I'll try my best not to kidnap you," she said, as they both got out of the car.

On the elevator ride up to the thirty-fifth floor, Robin could feel her heart pounding in her chest. She was yearning to feel Kevin's soft red lips pressed against hers. When they entered into the elegant condo, Kevin stood there admiring the place.

"This is a very nice spot," he said, checking out her state-of-the-art entertainment system.

"Thanks, I decorated it myself," Robin said, as she sat her small shopping bag down on the floor. "Music?"

"Yeah, that would be nice," Kevin said, walking over and taking a seat on the sofa. Robin walked over to the CD player and turned it on.

"What do you like?" she asked.

"Something smooth and laid back."

"Got you!" Robin said, going through her plethora of CDs. Suddenly, the smooth, soulful voice of Maxwell flowed out of the speakers. Robin's body was burning with desire, but she was trying her best to remain calm.

When she walked over to the sofa, Kevin stood up and said, "Let's go out on the balcony."

"Great idea," Robin agreed, as she grabbed his hand and walked him out onto the balcony.

"It's a beautiful night, isn't it?" Kevin said, looking out at the full yellow moon and bright shining stars.

"Perfect, if you ask me," Robin said, as she wrapped Kevin's strong tattooed arms around her waist. Staring into Kevin's eyes, Robin asked softly, "Can I please have a kiss?"

With a smile on his face, Kevin leaned forward and they started passionately kissing. For almost five whole minutes, they kissed without a break. Kevin had Robin gripped inside his arms. As their lips danced in unison, they were both completely turned on. However, taking Robin to bed, and making love to her, was not what Kevin had in mind that night. I will not make the same mistake twice, he thought.

When Kevin pulled his lips away from Robin's, she had a perplexed look on her face.

"What's wrong?" Robin asked with concern.

Her body burning with desire, and her thong moist from sexual anticipation. Right then, she wanted Kevin more than she had ever wanted any man in her life. Kevin could plainly see it in her beaming eyes.

"I don't think this was a good idea for me to come to your place," he said.

"Why not?" asked Robin, as she wrapped her arms around his neck. "Is it me?"

"No, it's not you Robin, it's me."

"Please, Kevin, why don't you stay tonight and we'll just chill in each other's arms," she said with a smile.

"I can't, because we both know what will happen if I do that, and that's not why I came up here. I have respect for you Robin, and I have bigger respect for myself."

Robin looked into Kevin's serious eyes and knew there would be no changing his mind. He was more of an enigma than she had thought. This only made her want him more! Still, her burning desire and persistence wouldn't give up.

"Please stay! I promise you that nothing will happen between us, just keep me company. Please," she begged.

Kevin smiled and kissed her gently on the lips.

"No. If I stay, not even a pack of wolves could keep me off of you," he said.

"Well, just tell my why? Why won't you stay, Kevin?"

"Because I want whatever we have to be more than just sex. Sex is a beautiful thing when two people are on that same emotional and spiritual level of understanding. But sex can also be the beginning of a relationship's downfall. What I'm saying is, why sex each other now when we can take our time and maybe one day, make love to each other in the future?"

Robin stood there, feeling the profound words sweeping through her entire body. Kevin could feel her body shivering inside his arms. Robin had never had a man turn down anything she offered—until Kevin Taylor entered her life. Kevin watched as tears fell down from the corner of her eyes.

"Where did you come from?" she muttered softly.

Kevin wiped her tears away with his hand, kissed Robin on the lips, and whispered, "Prison."

Then they both started laughing. Minutes later, they were pulling up in front of Kevin's mother's house. After a long, passionate kiss, Kevin grabbed the bag of new stuff that Robin bought him and opened the car door.

"I really enjoyed myself tonight," he said.

"Me too. Can I see you tomorrow?" Robin asked, holding on to his hand.

"No, not tomorrow, I have a few things to do with my mother," he said.

Robin frowned like a little child.

"How about Sunday, after I come home from church?" Kevin asked.

"Church?!" Robin said, in a shocked voice.

"Yeah, what's wrong with Church?"

"Nothing, I just never figured you to be the church type, that's all."

"I'm full of surprises, hopefully one day you'll see," Kevin grinned. "Oh, I almost forgot," Kevin reached into his pocket and pulled out a folded piece of paper.

"What's this?" Robin asked, as Kevin passed her the paper.

"A poem I wrote for you last night. I hope you like it," Kevin said, stepping out of the car.

"I'm sure I will." Robin watched as Kevin waved goodbye and walked to his front door.

"Since you got my phone number now, call me when you get in the house, so I'll know you're okay."

"I will," Robin said, as she started her car back up and drove off down the street.

With a big smile on his face, Kevin opened the front door and went inside the house.

~

On the drive back home, Robin couldn't get Kevin off her mind. She still couldn't believe that she had shed tears in front of him. Robin could feel her heart being slowly stolen away. There was nothing she could do about it. She looked at the small folded up piece of paper and smiled. It was the first poem that anyone had ever written for her, and she couldn't wait to get back home, lie in bed, and read it.

Robin called Tammy on her cell phone, but she didn't answer. She wondered who the lucky guy was tonight. Tammy always kept one on speed-dial.

After Robin got back home, she called Kevin to let him know that she had gotten in safely. They had a brief conversation, and hung up their phones. Robin went and took a relaxing hot shower. When she finished, she put on lotion and a white Vera Wang silk-chiffon nightgown, and climbed into bed. In the tranquility of her cozy master bedroom, only the soulful voice of Luther Vandross could be heard, coming from the two bedroom speakers. Robin reached over to the nightstand and grabbed the folded-up piece of paper. She got herself more comfortable in bed, then unfolded the paper and started reading.

"Your beauty saved me

When I looked into your eyes, I could honestly feel a strange, wonderful feeling entering into the depths of my hurting soul; a soul that had been yearning to be loved cherished and set free from the chains of loneliness and anguish.

Your beauty saved me from a world of ugliness. And your beauty rescued me from drowning in my own ocean of tears.

Your beauty saved me

Your beauty saved me from the darkness and showed me light

Your beauty saved me.

But the beauty I am talking about is not of the outer flesh, but of that lovely magnetic spirit that lives inside of you. I can see and feel what you can't.

Thank you for saving me and sharing your true inner beauty.

Thank you for saving me and following your intuition.

Thank you for saving me and listening to the inner voices inside your soul.

What I see inside of you is much more beautiful than what my eyes see on the outside. I just hope that one day you'll see the same thing in me."

Robin sat there as a stream of tears fell down her face. She sat on her bed completely still, lost in a world that she had never known existed before. The words from Kevin's poem had made love to her soul; bringing orgasms to her yearning spirit. The feeling was more wonderful than any sex she had ever had.

Robin tearfully reached for her phone. When she called Tammy, there was still no answer.

"Damn, Girl, who the hell got you up all night?" she said, before hanging up the phone and lying back on the bed.

What Every Woman Wants

As she stared up at the ceiling, she smiled. Robin knew that the handsome stranger she met at the bust stop was definitely her soul mate.

What Every Woman Wants

Chapter 9

New York City...

Inside the Hilton Hotel, the group of naked men and women were inside a large private suite, enjoying their weekly orgy party. The lights were dimly lit all throughout the suite. They were people of all different races: white, black, Indian, Spanish, and Asian K and they all had two things in common; they were all rich bisexuals. They were thirty-five members of a secret bisexual organization that traveled and met up all around the country, for their bisexual orgy parties. Their group had private spots in Miami, New York, Philly, Chicago, L.A., San Francisco, Atlanta, and New Orleans. The name of their secret organization was D.W.A.M. - the acronym stood for "Doing Women And Men". The thirty-five member secret society consisted of lawyers, judges, doctors, stock brokers, and real estate investors. For over five years, they had been meeting almost every week, faithfully, at different locations all over the country.

Nathan was standing on top of a blue floor mat, with an attractive older blond-haired woman, fucking her hard from behind. Her loud moans filled the air as naked men and women were walking around, sipping on glasses of champagne. Nathan had the woman's long blond hair wrapped around his hand, He gave her long powerful strokes from behind. Out of all the members of D.W.A.M., Nathan was her favorite. When Nathan glanced over to his side, he winked and smiled at the three naked men on the floor beside him. His business partner and friend, Charles, was pleasing a short Asian man with oral sex. While at the same time, an older white man had Charles straddled from behind, fucking him in the ass.

Since they were juniors in college, Charles and Nathan had been secret bisexual lovers. Until joining D.W.A.M., they had kept their dark secret all to themselves. Both men had had many partners, but Nathan was a married man with two children.

Still, Charles was deeply in love with Robin, and he was determined to one day make her his wife. He felt that once she became his wife, he could tell her the truth and Robin would accept who he really was. That was one reason why he didn't worry about the other people Robin slept around with; Charles knew it was only sex K nothing less, nothing more.

For years, Charles and Nathan had been living secret double lives. They were two bisexual men whose only concerns were establishing connections for more wealth, power, and sex. If their secret were ever exposed, it would cause a lot of people hurt and devastation. This would not only destroy them, but the people who truly cared about them.

When Charles had got up off the floor, he walked over to Nathan, who was now standing over by a wall in the corner.
"Enjoying yourself today?" Nathan asked.

"Always. I can't wait to meet out in L.A. next." Charles replied.

"That's next Thursday and Friday. Remember, Friday's Robin's birthday."

"I know, but I already bought her a gift. She'll get it, and I'll give her another excuse on why I can't be there to share her birthday with her." Charles smiled.

"Like what?"

"Like I have a very important meeting in L.A. and it's mandatory that you and I be there," he said. They both started laughing.

~

Saturday Morning...
The sound of the ringing telephone woke Robin up from a peaceful dream she was having.

"Hello," she answered.

"Girl, wake up, it's almost 10 o'clock," Tammy said.

"Why ain't you answer the phone? I was trying you all night," Robin said, sitting up in bed.

"That's why I'm calling you now to tell you all the good news," Tammy said, excitedly.

"What good news?"

"Hakeem! Girl, he was a maniac last night!" Tammy said, enthusiastically.

"You fucked Hakeem already?"

"It wasn't supposed to turn out that way, but you know how shit happens."

"Okay, tramp, run it down," Robin said, then listened eagerly.

"Well, that was Hakeem who I was talking to on my cell phone last night. He asked me to come by and pick him up, so we could go for a ride and talk. We drove down to Penn's Landing and just kicked it and talked. Then I asked if he wanted to come by my house for a little while."

"Uh ha!" Robin interrupted.

"Just listen. Anyway, we watched a DVD and cuddled up on the sofa. I swear, Robin, I had no intention of sleeping with Hakeem, but once he started kissing me around my neck, girl you know that's my spot, I just couldn't resist his fine ass. The man sucked my toes and had me crawling all over the couch."

"And what else?" asked Robin; now wide awake and all ears.

"After he undressed me, right there on the sofa, Hakeem got down between my legs and ate the shit out of my pussy. Girl, the man ate my pussy like it was the last oyster in a seafood restaurant!"

"Oh shit!" Robin laughed out.

"Then we sexed all over the living room. We ain't even make it upstairs to my bedroom! Not only is Hakeem packing, he know just how to work it. Robin, I'm telling you girl, it's something in that ghetto water they be drinking. Last night, Hakeem took me way past cloud nine, and I'm still trying to catch a ride back to Earth!" Tammy said, as they both started laughing.

"So you must really like him, huh?"

"Yeah, a lot, I'm seeing him again today," Tammy said, with a smile.

"Okay tramp, now tell me the bad news," Robin said seriously.

After a long sigh, Tammy said, "He has a 3-year-old daughter and a baby-mama he can't hardly stand. Plus, he just got laid off at his post office job. Now he is renting out a bedroom at his cousin's house on Lansdowne Avenue."

"Do he have a car?"

"Yeah, but it was towed a few weeks ago because of some overdue parking tickets he never paid. Damn, Robin, what happened to us?"

"What do you mean?"

"I mean, look at us. I'm twenty-nine, about to turn thirty, and you'll be thirty-one next Friday. Every man that I have ever slept with, before Hakeem, has made more money than me. Most of them are college graduates who own their own companies or work at Fortune 500 companies with high-paying executive positions. Since college, I've been dating only professionals, while I search for my D.L.M. that I've never come close to finding. Now, I meet this fine twenty-four year old man who has nothing to really offer me but some good sex. I feel more comfortable with him that all of them other men I have ever known. Last night, after we had finished, for the fourth time—I might add," Tammy giggled, "I laid across the sofa listening to Hakeem tell me about his life. When he had finally finished, I swear, Robin, I could feel all of his pain. He was honest about everything, and for the first time in my life, I didn't hold it against him as a person. I honestly could feel Hakeem's heart speaking to me," Tammy said, seriously. "Look at you, Robin, you have one of the most successful black real estate investors in the country breaking his neck to give you a world of luxury and you can't get Kevin off your mind. This guy is an ex-felon who lives with his mother, for God's sake! What's going on?"

"I don't know, Tammy, I really don't know," Robin muttered softly.

"This wasn't supposed to happen, Robin!"

"Maybe it was, Tammy. Maybe all this time, we were searching for the right men in the wrong circles?"

"So what happened with you and Kevin last night? And don't hold nothing back," Tammy said.

"We kissed."

"And?"

"And we talked."

"And?"

"And then he asked me to take him back home."

"What? Stop lying! Ain't no way you ain't get that man in your condo and didn't take him to bed. No way!" Tammy said, seriously.

"It's the truth, Tammy. We talked and kissed and that was it. He asked me to take him home because he didn't want nothing to happen."

"Hell no! Hell no! Hell no! You mean to tell me that a man turned down a chance to sleep with the beautiful Robin Davis? No fucking way!" Tammy shouted.

"He ain't gay, is he?"

"No, he ain't gay," Robin laughed.

"I thought you told me that Kevin just got out of prison?"

"He did."

"You mean to tell me that a man who had just finished doing almost ten years in prison didn't want to have sex with you?" Tammy said, clearly confused.

"Yup! After he explained why, I understood," Robin said.

"Okay, why didn't he?"

"Because, Tammy, Kevin wants more than sex! Sex is not everything to him, and plus, he's been hurt before, by the little tramp who left him and ran off and married his cousin. That's why," Robin said, "but he did "

"He did what?" Tammy interrupted.

"Kevin wrote me a poem," Robin said, with a smile.

"A poem?"

71

"Yes, Tammy, a poem and it's nice, too. I read it about five times last night. "

"Damn, ain't nobody ever wrote me a poem," Tammy said.

"What do it say?" Robin reached over to the nightstand and grabbed the folded up piece of paper. After reading the poem, Tammy said, "Wow! He's deep, girl. That poem is serious. Did you cry?"

"No," Robin lied. "What time are you and Hakeem getting back together?" Robin asked, changing the subject.

"I'm picking him up around seven-thirty, why?"

"Just asking."

"Are you seeing Kevin today?"

"No, he told me that he had some things to do with his mother today. I'm going to see him on Sunday after he gets out of church."

"Church?!" Tammy said, surprised.

"Yes, Tammy, you heard me correct, church."

"Kevin goes to church," she stated as a matter of a fact.

"Yes, Tammy, now drive over and I will tell you all the rest on our way over to Starbucks," Robin said, cutting her off.

"Why do we have to go to Starbucks?"

"Because it's Saturday, the two maids will be here soon to clean up the place. Now, let me hurry up and get myself ready, bye."

"Bye," Tammy said, as they both hung up the phone.

What Every Woman Wants

Chapter 10

A Short While Later...

Robin and Tammy left Starbucks and got back into Tammy's Lexus. They then headed over to the Gallery Shopping Mall, on 9th and Market Street. While inside the mall, they were constantly being hit on by men. Young, old, black, and even a few white man had tried their hand, but none were successful. Robin and Tammy were both used to being hit on by men. They were two attractive black women, whose beauty demanded attention. But today was much different from all the other times they went shopping together. Today was the first time in years that neither one of them had taken or given a man their phone number. There were several reasons for this strange occurrence. Robin couldn't get Kevin from out of her system no matter how hard she tried, Tammy, was also caught up and indifferent. She was feeling her young lover, Hakeem, more than she had expected.

An hour later, they walked out of the Gallery Mall, with two shopping bags each. After getting back into Tammy's car, Tammy drove Robin back to her plush downtown condominium; they parked just a few feet away from the garage elevator.

"Since you're not seeing Kevin today, what else do you have planned?" Tammy asked Robin.

"I'm just chillin' today. I'll probably go in and surf the net, check out my email and a few sites, then lay back and listen to my music. I just bought that new Ericka Badu CD that I've been looking forward to listening to," Robin replied.

"Well, I'm going back home to take me a nice long bubble bath. Then I'll get myself ready for Hakeem tonight." Tammy smiled.

"Oh, I almost forgot to tell you, I talked to T.J. yesterday, she'll be back in town on Monday."

"Where is she now?"

"She called from New York."

"Wow, I bet that's a lot of fun, having a job that takes you all over the country for free. Maybe we should have been airline stewardesses," Tammy said, jokingly.

"I'm sure she meets a lot of different types of people. However, I'm fine with my two or three airplane trips a year," Robin said.

"Well, just remember, one of those trips is how y'all two met," Tammy said, with a grin.

"Do she know about Kevin?"

"I told her, she said she was happy for me. I'll tell her more Monday," Robin blushed.

"That's nice that you and T.J. have a good relationship like that. That's the reason y'all two get along so well, because y'all are both very honest with each other."

"And I enjoy talking to her just as much as I enjoy having sex with her," Robin admitted, truthfully.

"Anyway, let me know how your date with Hakeem turns out. Call me when you get in tonight."

"How about I just call you in the morning?" Tammy asked, with a smile.

"Okay, Miss Hot-ass, just make sure your new young thug strap up," Robin said, as she grabbed her two bags and got out of the car.

"Always! I ain't ready to be nobody's mother, and I damn sure ain't ready to die young," Tammy said, in a serious tone.

After Robin had shut the door, she watched as Tammy waved goodbye and drove out of the garage. With the two shopping bags in her hand, she walked over and got on the parking lot elevator. When the elevator had stopped on the thirty-fifth floor, Robin stepped off and walked over to her condo unit. When Robin opened the door, the pungent scent of burning strawberry candles filled the air. She looked around at the vacuumed carpet and shining glass coffee table. Once again, Maria and her niece, Carla, had done a terrific job. With a big smile plastered across her face, she carried the two shopping bags back towards her cozy bedroom.

West Philadelphia...

Kevin was lying across the bed, staring up at the ceiling. He was thinking about two things; finding himself a job, and his new beautiful friend Robin. Kevin thought about how he had to suppress every sexual urge inside of his body when they were together inside Robin's condo. Her kisses alone had sent chills all throughout his body. He was positive that the sex would've done the same; but Kevin wanted more than sex.

While serving time in prison, Kevin had made a promise to himself. The next woman he invited into his heart would be a woman that loved him unconditionally. She would not be a woman who would abandon him as soon as things got a little rough, but a God-fearing woman who would love him if he was rich or poor—a soul-mate. The tap on the door snapped Kevin away from his daydream.

"Come in, Mom."

Mrs. Silvia opened the door and stuck her head inside.

"Kevin, you have a visitor downstairs," she said, then turned and walked away.

Kevin quickly got up and slid into his bedroom slippers. He wasn't expecting anyone to come by and see him. With a smile on his face, he had a good idea of who the person was. Kevin walked out of his bedroom and rushed down the stairs. When he saw who it was that was waiting for him, the smile faded from his face. Standing there with a strange look on her face was his ex-girlfriend Vera. She was by herself.

Kevin slowly walked up to her and said, "What's up, where's your husband?"

"He's at home, I told him that I needed to make a quick run," Vera replied, staring deep into Kevin's brown eyes.

"Kevin, I'm sorry! Please believe me!" Her eyes welled up with tears.

"You left me for dead, Vera! You let ten years scare you away."

"Kevin, back then I was confused. A lot was going on around that time. Kevin, ten years sounded like forever. I was twenty-seven years old, and I was going through a lot of personal problems with you, my job, my family "

"You left me, Vera! All those years we shared together meant nothing to you! Our love was a joke," Kevin replied, "and not only did you leave me, but you married my own cousin!"

Kevin looked deep into Vera's eyes, watching as the tears streamed down her beautiful face.

"Kevin, I never stopped loving you! Believe me, I thought about you every single day you was away," she cried.

"Vera, stop lying to yourself! You were out here living your life; partying and doing everything else you wanted to do. I heard all about you, so save it!"

"They were all lies!" she yelled, wiping her tears away.

"So was marrying my cousin a lie, too? Huh?!" Kevin snapped back in anger.

"Kevin, please, Gee was there for me after you went to prison."

"Save it! Please, just save it, Vera. You've run out of excuses and I'm done hearing your sob story. I'm free now! Free of you and people like you. You made your bed, now go lay in it with my cousin," Kevin said, walking over to the front door.

"Kevin, please!"

Kevin opened the front door and stood there, waiting for Vera to leave. When she approached the door, he grabbed her arm; her eyes were filled with an ocean of hurting tears.

"Do you remember that Regina Bell song you would always sing to me?" he asked.

"True love will never die, long after the sun has lost its shine," Vera recited softly.

Kevin stared deeply into her eyes and said, "You were absolutely right, Vera, true love never dies, only the phony "

When Vera walked out of the house, Kevin slammed the door and walked back upstairs to his bedroom.

What Every Woman Wants

Inside her cozy bedroom, Mrs. Silvia was sitting on the bed with a big smile on her face. It wasn't that she didn't like Vera; that was not the case at all. She had only wanted the best for her son and she knew that his ex-girlfriend wasn't the right person for him.

~

Later That Night...

After brief conversations on the phone with Charles and Trey, Robin walked out onto the balcony, holding a glass of white Zinfandel wine. The tranquil night sky was filled with stars. Robin sipped on her wine and stared out at the magnificently lit city that surrounded her. At night, the city of Philadelphia was a marvelous sight to see. This was far from the first time that she had stepped out on the balcony and enjoyed its wonder.

After drinking all of the wine in her glass, Robin turned and walked off the balcony. She looked over at the shopping bag by the door; it was filled with all the new stuff she had bought for Kevin. When she was at the mall, Robin had bought Kevin over a thousand dollars worth of gifts. She purchased a black leather jacket, jeans, shirts, belt, hat, and a new cell phone.

Robin walked over to the stereo and searched through her rack of CDs. When Robin found what she was searching for, she slid the disc into the CD player and pressed the play button. Instantly, Marvin Gaye's classic, "Sexual Healing," flowed out of the speakers. The smooth sound of Marvin's soulful voice filled the room as she walked over and relaxed herself on the soft leather sofa. The wine had her feeling tipsy, and in the mood for some sexual healing of her own. Robin set the empty glass on the coffee table. She then closed her eyes and slid her right hand down into her moist pink Victoria's Secret thong. In the privacy of her living room, Robin fantasized about Kevin,. She sat back and pleased herself until her body was taken over by a wonderful orgasm.

"Oh yes! Yes, Daddy, fuck me harder! Harder!" Tammy yelled out.

Hakeem was standing, holding Tammy's body in his muscular arms, her legs wrapped around his hips. Running sweat covered both of their naked bodies.

After they had enjoyed a wonderful dinner and movie, they got back inside Tammy's car and drove straight to her South Philly townhouse. Now, Tammy was being blown-away by her young, skilled lover; Hakeem was like no man she had ever had. For the first time in Tammy's life, she had met a man who was more sexually aggressive than she was K a man that Tammy thought she would never find.

They made love inside every room in the house; even down in the basement, where Hakeem had sat on the washing machine on spin cycle, to add more vibrations to their passionate love-making. Tammy was on cloud nine, she came two times before the machine had stopped. For three straight hours, Tammy's cell phone and house phone had both been ringing off the hook. Whoever it was had called her at a bad time, because tonight her gifted young lover was getting all of her undivided attention.

"Oh Hakeem! Fuck me harder! Harder!" Tammy grunted as her body bounced up and down on his dick.

Hakeem walked Tammy out of the bedroom, and down the stairs. She was still wrapped tightly around his body, resting her head on his sweaty chest. When they entered the living room, Hakeem knocked off everything that was on the large wooden living room table. Then he gently laid Tammy's body across the table, on her stomach. Tammy didn't say a word as she watched him climb on top of the table and kneel behind her. Hakeem reached out and grabbed a handful of Tammy's long black hair. Then, in one smooth motion, he slid his dick back into her wet love tunnel. Once again,

Tammy was lost in ecstasy; and if she never returned to Earth again, it would be just fine with her.

Chapter 11

Sunday Morning...

"Robin, he's amazing! And he's so mature for his age, it's scary!" Tammy gushed.

"So, did you get any sleep?" Robin asked with a grin.

"Yeah, we got a few hours in, but then we were right back at it again. We did it twice this morning!" Tammy said, excitedly.

"Where is your young stud at now?"

"He's in the bathroom, taking a shower."

"And you're not in there with him?"

"No, I'm trying to save my energy for tonight," Tammy chuckled.

"Tonight?"

"Yeah, Hakeem's staying over here tonight, I'll drop him off at his cousin's on my way to work in the morning."

"Do y'all two have any other plans for today?" Robin asked.

"I'm about to cook us a nice breakfast and then I'm gonna drive over to his child's momma's house so he can give her some money, and see his daughter."

"Damn, I can't believe I'm hearing those words coming out of your mouth. Cooking breakfast and driving over to his baby momma's house; who would ever believe it?"

"Yeah, tell me about it! I can hardly believe it myself. But at the same time, I'm wondering where the hell this man has been all my life," Tammy said, as they both started laughing.

"So far, I got my D. and L., now I just gotta find a way to help Hakeem get his M. right, feel me?"

"All the way. I might end up in that same predicament with Kevin."

"So you think the sex is gonna be all that?" Tammy asked, curiously.

79

"I hope so, girl, especially after I keep hearing about you and Hakeem," Robin replied.

"So, Robin, are you still gonna do that?"

"Yup, I'm dressed and ready to go out the door."

"I wish I could be there to see their faces."

"Too bad, Tammy, I'll call you later. Love you."

"Love you, girl. Bye," Tammy said, as they both hung up the phones.

When Tammy hung up and turned around, Hakeem was standing there with nothing on but a white towel wrapped around his waist. "Since I still have about an hour and a half, I figured that we can get in a quickie before breakfast," he said.

Tammy lifted the white T-shirt over her head and said, "I'm all yours, Daddy." Then she ran over and jumped her naked body on top of the bed.

~

Southwest Philadelphia...

Inside his small two-bedroom apartment, Trey was straddled on top of Penny's white naked body, stroking her with everything he had.

"Oh! Ahh! Ohh! Ooooh! I'm coming again Trey! Oh Trey!" Penny yelled out in ecstasy.

Moments later, they both came at the same time. Trey slumped down on Penny's petite white body.

"I love you, Trey! I swear, I love you and that big black dick of yours!" Penny said, as she rubbed her hands up and down his sweaty back.

Trey didn't say a word. He knew he had Penny strung since the first time they had sex a month earlier. Not only was Trey sleeping with Robin and Penny, but the young handsome stud was also sleeping with Sherri Star, the radio station's new afternoon disc jockey. None of the women at his job had known that Trey was sleeping around with other coworkers, but none of the other women in Trey's life had him open like Robin did. She was the only woman that Trey couldn't control, and it had made him want her even more.

"I'm hungry, go make me something to eat!" Trey said, as he rolled over on the bed. Penny quickly sat up and grabbed a yellow T-shirt off the floor. Then Trey watched as she put it on and joyfully walked out of the bedroom. With his hands behind his head, Trey felt like a king inside his own castle. The sex with Penny was good, but deep down he wished the pretty young snow bunny was the beautiful Robin Davis instead.

~

West Philadelphia...

The Mount Pleasant Baptist Church was filled to capacity. People were crying and calling on the Lord. The church was large and spacious, and the home of so many believers who showed up faithfully every Sunday. In the middle row, Kevin and Mrs. Silvia were seated with their Holy Bibles inside their hands. A short, older, dark-skinned preacher was on stage delivering another moving sermon, and people were feeling the Holy Ghost everywhere. The twelve-member choir stood over to the left of the preacher, watching and listening to all his poignant words.

"The Bible tells us that adultery is a sin, but every day, everywhere you look there's someone sleeping around with somebody else's husband or wife! The Bible says to love your neighbor like you love yourself, but people are sleeping with their neighbor's wife and then shooting the man in the back! Women are divorcing their husbands a year after vowing to God, till death do us part!' The Devil is alive and well, ladies and gentlemen! He's sneaking around, snatching up the souls of the weak!" The preacher shouted excitedly.

"Amen!" a man shouted, as people stood up in their chairs, clapping and feeling the power of the Holy word.

What Every Woman Wants

Robin was standing in the back of the church, holding back tears. This was the first time she had been to a Baptist church since the death of her parents, when they would all get dressed and go to church together. That was thirteen years ago, when she was an eighteen year old freshman student in college.

It had felt like every word the preacher was speaking was directed to her. Robin got her composure together and slowly walked down the middle aisle. Like always, she was looking as glamorous as ever. She was dressed in a white Versace jacket and matching pants, with a pair of white Versace open-toed heels that showed off her freshly pedicure toes. She had small pearl studs in her ears, with a matching pearl necklace around her neck, and her long silky black hair was tied in a small knot and hanging in a small ponytail. Wandering eyes watched as the beautiful black woman took her time walking down the aisle. When Mrs. Silvia spotted Robin walking down her row, a big smile came to both of their faces. Kevin was too busy reading his Bible to notice; focused on the deep scriptures in the book of Ecclesiastic. When he finally looked up, Robin was grinning and sitting down beside him.

"How did you know?"

Robin put her finger to her mouth and silenced him. Then she put her mouth to his ear and whispered, "When a woman wants something really bad enough, she finds a way to make it happen." Then she turned to Mrs. Silvia and winked her eye.

As the pungent scent of Robin's Vera Wang perfume escaped into the air, she reached down and grabbed Kevin's hand. She then leaned over once again and whispered into his ear.

"That poem was amazing. Furthermore, I believe you're helping to save me also," she said.

"From what?"

"From myself," Robin said, with a serious look in her eyes.

After church had ended, they all walked outside together. Kevin still couldn't believe that Robin had shown up at his church. He just couldn't figure this woman out.

"How did y'all get down here?" Robin asked, as they stood around watching the church goers moving in every different direction.

"We caught the bus," Mrs. Silvia replied.

"Well, my car is parked right around the corner, how about we all go get something to eat and then I drop y'all off back at home? My treat," Robin offered.

Kevin just stood there, staring at Robin. So many thoughts were running around his confused head. Where did she come from? Wow, she's beautiful! But does she think she can just buy my love? Is she another Vera in disguise? Whatever it was, Kevin was sure that he would find out soon. This time, giving his heart away to a woman wouldn't be as easy as before.

"What did you have in mind?" Kevin asked.

"There's a Denny's and an I.H.O.P. on City Line Avenue, you decide," she said, as they started walking down the street.

"Denny's is fine with me," Kevin said.

"Then Denny's is it," Robin agreed, as she reached and grabbed Kevin's hand.

Mrs. Silvia smiled and watched as Robin did her thing. She knew that Robin was the type of woman that her son needed in his life—a woman who wasn't afraid to take control. Robin had reminded her of herself when she was around that age. Now, all she could hope and pray for was that Robin wouldn't make the same costly mistakes that she had once made. One thing was for sure, Mrs. Silvia would try her best to make sure that the beautiful young woman didn't. For her only child, she felt there was no limit to helping him finally find some happiness in his life.

~

North Philadelphia...

The blue Lexus pulled up and parked in front of a small row house on Eighteenth and Diamond Street. Two young black women were sitting outside on the small concrete steps. Hakeem

83

opened the door and got out of the car. The two young women were staring at Tammy, who was sitting behind the wheel, not paying them any mind at all. Inside her yellow and white Chanel bag was her licensed-to-carry three eighty pistol. And if her life was threatened, Tammy would not hesitate to bust a cap in the first hood rat's ass who got up in her face.

Tammy pushed in her Jaguar Wright CD and reclined back into her soft leather seat. Even with both of her eyes closed, she could still feel the piercing eyes of hate and jealousy watching her very closely.

Hakeem followed one of the women inside the house. As soon as she shut the door, she said, "Nigga, who that bitch you got outside my house?"

"She ain't no bitch, Keisha, and it's none of your business who I'm with!" Hakeem said.

"Nigga, you some shit! That's why I can't stand your sorry, broke ass!" Keisha yelled.

Hakeem looked at the mother of his child and just shook his head in total disgust. Even though he loved his daughter more than anything else in the world, he sometimes wished that he never had conceived her with Keisha. Keisha was a twenty-one year old hood rat, with a pretty face and a fat ass. She's a high school dropout. She never made it passed the eleventh grade. She was the type who sat around watching daytime soaps and smoking weed with her hood rat girlfriends.

"So is this bitch your new girlfriend?" Keisha pressed on.

"I told you that she's not a bitch. Now, where's Hakeemah?"

"She's upstairs, sleeping. Now answer my question Hakeem, who is your new bitch, and how long you gonna keep this one?" Keisha said, following Hakeem up the stairs.

Hakeem didn't answer her, he just walked straight into the bedroom and over to his beautiful sleeping child. Seeing his daughter lying on the bed, peacefully sleeping, brought a big smile to his face. Hakeem leaned down and kissed her softly on the cheek. When he turned and walked back out of the room, Keisha was waiting in the hall with her face frowned up and arms crossed over her large breasts.

"What is it now, Keisha?"

Keisha blocked Hakeem from walking downstairs. She stared deep into his face. Her eyes welled up with tears as she said, "Hakeem, why do you do me like this?"

"Like what, Keisha?"

"Disrespecting me by bringing some bitch by my house!" Keisha vented.

"She's a friend, Keisha, and she only drove me over here to see my child and give you this," Hakeem said, going into his pocket and pulling out two brand new hundred-dollar bills.

"I like her, a lot Keisha, so get used to seeing us together."

Keisha took the money from him and stuffed it down her bra. She then grabbed Hakeem's arms and tearfully said, "Hakeem, why can't we be together; me, you, and our daughter? Tell me why?"

Hakeem looked straight into her crying eyes and said, "Do you really want to know, Keisha? Because, there are so many reasons, too many to even name... Let's start at reason number one.. I told you to go back to school and get your G.E.D. Two, you tricked me and said that you were on the pill! Three, all you do is get high and hang around with other lowlife hood rats who gossip all day long! Four, when we were together, you cheated on me and gave me gonorrhea! And five, you have a drug dealer boyfriend who lives right around the corner from you!"

"But I don't love him, I still love you!" Keisha protested.

"Keisha, when you had me, you didn't know how to love me. We haven't been together in over a year, it's time for you to start moving on and accept that me and you will never be together. I love you for giving me a beautiful daughter, but that's it!" Hakeem said, as he knocked her arms away and walked back down the stairs.

Keisha stood at the top of the stairs and cried like a lost child, knowing that she had let a good man slip right through her hands.

When Hakeem had got back into the car, Tammy noticed the sad look in his eyes.

"Are you okay?" she said, pulling her car off down the street.

"Yes, Sweetie, I'm fine," he said.

Tammy could tell that something was wrong, but she didn't want to press the issue.

"Thanks for the money, Tammy, I promise I'll pay you back," Hakeem said.

"Don't sweat it, Handsome, just pay it back whenever you can," she said, with a smile.

Hakeem looked into Tammy's eyes and said, "I'm serious Tammy, you'll get every penny, I'm no leach."

Tammy smiled and said, "I believe you, Hakeem. If I didn't, I wouldn't have given you two hundred dollars."

Hakeem reached over and grabbed her free hand.

"Thank you."

"You're welcome. Now, how about we go by the supermarket and pick up some chocolate syrup, whipped cream, strawberries, and cherries?" Tammy said.

"For what?" Hakeem asked curiously.

"I want to be your human desert," Tammy flirted.

"That sounds good to me!" Hakeem replied, with a grin.

~

West Philadelphia...

As Robin's Mercedes pulled up in front of the house, Mrs. Silvia saw another car parked across the street from her house and said, "Not again, what the hell do she want now?"

When Kevin saw Vera sitting behind the wheel of a brand new pearl-colored Audi sports car, he just shook his head. At Denny's, they had both told Robin all about Vera's unexpected visit to the house the day before. So when Robin saw her inside the car, her face quickly clenched up. The one thing that Robin didn't like was competition, especially with an ex-girlfriend that was still in love.

86

"I'll handle it," Kevin said.

"No, Sweetie let me, please," Robin said, parking her car and quickly turning it off.

"Please, I promise that it won't take long at all," she grinned devilishly.

"Are you sure, Robin?"

"Positive. Now y'all two go in the house and wait for me, I'll be right there." Robin watched as Kevin got out of the car. Mrs. Silvia was right behind him, smiling from ear to ear.

After a long sigh, Robin got out of the car, shut the door, and walked across the street toward Vera's car, while Kevin and Mrs. Silvia both walked inside the house. Robin approached the driver's side window and looked at the confused woman inside the car.

"Yes, can I help you?" Vera said, staring up at the taller woman in front of her.

Robin looked at Vera with a cold stare and said, "Look bitch, you had Kevin and you let him go! You then turn around left the man while he was in prison, and then had the audacity to marry his own cousin! All the love that he once had for you is dead and gone. The only one you have to blame is yourself! What stupid bitch leaves a man who she's supposed to be there for in his darkest and weakest time? You! A dumb, confused bitch, and now you realized that you lost a good man!"

Vera sat there, staring at Robin and not saying a single word. "Look here, Vera, I'm not a violent woman, but for Kevin, I will take off my Versace heels and whip your little ass. So do us both a big favor so I don't break my freshly manicured nails on your pretty face. Go home to your husband and stay the hell away from Kevin. And yes, that's a threat!" Robin said, staring straight into Vera's scared eyes.

"I just wanted to "

"Bitch, you stay here for one more minute or I'm gonna snatch your little ass out that car and make an example out of you!" Robin said, cutting Vera off.

Vera rolled up the window and put her car in drive. Seconds later, she was pulling off down the street. Robin walked over to the trunk of her car and opened it. Then she took out the shopping bag full of clothes that she bought for Kevin.

When Robin walked into the house, Kevin was upstairs in his bedroom and Mrs. Silvia was on the couch. She had watched everything from the living room window.

"What happened?"

"Put it this way; Vera won't be making any more unexpected visits around here, if she knows what's good for her," Robin said, as they both started laughing.

"Kevin's upstairs in his bedroom, go on up, it's straight back," Mrs. Silvia said, she got up and walked towards the kitchen.

Robin walked up the stairs and down the hall to the back room. The door was open and Kevin was sitting on the bed with his back to her, wearing a white tank top.

"Can I come in?" she said.

Kevin turned around, surprised.

"Sure," he said, jumping up and moving some clothes from off of a chair.

"You can sit here," he said, feeling a little embarrassed because his bedroom wasn't in order.

Robin smiled, walked over, and sat down.

"Here, these are a few things I got you when I went shopping yesterday," she said, passing Kevin the bag.

Kevin took the bag, but he didn't bother to look inside.

"Thank you."

"You're welcome," she grinned.

"Did you handle that?"

"Yup, she's gone and I don't think she'll be coming back."

"Thanks again," Kevin said, looking into her eyes.

"Can I ask you a serious question?" Robin said.

"Go ahead."

"Do you still love her?" Robin asked seriously.

"Not in that way anymore," he answered truthfully.

"Can I now ask you a question?" he said.

"I'm all ears."

"Do you always get everything you want?"

"No, but when it's something that I really want, I'll do everything in my power to get it. So if I don't get it, then at least I know I gave it my all," Robin said, honestly.

Kevin got down on his knees and crawled over to the chair.

"Thank you for everything you done for me, but I want you to know that you can't buy my love! Just be real, and let God do what he do," Kevin said, in a serious tone.

Robin stared deep into Kevin's eyes,

"Kevin, I am real, this is who I am, but I'm sorry, I don't think I can wait for God," Robin said, as she leaned forward and they began passionately kissing.

Chapter 12

Bryn Mawr, Pennsylvania

Later That Night...

Inside the elegant living room of his spacious home, Charles and Nathan were sitting around, talking with two older white men.

"So, Charles, did you enjoy yourself this weekend?" one of the men said, before sipping on the bottle of Heineken.

"Yes, Spencer, I had a ball in New York, I can't wait to get to L.A. next. How about you?"

"I always enjoy my getaways with the other D.W.A.M. members," Spencer said.

Spencer Lloyd was a 54-year-old federal judge from Miami; he was also one of the founding members of the D.W.A.M. organization.

"I'm looking forward to going out to L.A. too," the other white man said.

"Thomas, you look forward to going to all of them," Nathan said, as they all started laughing.

"How's that pretty girl of yours, Charles?" Spencer asked.

"She's doing fine, I haven't called her and told her that I was back from New York yet. I'll pop up and surprise her on Tuesday," Charles said, with a smile.

"Why Tuesday?" Thomas asked.

"Because Charles and I are catching a late night flight to Baltimore tonight," Nathan interrupted.

"You might be finished partying, but we're not," Charles said, grinning.

"I don't know how you two do it, but my wife would lose her mind if I stayed away for four or five days at a time," Thomas replied.

"Well, my wife understands that if she wants to keep living in the beautiful suburbs of Philadelphia, then I'm gonna have to keep working my ass off," Nathan said, joking.

"She has everything she wants or could ask for. She drives a Mercedes, owns two homes, and she has our two children to look after K so she stays busy and so do I," Nathan said, winking his eye at Charles.

"So, Charles, do you ever plan on marrying that pretty girl of yours?" Spencer asked curiously.

"Yes, I do! Sooner or later, she'll give in," he answered.

"Will you still continue to be a member of D.W.A.M.?" Thomas asked.

"I'm D.W.A.M. for life, that will never change," Charles said, as he stood up and raised his bottle of Heineken up in the air. The other three men all stood up, raising their beer bottle sin the air.

"D.W.A.M. for life!" Charles said loudly.

"D.W.A.M. for life!" they all cheered in unison.

After Spencer and Thomas got into a limousine and left, Charles and Nathan got inside of Nathan's white BMW and headed for the Philadelphia International Airport.

~

Tammy's naked body way lying across the bed, tired from a two and a half hour sex session with her young handsome stud. She was covered in red strawberry stains and brown spots from the Hershey's chocolate syrup. As she laid there catching her breath, she watched as Hakeem stood a few feet away, talking on his cell phone.

"Keisha, I said that I will pick up Hakeemah from the daycare tomorrow, now will you please stop calling me!" he said, pressing the end button on his phone. Hakeem sat his phone down on the dresser and walked over and got back into bed with Tammy.

"I'm sorry, Tammy, I know I said I wouldn't answer it anymore, but Keisha put in the emergency code for my daughter."

"I understand; she's just using y'all child to stay close to you." Tammy interrupted.

"Me and all my baggage, huh?" Hakeem said, in a serious tone. Tammy rolled over and climbed on top of Hakeem's muscular naked body.

"Don't worry, Sweetie, if Keisha think that's gonna run me away from you, then she's in for a big surprise," Tammy said softly.

"I'm still confused on why you even put up with this when you really don't have to," Hakeem said.

"Because, when we first met, you were totally honest and up front about everything; your child, baby-momma drama, getting fired from your job, and getting your car impounded for not paying your tickets. You didn't have to tell me any of that stuff, and you could've lied just like most men would've done. Hakeem, you were truthful, and to me that means a whole lot. I'm twenty-nine years old with no children and no husband. That's because I've never found one good man who was truthful. Every man that I've ever known has turned out to be one big lie. You'd be surprised to find out just how many lonely women are out there hoping to find that one good man to call her own." Tammy said.

"So me being broke and jobless with a child didn't turn you off?"

"Yes, it did! But you being totally honest about your situation had turned me on even more," Tammy said, as she leaned down and gently kissed his lips.

"Look, maybe its destiny, Hakeem. We are two people from two different worlds who are very compatible on many levels. It was meant for us to meet, that's why you're here now."

"So being truthful was all it took?" Hakeem asked, and grinned.
"Yup, plus you're so damn fine, and all these muscles ain't hurt either," Tammy said, squeezing his arm. "And the sex! Boy, if I could put your love-making skills in a bottle and sell it, we would both be rich!"

"Well, let's not talk about it," Hakeem said, as he rolled Tammy around and laid on top of her. "Destiny, huh?"

"That's right, Handsome, destiny," Tammy smiled. Then, in one smooth motion, Hakeem spread her legs far apart and entered his hardness deep inside of her inviting paradise.

~

After enjoying a delicious home-cooked chicken dinner, Mrs. Silvia and Robin cleaned up the dishes while Kevin went upstairs to his room and changed clothes. When Kevin came back downstairs, he was wearing a brand new white sweat-suit and a new pair of white Nikes. Robin stood there with a smile on her face, admiring her taste in picking out men's clothes.

"I'll see you later Kevin; and Robin, don't forget to call me," Mrs. Silvia said, walking over to the stairs.

"I won't, Mrs. Silvia," Robin said, waving goodbye.

After Mrs. Silvia went upstairs, Robin and Kevin walked out the front door.

Once they got inside Robin's car, Kevin asked, "So, are you gonna tell me what your special surprise is or not?" he blushed.
"Nope," Robin replied before she started up her car and pulled off down the street.

The whole time they ate dinner, they couldn't keep their eyes off of each other. A few times, Mrs. Silvia had to say something just to break their stares.

A half-hour later, they were inside the elevator that carried them to Robin's condo on the thirty-fifth floor. When they walked into the condo, Robin grabbed Kevin's hand and walked him into her master bedroom. With a serious look on his face, Kevin didn't say a single word.

'She still doesn't get it. She doesn't understand me.' Kevin thought to himself.

"Sit on my bed, I'll be right back," Robin said, as she grabbed a small black bag, then rushed into the private walk-in bathroom.

Moments later, Robin walked back out wearing a red Victoria's Secret bra and matching thong, with a pair of red Manolo Blahnik heels on. Robin had cherry lipstick on her lips and a long red silk scarf wrapped around her neck.

"You like?" Robin asked, walking over to Kevin and getting down on her knees.

When Robin moved her hand toward Kevin's dick, he stopped her and said, "So, your special surprise was to bring me over to your condo to seduce me?"

Robin saw the serious look in Kevin's eyes and said,

"Yes, that was my intention. Kevin, I want you more than any man I've ever wanted in my life. My body has been yearning for yours since we met. I can't stop thinking about you being inside of me," Robin said, with a serious look in her eyes.

Kevin stared into her beautiful face and said, "Robin, we are not making love tonight, because this is not all about you. Your body is burning for sex, mine is not. Robin, you are a very beautiful woman, inside and out, but you're also very spoiled and used to getting whatever you want. Well, Beautiful, I'm not that easy. And no, I'm not a fagot and I don't have any diseases. Like I said, Sweetie, this is not all about Robin Davis. But I will tell you this," Kevin said, as he reached out his hand and placed it under her chin, "When I decide that you're ready and that special day does come, I'm going to take you to a place that you'll never want to leave, and that's a promise."

Robin could feel herself getting soaking wet. The thing about Kevin was that he exuded confidence. There was no doubt, in Kevin's eyes, that he wasn't telling Robin the truth, and she knew it. When Kevin grabbed her hands and helped Robin to her feet, he could feel her whole body start to tremble. Kevin's soft touch and confident words had made her come on herself.

"I feel so embarrassed," Robin said. Kevin wrapped his arms around Robin's trembling body and looked her straight into the eyes.

"Don't be, Beautiful, this is only the beginning," he said, as they started passionately kissing.

After their long, passionate kiss, Kevin stepped back and said, "I want you to take everything off."

Robin smiled and did as he said. First, she unsnapped her bra and threw it on the bed. The nipples on her plump, full breasts were sticking out like thorns. Then, Robin slowly slid down her wet thong and stepped out of it. Her pubic hairs were shaved off completely.

"Shoes too?" she asked, with a smile.

"Everything," Kevin said, as he stood there with a serious look on his face.

Robin took her heels off and kicked them over to the side. Then she snatched the red scarf from around her neck and tossed it into the air. When she was totally naked, Kevin walked up to her and let his eyes scan her flawless brown body. He slowly walked around her in one full circle. Robin stood there like a mannequin at Macy's, wondering what was going on in Kevin's head. Kevin made sure that he sized up her body completely. Broad shoulders, slim waist, a nice round ass, plump breasts, long neck, long legs, and perfect little toes. Robin's body was a fine work of art, he thought. When Kevin had faced her once again, he looked into her beaming eyes.

"Okay, Beautiful, you can get dressed. I'll be waiting for you in the living room," he said. Then he kissed her on the top of her nose and walked out of the bedroom. Robin stood there, naked and dumbfounded. Her pussy was wet and throbbing out of control. She stood there feeling her heart pounding inside her chest; captivated and confused at the same time. Robin knew that Kevin was a different kind of man. Her trembling body was burning with desire that could burn a house down to the ground. Kevin was the only one who possessed the power to put out the burning flames. After a long sigh, Robin turned and walked into the bathroom, more captivated and confused than she had been in her entire life.

What Every Woman Wants

Inside the plush living room, Kevin was sitting on the sofa with a big smile on his face. He knew exactly what he was doing; mastering the art of total seduction. Since the moment they met, Kevin had started making powerful love to Robin's mind; something that Robin had known nothing about. Without even touching her, he was giving Robin powerful orgasms that swept through her mind, body, and soul. When the time was right, Kevin was going to give Robin everything she had ever imagined, and a whole lot more.

What Every Woman Wants

Chapter 13

Monday Afternoon...

Inside Jennifer's office, Robin and DJ Love-Daddy were standing around, listening to Jennifer talk.

"Overall, the radio industry has got a major problem," she said, sitting down at her desk.

"Why do you think that?" Love-Daddy asked.

"Because although we have millions of loyal listeners that tune into Power 99 on a daily basis, it's getting a lot tougher to hold our listener's attention," Jennifer replied.

"But I have the top-rated program in my late night time slot," Love-Daddy said, proudly.

"I understand that, Love-Daddy, but everyone else's ratings have gone down a few points."

"But Jennifer, there's not too much we can do about it. We are facing flat revenues, and competition ranging from iPods to music phones, satellite radio, or the new HD format; it's got the radio industry scrambling to reinvent itself. There are now so many different choices for a person to tune in each day. They can either choose to hear their favorite over-caffeinated DJ, or catch those rush hour traffic updates," Robin said.

"She's right, Jennifer, the overall competition is getting worse by the day, so all us DJs can do is what we've been doing, and hope that our loyal listeners don't go astray," Love-Daddy said.

Jennifer sat at her desk, nodding her head. She knew that everything they said was the truth. After the meeting, Robin and DJ Love-Daddy walked out of Jennifer's office and shut the door. As Robin was walking back towards her office, he noticed Trey talking to the new afternoon DJ, Sherri Star. Sherri Star was a short, pretty woman with a light-skinned complexion. Robin noticed the two DJs smiling and laughing as she walked inside her office and closed the door.

When Robin sat back down at her desk, she couldn't get Kevin from out of her mind. After dropping Kevin back off at home last night, Robin rushed back to her condo and quickly undressed. Then she lay across her bed and started playing with herself, until her body exploded with a powerful orgasm. The sound of the phone ringing snapped Robin from her sexual thoughts. She picked up the phone and said,

"Hello, Robin Davis."

"Hey, Beautiful," a soft voice said.

"Hey T.J., are you back in the city?" Robin asked with a grin.

"Yes, I got back early this morning. I've been running around all morning, catching up on a few important things. Is it still on for tonight?"

"Definitely!" Robin said, excitedly.

"Good, cause we need to have a serious girl to girl talk," T.J. said.

"About what?" Robin said, already knowing the answer.

"About this new handsome stranger that got you all screwed up." T.J. said, as they both started laughing.

"Don't worry, I'll tell you everything, I'll see you later tonight," Robin said. They both hung up.

When Robin turned back to her computer, she was interrupted once again by a soft tap on the door.

"Come in."

The door opened and Trey walked in and closed the door behind him.

"What's up, Beautiful?"

"Nothing much, just trying to finish up my work," Robin replied, folding her arms across her chest.

"I see that you get around," she said.

"Huh?"

"Don't 'huh' me, Trey, I be seeing you up in all the women's faces around here. You got Sherri Star's eyes and nose wide open and she ain't been here a whole month yet."

"We're just friends," Trey said.

"Yeah, okay Mr. 'Just Friends'."

Trey walked up to the desk and said, "So, Robin, when can we get together again? I've been missing you like crazy."

"Is that right?" Robin said, blushing.

"You know it's right. So what's up, when can I see you?"

"Not tonight, Handsome, I'll be very busy, But I'll definitely try to fit you into my busy schedule sometime this week. Maybe I'll invite you over to my place again," Robin said, teasing him.

"I have a strange feeling that someone is starting to get all of your attention. It must be that super-rich boyfriend you got."

"Nope, you're wrong, and I told you so many times that Charles is not my boyfriend; he's a friend, just like you."

Before Trey could say another word, the tap on Robin's door stopped him.

"Come in," Robin said.

The door slowly opened and a short white man, dressed in a brown jacket and pants, walked into the office. The man was carrying a small bouquet of fresh new roses. Altogether, there were a dozen roses; eleven yellow and one red one.

"Excuse me, but these are for you, ma'am," the man said, walking up to the desk and passing Robin a small folded-up piece of paper.

"Thank you," Robin said, with an excited look in her eyes.

After the man had turned and walked out of the office, Robin looked up at Trey and said, "Alright, I'll talk to you later, I have my work to do."

"Aren't you gonna read what's on the paper?" he asked curiously.

"No, not in front of you, bye, Trey," she said, laying the roses down on her desk.

"This week, right?" Trey said, walking over to the door.

"I said that I'll try; now bye, I'm sure Penny or Sherri Star are waiting for you somewhere."

Trey smiled and shook his head, then walked out of the office, shutting the door behind him.

As soon as Trey had shut the door, Robin sat back comfortably in her chair and opened up the folded piece of paper. With a big smile on her face, she started reading:

Hey beautiful,

I don't have much to give you financially, but I do have this poem to share with you, hopefully it will last just as long as all the diamonds you own.

I only want everything, nothing less, and I only will settle for your very best.

I will not chase an illusion, or run after a dream, and I only will do what my heart truly believes.

The game of true love is not to be misused, even though love plays many tricks and has us all confused.

So just follow your heart and the spirit within, and keep God close and you will always win.

Listen to your yearning soul and you will never fall.

Remember, I only want the very best or nothing at all.

Sincerely,
Kevin

After reading the poignant poem, Robin started wiping the tears from the corner of her eyes. She sat still in her chair.

"Damn, Kevin, what are you doing to me?" she mumbled to herself. After a long sigh, Robin folded up the piece of paper and put it inside her Versace handbag. Then she took out the single red rose and placed it to her nose.

"Kevin... Kevin... Kevin..." she said, softly.

At 3:59, Robin was finished with work and walking out the front door. Out in the parking lot, she spotted Trey and DJ Sherri Star standing beside his Navigator truck, conversing. Robin smiled and winked at Trey before she got inside her car. When she started up her car and drove out the parking lot, Robin noticed Penny, the station's secretary, standing in the doorway, staring at Trey with a disappointed look on her face.

On her way over to Kevin's house, Robin drove by the bank and picked up Tammy. They cruised down the street with the convertible top down, Tammy talked about her amazing night she had with Hakeem. When Robin told Tammy about her night with Kevin, Tammy just shook her head and said, "Damn, Robin, you have finally found your match."

"I ain't the only one," Robin said, as she drove her car down Market Street, "It seems like your new young boy-toy got you on cloud nine too." When Robin glanced over, Tammy had the biggest smile on her face.

Robin pulled her car up in front of Kevin's house and saw him sitting on the front step, talking to two dark-skinned, rough-looking men. Tammy had spotted Hakeem as soon as the car turned on the street. Both women got out of the car, each one headed in a different direction. While Robin was walking towards Kevin, Tammy was grinning and walking up the street to go see Hakeem.

"Just think about it, Kev, being broke is for the birds!" one of the men said, before he and his friend shook Kevin's hand and walked away. After the two men had walked away, Robin smiled and sat down on the step beside him.

"Hey, Handsome, you okay?" she said, seeing the perplexed look on his face.

"Yeah, I'm okay. How was your day?" Kevin asked.

"Wonderful! Thanks for the roses and that wonderful poem," Robin said, leaning over and kissing Kevin softly on the lips.

Robin looked into Kevin's eyes and could tell that something serious was on his mind.

"Who were those two guys?" she asked.

"Some old friends of mine."

"What did they want?" Robin asked curiously.

"They want me to do something, but I told 'em that I'm not sure; that I'll let 'em know."

"I hope it's nothing bad," Robin said, in a serious tone.

"Sometimes a man is forced to do things that he don't want to do, Robin. It's hard out here, in my world. Remember, I'm an ex- felon who can't seem to find a job nowhere. This morning I got three more 'don't call us we'll call you' to add to my long list. This is worse than being in prison. If I don't get my hands on some money real soon, I don't know what I'm gonna do," Kevin said, clearly upset at the situation.

"Kevin, please don't do something stupid that will send you back to prison. Everything will work itself out. Is there any way that I can help you?" Robin said, reaching over and grabbing his hands.

Kevin looked deep into Robin's eyes and said,

"You've done more than enough, Robin, I have to be a man and do the rest by myself."

"Please, just let me help you!" she said, begging him.

"You helped me enough," Kevin replied.

Tammy and Hakeem were standing on the corner when the two rough looking men strolled by them.

"Hakeem, do you know those guys?" Tammy asked.

"Yeah, and they're nothing but trouble," he said.

"Why? What is it that they do?"

"What don't they do? Their street names are Black and Noonie, they are nothing but trouble.

Those two guys are into everything from selling drugs to loan-sharking, kidnapping people, and even extortion."

"Do you know Kevin?" Tammy asked.

"Yeah, I know Kevin pretty well. That's who your girlfriend be coming down here to see, right?"

"Right. I just saw those guys talking to Kevin when me and Robin pulled up in her car."

"Well, I hope Kevin don't get caught up in nothing stupid. He's a cool guy, everybody likes Kev. Before he went to prison, Kev was the man around here. But that was almost nine years ago, things have changed; and now Kev seems like he's a little down on his luck."

"Do you think those two guys want Kevin to do something with them?" Tammy asked, concerned.

"Probably. Let's just hope Kevin is smart enough to just say no."

"Come on, let's walk down to Kevin's house and see what's up with them," Tammy said.

"Oh, you can still walk after last night?" Hakeem joked.

Tammy playfully punched his shoulder and said, "Barely, I'm gonna have to see a chiropractor this week, and you're paying for it!"

"Okay, just add it to my bill, because after tonight, you might need back surgery," he said, with a smile.

Tammy grabbed Hakeem's arm and said, "Don't wear yourself out, cutie."

"Baby, with you there's not enough hours in the day."

Chapter 14

The four of them had all climbed into Robin's car, and headed down to Pat's Famous Cheese steak Restaurant in South Philly. After they had all enjoyed a cheese steak and cold bottles of Pepsi, they got back into Robin's car and drove out to the lovely Fairmount Park. While Robin and Kevin walked over to a small pond, Tammy and Hakeem were sitting on the park bench, locked in a long, passionate kiss.

"Look at them," Robin said.

"Yeah, I think those two might have found something very special in each other," Kevin said.

"Like us?" Robin asked, wrapping her arm around his.

"The verdict is not in yet, only time will tell," Kevin said.

"So, how long will it take for a jury to decide?" Robin said, staring into his eyes.

"When the judge is ready."

"Are you like this with everything, Kevin, or is it just me?"

"I'm cautious with everything, Robin. I have to be."

"Can I ask you something?" he said.

"Anything."

"When was the last time you told a man that you loved him?" Kevin asked.

Robin stood there thinking about the question. After about a minute, she said, "The only men that I ever said 'I love you' to was my father and my brother—no one else."

"Nobody?"

"Nope, not one. I never met a man who had made me feel that way. That was until I met " She stopped herself.

Kevin put his arm around Robin's shoulders and kissed her on the cheek. Then, without saying another word, they walked over to Tammy and Hakeem.

"Okay, y'all two, it's getting late. Tammy, I'll drop you and Hakeem off at your car," Robin said, as they all walked over to Robin's car and got back inside.

After Robin had dropped Tammy and Hakeem off at Tammy's car, she drove Kevin back to his house. Robin went inside the house and had a nice brief conversation with Mrs. Silvia. When it was time to leave, Kevin walked Robin outside to her car. The sky was dark and tranquil, and the street was quiet with only a few people standing around outside.

"I'll call you as soon as I get in. I'll be back by here to see you tomorrow," she said.

"Alright, you be safe," Kevin said, as he leaned down and kissed Robin softly on the lips.

Kevin walked over to the steps and watched as Robin waved goodbye and drove off down the street.

When Robin had reached the corner, she saw the two rough looking men from earlier walking towards Kevin.

"Be strong, Baby," she mumbled, before turning the car and driving off the block.

Robin looked at her gold watch and noticed that the time was eight forty-seven. T.J. was going to be at her condo at ten.

After driving down Girard Avenue, Robin hopped on the expressway. At nine o' eight, she walked into her condominium and went around lighting up all the scented candles around the apartment. Robin walked over to her state-of-the-art stereo system and turned it on. She grabbed a CD from the tall CD rack, and slid it into the CD player. The disc was filled with songs from all of her favorite male R&B singers. She had all the hits which included Maxwell, Jaheem, Musiq Soulchild, Joe, Gerald Levert, Johnny Gill, D'Angelo, Babyface, Silk, Jodeci, Boys II Men, Frankie Beverly & Maze, Lionel Richie, and her favorite of them all, the talented singer known as Prince.

After Robin had taken a quick hot shower, she slipped into a white Moschino bra and thong set. As the music flowed out of the bedroom speakers, Robin lay across her oval-shaped bed and waited on T.J. to arrive. Inside, she wished that it was Kevin coming over instead; but tonight, her bisexual lover, T.J., would have to do.

~

An Hour Later...

"Fuck me, Baby! Fuck me harder! Harder!" Tammy grunted out loudly.

Hakeem had Tammy's naked body bent over the bed, fucking her aggressively from behind. The instant they walked into the house, they attacked each other like two wild savages who had just caught their sexual prey.

"Ahhh! Ohh!" Hakeem moaned out as he exploded into the condom. Hakeem slumped down on Tammy's back, feeling her body trembling beneath his. Then, he slid out of her and rolled over beside her. Both of them were breathing hard. Tammy lay there in total silence. Since meeting Hakeem, she had felt young and vigorous, while having some of the best sex she had ever had in her entire life. Tammy knew that the young stud was quickly becoming her weakness. She was already feeling him more than she had realized. Hakeem was everything that Tammy had ever wanted in a man. He had the looks, a great personality, and an unbelievably high sex drive. That's why Tammy no longer cared about Hakeem having a young child, or his baby-momma drama. Her feelings for him were becoming stronger by the day. Hakeem had turned out to be a surprisingly wonderful blessing. He made Tammy feel like no other man, older or younger, had ever done before. He made Tammy feel totally happy. Tammy rolled over on the bed and stared into Hakeem's satisfied eyes.

"That's it, Stallion, if we keep this up, I'll never make it work in the morning," she said softly.

Hakeem leaned forward and kissed her gently on the lips. He then said, "Just one more time, then we can go take a shower together and call it a night."

Tammy smiled, shook her head, and said, "Okay, Baby, just one more time," she said.

Then she watched as he reached over to the dresser and grabbed another condom.

~

Inside Robin's condo, her and T.J. were lying on top of the silk sheets. After an intense round of blissful sex. Their two beautiful naked bodies lay side by side. The music from the stereo was turned down low, but the smooth soulful voice of D'Angelo could still be clearly heard.

"T.J., the man is a mystery that I just can't seem to solve. And he's just so damn fine that I actually get goose bumps when I'm near him. And every time we kiss, I feel like I'm coming on myself; a few times, I actually did!" Robin said, as they both started giggling.

"Robin, the way that this man sounds, you better be extra careful. A man like Kevin can only turn out to be one of two things," T.J. said.

"What's that?"

"The perfect man for you, or a handsome scheming manipulator that's playing you like a flute. Remember, the man is an ex-felon who's down on his luck; he'll say and do anything to keep you close. Don't forget, Robin, you have everything that a man could want. Especially a man who has nothing," T.J. said, with a serious look on her face. "I just want you to be safe. We're friends, and no matter what, I always have your back."

Robin lay there with a perplexed look on her face.

"T.J., maybe you're right, but I feel in my heart that Kevin might be the perfect man for me. Hell, he maybe even my soul mate."
"And what about Charles and Trey?"

"Trey is still a boy, I just have my fun with him but that is it. Charles gives me the world, but can't satisfy me in bed. But Kevin has everything. Everything I ever wanted in a man except

107

'Money', that's why you need to watch him, Robin," T.J. interjected.

"But T.J., with Kevin, it's not about money, it's more!" Robin said, defending him.

"Robin, is there something you're not telling me? Is there more to this guy, Kevin, that you're not telling me?" T.J. asked.

"Like what? Robin asked, defensively.

"Are you in love with this man?"

Robin didn't respond to the question, she just lay there in total silence, looking into T.J.'s serious eyes.

"You're in love, aren't you?"

"T.J., I don't know what I feel. I've never been in love before, but with Kevin, I just can't explain it." Robin said.

"Answer this question, then I'll know if you're really in love or just super-infatuated," T.J. said, with a smile.

"What is it?"

"Since meeting Kevin, have you sat back and cried while thinking about him?"

"No!" Robin lied.

"Then you're not in love yet. But the way it sounds, you're almost there. Just be safe."

"I will."

"Do you have a picture of this guy?" T.J. asked, sitting up on the bed.

"No, but I have a picture of Charles and Trey. Do you want to see them?" Robin answered.

"Yeah, why not," T.J. said, as she watched Robin get up from the bed and walk over to the dresser.

Robin slid open the top drawer and took out two color photos. She then closed the drawer and walked back over to the bed.

"Here, this is a picture of Trey." She passed the photo to T.J.

T.J. looked at the picture, "He's cute. Young; but very cute," she said.

"Yeah, that's my lil' boy toy, I'm getting him ready for his future wife," Robin said, as they both started laughing.

"Here, this is Charles, that's us together in Costa Rica. He took me there last year for a quick weekend getaway."

T.J. stared hard into the photo. Robin studied her face and said, "What's wrong?"

"I've seen this man somewhere before. His face looks so familiar," she said.

"He travels a lot, remember? I told you, Charles is a real estate investor who flies all around the country buying property with his partner, Nathan. You've probably seen Charles on one of your flights; he's always on the go."

"You're probably right, but I've seen him somewhere else before, I'm sure of it." T.J. handed the photo back to Robin.

"So, T.J., where will you be traveling to next?"

"For the next few weeks, I'll be very busy. New Orleans, Detroit, Atlanta, L.A., Miami, and Charlotte," T.J. said.

"So that means after tonight, it will be a little while till the next time we get to see each other?"

"Exactly," T.J. smiled, "By then you'll know the real scoop on this guy, Kevin. Like they say, no lie lasts forever. But for you, Robin, I honestly hope everything turns out for the better."

"And if it does, you won't be mad?" Robin asked.

"Why should I? We both agreed on this from the very beginning. If you found your true soul mate, then we would both go our separate ways. If that was to happen, believe me, it would hurt, but I have enough friends out there to keep me smiling," T.J. said, with a big grin on her face.

"I bet you meet a lot of exciting people."

"Being an airplane stewardess, you can't help but meet a lot of different exciting people from all over the world. I have a good friend in Miami, he's a judge; another male friend from Chicago that's a NBA player for the Bulls, and his wife," T.J. said.

"His wife, too!" Robin said, shocked, "You be doing both of them?"

"Not at the same time. Neither of them knows that I'm sleeping with the other," T.J. said, as both women started laughing.

T.J. reached over and grabbed the 8-inch strap-on dildo from the floor. After she wrapped it around her waist, she laid Robin gently down on her stomach. Robin tossed the two pictures to the floor, and spread her legs and arms. T.J. slowly entered her wetness from behind; Robin had her eyes tightly shut, with a vivid picture of Kevin inside her mind.

Chapter 15

Tuesday Afternoon –

Robin had requested the afternoon off, she walked out of the radio station's office and got into get car. Before she headed downtown to go see her brother, Billy, she called Kevin on his new cell phone and told him that she was on her way to pick him up.

When Robin pulled up in front of Kevin's house, he was standing out front, talking to the same men that she had seen before. Kevin smiled, walked over, and got inside the car. Robin leaned over and they kissed each other on the lips.

"So, what's the emergency?" he asked curiously.

"I want you to meet someone," she said, with a smile.

"Who?"

"My older brother, he's waiting for us down at his office," Robin said, pulling off down the street.

"So, I see you were talking to your two friends again," she said.

"Yeah, they just came by to say what's up," Kevin replied, nonchalantly.

Tammy had already called Robin at work and gave her the whole scoop on the two lowlife thugs. Robin knew that both men were nothing but trouble.

"I have to run by my place for a quick second. I want to change out of these clothes," she said stopping the Mercedes at a red light.

"Fine with me," Kevin replied.

Robin was dressed in a dark-blue Donna Karen cotton dress and a pair of matching heels. When they pulled up in front of her condo building, Robin parked her car and said, "You can wait out here, I'll just be a minute."

Kevin watched as she grabbed her black DKNY leather bag and walked towards the front entrance of the building. He settled comfortably in his seat and finished listening to the soulful voice of Stevie Wonder coming out of the car speakers.

Robin walked into the quiet, spacious lobby of her apartment building; she was approached by a tall, slim white man.

"Ms. Davis, how are you doing today?" he asked politely.

"Fine, and yourself?" she asked walking towards the elevator.

"I'm doing well. Are you satisfied with the cleaning service?"

"Oh, yes, Mr. Wesley, the maids are wonderful," Robin replied.

"Good, they cleaned up your apartment a few hours ago."

Mr. Wesley was the head manager of the entire building. He was a tall white man in his early fifty's who made sure everything was running smoothly in the condominium complex.

"Maria and Carla have been doing a wonderful job. Why, is there a problem?" Robin asked.

"No, we've had a few minor complaints, but nothing to worry about," he said.

"Well, I don't have any complaints," Robin said, as the elevator door swung open and she stepped inside.

"Okay, Mr. Wesley, you take care," she said, before the elevator door closed.

When Robin had entered into her lavishly cleaned apartment, she rushed into the master bedroom and quickly changed her clothes. She took of her dress and heels, and put on a pink Baby Phat sweat suit and a pair of pink and white Nike Air running shoes. Moments later, Robin was walking back out of the front entrance, and rushing over to her car. Kevin looked at her and said, "Your cell phone has been ringing like crazy."

Robin got into the car and checked the messages on her voice mail. Charles had left two messages.

"Just one of my friends," Robin said, as she started up the car and drove down the street with a big smile plastered on her face. Billy's private law office was just a few blocks away from Robin's Condo. Robin pulled up and parked her car, she and Kevin

112

got out and headed towards the tall downtown office building. They walked into the crowded lobby and got into one of the four elevators. Robin pressed the button for the eighteenth floor. After the elevator stopped at their destination, they stepped off into a small, nicely decorated lobby. Robin walked up to an attractive white woman who was sitting at the front desk, typing on the computer.

"Hey Robin, Mr. Davis is back inside his office waiting on you," she said cheerfully.

"Thanks, Amy," Robin said, noticing how she was eyeing Kevin down from head to toe.

"Is the gentleman with you?" Amy asked curiously.

"Yes, he's with me," Robin answered, before turning around and saying, "Come on, Kevin, follow me."

Amy watched as Robin and Kevin walked down the hall. She never took her eyes off Kevin until he disappeared from her sight. While they walked down the hall towards Billy's office, Robin had noticed all the women watching Kevin closely. A few of them didn't even try to hide it.

"Damn, you see him?" Robin heard one of the women whisper to her girlfriend.

Robin knew that Kevin was an extremely handsome man who women showed a lot of attention to, but she also knew that Kevin was into her just as much as she was into him. So all the other women could do was watch and lust.

When they entered the large private office, Billy walked up and gave his younger sister a long, warm hug. Billy was a large light-skinned man who stood 6'3" tall, and weighed 265 pounds. He looked more like a NFL middle linebacker than the Philadelphia criminal lawyer that he was.

"Kevin, this is my brother, William," Robin said, introducing them.

"Just call me Billy," he said, as they shook each other's hand.

Billy had been a criminal lawyer for 23 years. He was a 49-year old single man who looked nowhere near his age. And even though

Robin was his younger sister, Billy was old enough to be her father. Their parents had Robin when Billy was a 19-year-old law student at the University of Pennsylvania. Still, they were as close as any siblings could be.

"So, Kevin, you're the guy who got my little sister all excited?" he asked, smiling.

"Billy!" Robin said, punching him on his shoulder.

"Okay, okay!" Billy said, seeing his little sister blushing with embarrassment.

"Robin told me that you were looking for some work," Billy said.

Kevin looked over at Robin with surprised look on his face. He had no idea that Robin had set him up with a meeting with her brother. Robin smiled and winked at him.

"Yes, I just got out of prison and – "

"Robin told me everything. What can you do?" Billy said, cutting him off.

"Well, I'm pretty good with my hands, I can fix almost anything. I learned a lot of different skills while in prison."

"I actually have a job opening for the office janitorial position. If you're interested, you can start tomorrow morning. It pays well, you will be scheduled to come in every morning before the staff arrives, and get off around one o'clock," Billy said.

Kevin's eyes lit up with excitement. It wasn't that the job was exactly what he had wanted; but it was a job, and a way for him to start making his own money. Besides, anything was better than being broke and dependent on others, he thought.

"Yes, I would love to have the job," Kevin said, enthusiastically.

"Good! Robin already have me all of your information. Now all I'll need is your social security number, That and of course, for you to show up at 5am tomorrow morning. I'll meet up with you and show you around the place, then I'll introduce you to the people you need to know," Billy said, as they both shook hands again.

"Thank you, Billy, I really appreciate this," Kevin said.

"Thank my little sister, she's the person who begged me to find her future husband a job," Billy said, laughing.

"Billy!" Robin said, punching his shoulder again.

Kevin didn't know what to say. He just stood there with an excited look on his face.

"Thank you," he said, giving Robin a kiss and a hug.

"Kevin, can I ask you something?" Billy said, in a serious tone. "Yes, Billy, what is it?" he said, standing there, holding Robin's hand.

"Do you have any other plans for your life? I'm sure you don't want to be a janitor forever," he said.

"Well, to be honest, Billy, once I get myself back on solid ground, I want to go back to college and finish my degree in Business Management. I was enrolled in college while I was in prison, and my grades were all pretty high. So I do plan on going back to college and finishing up my degree," Kevin said, seriously. Billy shook his head and said, "Well that's good to hear, you seem like you have a good head on your shoulders, I'll see you in the morning."

After shaking Kevin's hand again, Billy hugged and kissed Robin. He then watched as they both smiled and walked out of his office. Inside the elevator, Robin and Kevin were locked in a long, passionate kiss. When they got back inside of the car, Kevin asked, "Where to next?"

"Shopping; what else?! You're gonna need some nice new work clothes and boots for your new job," Robin said, as she started up the car and pulled off down the crowded downtown street.

"Future husband, huh?" Kevin said, with a grin.

"Oh, don't pay my brother no mind," Robin blushed, as she drove down Walnut Street.

"Well, if that was true, then we might as well wait to make love on our honeymoon," Kevin said, jokingly.

Robin looked at Kevin's smiling face and said, "Kevin, you better stop playing with me!"

Kevin didn't say another word; he just sat back in his seat, smiling from ear to ear.

Inside her office at the Philadelphia Federal Credit Union, Tammy was at her desk going over some important paperwork, when a tap on the door startled her. When she saw Nathan standing at her door, a big smile came to her face. She quickly waived him in. Nathan walked into the office and closed the door behind him. Tammy then stood up from her desk and walked over and gave him a hug.

"I missed you, Sweetie," he said, as they kissed softly on the lips.

"How was New York?"

"Work as usual, nothing to really talk about. You know, just me and Charles doing what we do," he said. "Can I come by and see you tonight? I really would like to show you just how much I miss you," he said, teasingly.

Tammy stared into Nathan's dark, handsome face and didn't know what to say. Every time they had sex, it was great, she thought.

"Where's your wife?"

"At home, where she's supposed to be," Nathan said, feeling that something was wrong. Tammy looked at Nathan's tall, dark body and couldn't help but imagine it grinding up against hers.

"Yeah, you can come over tonight. How about around eight?" she said.

"Perfect. And don't worry, I'll bring the pizza and a pack of condoms," he winked. After giving Tammy a kiss and a hug, Nathan walked out of her office. Tammy sat back down at her desk and thought about Hakeem. Her mind was racing with thoughts. Hakeem made Tammy feel like a totally new woman every time they were together. But with Nathan, it was nothing but sexual lust and tonight, she wanted it.

Tammy continuously tried to call Hakeem on his cell phone; once again, she didn't get an answer. She had been trying to call him all morning, but kept getting his voice mail. Tammy needed to tell Hakeem that she wouldn't be able to see him tonight. She had other plans, and she needed to get her lies in order. Better safe than sorry, she thought.

What Every Woman Wants

Chapter 16

Later That Evening –

Robin and Kevin had driven out to the King of Prussia shopping mall. Everywhere they walked, Robin noticed how women couldn't keep their wandering eyes off of Kevin. Women of every race were attracted to Kevin's handsome, masculine looks. Since he had just come home from doing time in prison, Kevin had what was known as "the prison glow". While they were at the King of Prussia mall, they ate, shopped, took a few pictures together, and walked around holding hands. They were acting like two young teenagers caught up in their first crush. Robin had bought Kevin everything that he would need for his new job. She purchased him work-boots, gloves, hats, socks, shirts, and pants. She had also bought Kevin some leather loafers, a Nautica fall jacket, Abercrombie & Fitch cotton T-shirts, Calvin Klein briefs, Sean John and Ralph Lauren colognes, and a $500 Tag Hauer watch. Money was not an issue with Robin K she had more than enough. Not only was she well of on her own, but after her parents had died in the plane crash, Robin and Billy were the only two beneficiaries to their $3 million life insurance policy. So, even without the job at the radio station where Robin was making over $80,000 a year, she was set for life. Only Tammy and her brother, Billy, had known about her secret wealth.

On their way back to Robin's condo, they listened to music and laughed the whole ride. When Robin pulled into the underground parking garage, the first thing she noticed was Charles' blue Bentley, parked in her visitor's parking space.

"Oh shit," she mumbled under her breath.

Kevin heard her, and when he looked out and saw the tall, well-dressed black man leaning on his expensive set of wheels, he knew that the man was waiting on Robin.

After Robin parked her car beside the Bentley, she and Kevin grabbed their shopping bags and got out of the car.

"Charles, why didn't you call and tell me that you were back in town?" Robin said, with an uncomfortable look on her face.

"I wanted to surprise you; I've done it before," he said, giving Robin a hug and a soft kiss on the lips.

"Charles, this is my friend, Kevin," she said.

They reached out and shook each other's hand, eyeing each other down from head to toe.

"I see I caught you at a bad time," Charles said.

"No _ I mean, yes _ I mean, no, Kevin is just a friend," Robin said, stumbling over her words.

"Well, since your birthday is Friday, and I won't be able to make it, I just—"

"Why won't you be able to see me on my birthday?" Robin asked, cutting him off.

"Nathan and I have a very important business meeting out in L.A., and it's mandatory that we both be there. I'm sorry, but that's why I came by to see you today, and give you this," Charles said, as he went into his jacket pocket and pulled out a beautiful two-carat yellow diamond bracelet. Robin's eyes opened wide with excitement.

"Happy birthday, Beautiful," Charles said, passing the bracelet to Robin. Robin gave Charles another hug and kiss, while Kevin was standing there, feeling totally out of place. Kevin knew that Charles was showing off his wealth, but he remained cool and calm. He had seen Charles' type before: rich and arrogant, believing the world is all his.

"Can we have a minute alone?" Charles asked.

"Yeah, what's up?" Robin replied.

Charles grabbed Robin's arm and pulled her to the side.

"I want to see you later tonight, so can you get rid of your little friend and make that happen? I miss you like crazy, Robin."

"Charles, Kevin is a very good friend of mine _ "

"Can I see you or not? I'll be busy tomorrow and I leave for L.A. on Thursday," Charles said, in a demanding tone.

After a long sigh, Robin said, "Yeah, I can see you later tonight. Is ten o'clock fine?"

"Perfect!" Charles said, with a big smile on his face. After Charles had kissed Robin once again, he walked over to his car and paused before he got inside. He looked at Robin and Kevin standing next to each other, holding shopping bags.

"Kevin, it was nice to meet you," he said.

Kevin just nodded his head.

"Robin, I'll see you later tonight," Charles said, before he smiled and got back into his car.

Robin didn't respond. She knew that Charles only had said that to make Kevin upset and get under his skin. Regardless, Kevin stood there showing no sign of humiliation.

"You ready?" Kevin said, as he and Robin walked over to the waiting elevator.

Charles sat inside his car until they had disappeared into the elevator.

"Damn, he is a handsome man," he said, as he started up his Bentley and drove out of the garage.

~

Inside Robin's apartment, Kevin followed her back into the master bedroom, and they sat all the shopping bags on the floor. Robin looked at her beautiful bracelet again before she opened one of the drawers of her dresser and put it inside. When she turned and looked at Kevin, he was standing there with a serious expression on his face. Robin walked up to Kevin and put her arms around him.

"Charles is just a good friend of mind, he's—"

"You don't have to explain yourself to me, Robin," he said, cutting her off, "I'm sure you had many friends before I came into the picture."

"It's nothing serious."

"Robin, can you please leave it alone? I'm not worried about your friend, believe me," Kevin said confidently. "Are you ready to drop me off back home?"

"I thought you were gonna keep me company for a while?" Maybe we could order out and watch a movie together," Robin said, looking into Kevin's eyes.

"Maybe we can do it some other time. I want to go home and get myself ready for work in the morning. Plus, you have a hot date tonight, remember?"

"Kevin _ "

Before she could get out what she wanted to say, Kevin leaned forward and gave Robin a long, passionate kiss. They held each other tightly, while both of their eyes were completely closed. Kevin ran his hands through Robin's long black hair, then moved his hands down and palmed the cup of her ass. The kiss lasted almost five minutes long. When they had finally finished kissing, Robin could feel the wetness in her thong. She stared at Kevin with beaming eyes, almost on the verge of tears.

"Kevin, what are you trying to do to me?" she said softly.
"Nothing! Now come on, I'm ready to go," Kevin said, as he grabbed her trembling hand and walked her out of the bedroom.

~

Hakeem hadn't heard from Tammy all day. This morning, when she had dropped him off at his cousin's house, Hakeem realized that he had left his cell phone inside her bedroom. And he didn't know Tammy number; he had it programmed into his cell phone because he wasn't good at memorizing numbers. He went about his daily business. He caught a ride with a friend to North Philly to go see his daughter and nagging baby momma. Afterward, he got himself a haircut and hung around the neighborhood with a few of his friends.

What Every Woman Wants

Earlier when Tammy had driven to his cousin's house, he wasn't there, so she drove around the neighborhood searching for him. When she pulled her car up on 42nd Street, Hakeem had just gone inside one of his friend's houses to play NBA Live on the Sony Playstation. Her timing was off and she had just missed him. Tammy looked at her watch and noticed that the time was 7:15. She knew that Nathan would be at her house at eight, on the dot. He was always prompt. With a worrisome look on her face, Tammy drove down the street and headed back home. On her way to her townhouse, Tammy could only hope that Hakeem wouldn't show up unexpectedly.

"Damn, where is he?!" she said, driving her car toward the expressway.

~

West Philadelphia...

Mrs. Silvia was standing on the porch when Robin's Mercedes pulled up and parked. She watched as Robin and Kevin got out of the car, carrying shopping bags. On the ride back to Kevin's house, they hardly said ten words to each other; both had been in deep thought.

"Hey, Mrs. Silvia," Robin said, giving her a warm hug and following her into the house.

"Hey Robin, your brother called and I gave him Kevin's social security number. Thank you so much for helping him to get a job."

"It was nothing, Mrs. Silvia, I just wanted to help."

Kevin grabbed all of the bags and took them upstairs to his bedroom.

"Mrs. Silvia, what are you doing on Friday?" Robin asked.

"Nothing, what do you have in mind?" she replied.

"Since Friday is my birthday, I would like to take you and Kevin out for dinner."

"Wouldn't you rather spend it with Kevin alone?"

"Well, my brother will be there also, I want to introduce you to him. What better birthday present is there than spending it with people you enjoy being around?" Robin said.

"If Kevin don't mind, it's alright with me," Mrs. Silvia said.

"If Kevin don't mind what?" Kevin said, walking down the stairs.

"You and your mother spending my birthday with me and my brother. I want to take us all out to a nice restaurant," Robin said, walking over and grabbing Kevin's hand.

"It's cool with me," Kevin said, looking over at his mother. Kevin had only agreed to get his mother out of the house. She hardly ever went out, and when she did, it was to go food shopping or to get her hair done at the neighborhood salon.

"I'll call you, Mrs. Silvia," Robin said, as she and Kevin walked over to the front door.

"Alright, Robin, you take care, Sweetie," Mrs. Silvia said, turning around and walking towards the kitchen.

When Robin had got inside her car, Kevin leaned over and gave her a soft kiss on the lips.

"Drive safe and call me when you get back home."

"I will," Robin said, wishing she didn't have to leave.

"Thanks again, Robin, for everything. I promise you that I'm going to pay you—"

"Kevin, I did it because I wanted to. You don't owe me anything.

And if you ever tried to pay me back, I wouldn't take it," Robin said truthfully. Kevin just nodded his head.

"Can I see you tomorrow, after I get off work?" she asked.

"Just call me," Kevin said, walking back toward the house. Robin could feel that something wasn't right. Kevin's attitude hadn't been the same since meeting Charles.

"Hey, Kevin," she called out.

"Yeah," he said, turning around.

"Check your new suit pocket," Robin said, pulling off in her car.

What Every Woman Wants

Kevin stood there and watched Robin drive down the dark street. When she had disappeared from his sight, he walked back inside the house. After Kevin walked into his bedroom, he reached into one of the shopping bags and took out his new Salvatore Ferragamo suit. When he reached into the left pocket, he felt something and pulled it out. It was five brand new hundred-dollar bills. Kevin smiled and sat down on the edge of the bed. He thought about Robin and the wonderful day they had together. Even though he knew that she was now on her way to go see another man a very wealthy one at that. Kevin felt it was getting harder and harder to not make love to Robin. The more he was around her; the more he wanted to just snatch off all of her clothes and give her all the sex she could handle. He had already sized Robin up from head to toe. He knew exactly how he would make love to her. He was almost sure that Robin Davis would be the first woman he touched in over eight years. Kevin knew that special day would be coming soon. He already had it all planned out.

Chapter 17

Tuesday Night; 9:23 PM —

Tammy's naked body was covered with small streams of running sweat. Nathan had her small, petite body pinned down to the bed, fucking her with everything he had.

"Whose pussy is this? Tell me whose pussy this is!" Nathan yelled out aggressively.

"Yours! It's yours, Nathan! Oh, yes! God, it's yours!" Tammy shouted out.

The loud sound of the doorbell instantly snapped Tammy from out of her sexual trance.

"Oh shit!" she gasped, pushing Nathan off of her.

Tammy quickly got off the bed and grabbed her robe. Nervousness was all over her face. She knew it was Hakeem. "Damn!" she cursed under her breath.

Tammy looked over at Nathan, who was lying on top of the silk sheets with a big smile on his face. The doorbell rang once again. "Just don't answer it," Nathan said.

Tammy walked over to the window and peeped out the curtain. Hakeem was standing out in front with something in his hand. Tammy's car was parked out in front, so Hakeem knew she was inside.

Once again, the doorbell rang. Tammy stood there thinking about what she should do. Once thing was for sure—she couldn't let Hakeem find out about Nathan.

"Nathan, you stay up here!" Tammy said, rushing out of the bedroom.

She nervously walked down the stairs, as the doorbell continued to buzz. When Tammy opened the front door, Hakeem was standing there with a smile on his face and a box of pizza in his hand.

"Hey, Sweetie, where you been all day?" Hakeem said, kissing her on the lips.

When Tammy didn't invite him into the house, Hakeem knew something wasn't right.

"Boo, what's up?"

"Hakeem, I tried to call you all day, I even drove to your cousin's house looking for you. Why didn't you answer your cell phone?" she said.

"Boo, my phone is under your bed, I left it there last night by accident. Plus, it's on vibrate," Hakeem said, seeing the concerned look in Tammy's eyes.

"Why didn't you call me?"

"I don't have your number memorized. Why, what's the twenty one questions all about?"

"Damn, Hakeem, damn!" Tammy said, standing there, sadly shaking her head. She was madder at herself than anything else; she knew better than anyone how much the truth hurts.

"Is this what you came here for?" A voice came from the stairs.

Tammy turned around and saw Nathan walking down the stairs, holding Hakeem's cell phone in his hand. The only thing Nathan had on were a pair of silk boxers.

When Hakeem saw the man walking toward them, his heart felt like it had stopped beating inside his chest. The first thing that Hakeem had noticed was the gold wedding band on the man's finger.

"Nathan, I told you to stay the fuck upstairs!" Tammy said, as she angrily snatched the phone from his hand.

"Just trying to help," Nathan said, as he smiled, then turned and walked back up the stairs.

"Hakeem, please listen _ "

"Boo, it's cool, I understand," Hakeem said, cutting her off. Tammy could see the hurt in his eyes. When she passed Hakeem his cell phone, the tears started to fall quickly from her eyes.

"Hakeem, just please listen, it's not what you think! He's nothing, believe me!" she cried out.

126

Hakeem stared hard into her watery eyes and said, "Is that what you tell him about me? Tammy, I thought we had something special."

"We do..."

"Hold up, let me finish," he said. "If what we had was special, then I would be up there, making love to you, and not your married friend. Tammy, I don't know what it is that you want in life, but I'll give you some good advice. You'll never find true love through sex alone. Sometimes, what every woman wants is right in front of their eyes, but they never know it until it's too late," Hakeem said, as he sadly turned around and walked away.

"Hakeem, please! Please don't do this!" Tammy pleaded, running behind him. When she grabbed his arm, Hakeem yanked her away.

"Boo, it's over. Just let it rest!" he said.

Tammy stopped and watched as Hakeem continued to walk into the darkness of the night. She had just lost her true soul mate. The worst part was, she had lost Hakeem over her own sexual lust. She had lost Hakeem for a married man who would never be hers.

When Tammy walked back into the bedroom, she looked at Nathan and shouted, "Get the fuck out of my house!"

Nathan saw the look in her eyes and said, "Calm down, Baby, just tell me what's wrong."

"Nigga, I said get the fuck out of my house. Now! I told you not to come out of my bedroom, you slimy motherfucker!"

"Tammy, let's talk, we've been seeing each other for a while _ "

"Nathan, get-the-fuck dressed and leave!" Tammy said, walking over and reaching down inside her Chanel bag and pulling out her loaded .380 pistol.

Tammy turned around and pointed the gun at Nathan's head.

"You got three fucking minutes to put your shit on and get out of my house!" she fumed. Nathan saw the serious look on Tammy's face and quickly started getting dressed. Two minutes later, he was rushing out the front door and getting inside of his white BMW.

What Every Woman Wants

From her bedroom window, Tammy cried and watched Nathan speed off down the street.

~

Sitting in the back of a SEPTA bus, Hakeem was deep in thought. From the moment he had met Tammy, he thought that she was the one. Now he realized that she was nothing but a beautiful sex fiend. A woman lost, searching for love in all the wrong directions. Just like so many other women.

When Hakeem walked into the house, his cousin was sitting on the living room sofa, smoking on a blunt.

"Yo Cuz, Tammy came by here looking for you earlier today. And she just called three times," he said, blowing a thick cloud of smoke into the air.

"If she calls again, tell her I ain't here," Hakeem said, walking up the stairs.

The phone rang and his cousin quickly picked it up.

"Hello? No, Tammy, he still ain't here," he lied, and hung up the phone.

Inside her bedroom, Tammy was sitting on the edge of her bed, lost in a puddle of tears. Nathan had called her on the phone and called her "a crazy bitch" before he hung up. Tammy just couldn't get Hakeem from out of her mind.

"What the hell was I thinking?!" she asked herself.

When she tried to call Robin, she got her voice mail. She called two more times, but each time, the voice mail came on.

"God, please don't let me lose him like this," Tammy whispered. She knew that if she ever got Hakeem back, she would cut every other man out of her life. The pain that she was feeling had told her everything she needed to know. It was a pain that she had never felt before. A pain that she had heard many stories about, from women who had let their true loves slip away. Now, this same pain had entered her. She once read in a magazine that everyone gets just one shot at their true love. Thinking about that had only made her pain intensify. As the tears continued to fall from her eyes, the pains of love and confusion swept all throughout her mind, body, and crying soul.

~

Robin was lying in bed under the soft silk sheets, staring up at the ceiling. Charles was sleeping peacefully beside her. They had just finished having sex. Like always, Robin had given one of her Oscar worthy performances. She made sure to give special effects, placing emphasis on fake moans, screams, and phony tears of bliss—all the things that Charles had loved.

The whole time that Charles was on top of her, she had envisioned him being Kevin instead. It was the only way she could climax. She looked over at Charles' sleeping body and just shook her head. She knew that Charles wanted to give her the world. He would do it in a heartbeat. It was for that reason alone that she had strong feelings for him. But Robin also knew that she wasn't in love with him, and never would be. Their relationship had always been about sex and gifts—nothing more. Unlike Kevin, Charles was not a challenge for her. He had always been predictable. Plus, he was a spoiled rich boy who didn't satisfy her in bed. Robin was sure that Charles was sleeping around with other women from all around the country. That's why they never had sex without a condom. She told Tammy to be the same way with his partner, Nathan. Robin never understood why they traveled around the country so much, but she had enough sense to know that every trip wasn't always about company business, like Charles kept telling her. When Robin looked at her vibrating cell phone, she thought about getting out of bed and answering it. She knew it wasn't Kevin because he had to be at work too early to be calling her this late at night. Ignoring the vibration, Robin looked back up at the ceiling. Once again, a clear vision of Kevin entered her mind. If Kevin didn't make love to her soon, she was going to lose it. Since the day they had met, her body had been yearning for all of his attention. 'How long will he make her wait?' she thought. Robin thought about all of the attention that Kevin had received from the women at the mall. Her mind flashed back to the lustful looks that the women had given Kevin at her brother's law office. She knew that a man as fine as Kevin could have almost any woman he wanted, including herself. So what if he was broke? He was handsome, humble, and God-fearing. What more could a woman ask for? Great sex, she thought, with a devilish grin.

Robin looked over at Charles again to make sure he was still asleep. Hearing his light snores let her know that he was lost somewhere in dreamland. Robin slowly reached under her thick quilted pillow and eased out her small black vibrator. She used one hand to spread apart her vagina lips, and with the other hand, she set the vibrator on the tip of her clitoris. After a long sigh, she looked back up at the ceiling and turned on the vibrator. Instantly, it brought her naked body a pleasing sensation.

"Kevin! Oh, Kevin!" she whispered softly.

As the powerful orgasm swept throughout her trembling body, the tears of bliss escaped from the corners of her eyes. Kevin had a spell on her heart that could only be broken by him. When she felt Charles body moving beside hers, she quickly put the vibrator back under her pillow. She closed her eyes, pretending to be sleeping. She listened as he went to the bathroom, flushed the toilet, and washed his hands. When he walked back into the bedroom, Robin continued to act like she was sleeping.

Charles stood over the bed watching, as Robin appeared to be sleeping peacefully. He thought about waking her up for another round of good sex, but changed his mind. He got back in bed, pulling the silk sheet back over his body.

With their backs turned against each other, they were both lost in deep thought. Robin was thinking about seeing Kevin again; Charles was thinking about Nathan, and going out to Los Angeles with the other members of D.W.A.M.

What Every Woman Wants

Chapter 18

Wednesday Morning –

Trey and DJ Love Daddy were standing outside of the main studio room at Power 99 FM., They were engaged in a friendly discussion over which of their music styles was the best.

"I'm a rap music addict! Rap rules the world. Look at Snoop Dogg, Dr. Dre, Jay-Z, and others like 50 Cent, T.I. I.C.H. "Inner City Hustlers"Lil Wayne, and Eve," Trey said.

"Boy, that ain't no real music. Can't nobody make a baby off of no Snoop Dogg!" Love Daddy said, with a laugh. "I'm talking about that real soul, baby-making music. The music that your parents laid down and made you to. Minni Rippleton, Shirley Murdock, The Isleys, Mikki Howard, Sade, Stephany Mill, Debarge, Teddy P., Anita Baker, James Ingram, and the Stylistics."

"The Styl-what?" Trey said.

"Boy, you need to check out some of the older classics and put that rap stuff down for a minute," Love Daddy said, before turning and walking away.

"Where you going at, Old head?" Trey asked.

"I'm going to go listen to some Donny Hathaway," Love Daddy said, as he walked down the hall.

Trey slung his backpack full of rap CDs across his shoulder, and walked out into the lobby.

Penny had just hung up the telephone, and said, "Trey, can I speak to you for a minute?"

Trey walked over to her desk and said, "What's up?"

"When can I see you again?"

"Damn, Penny! I just saw you Monday!"

"So what!" she said, upset.

"Look, don't start sweating me about always coming by to see you," Trey said, looking down at his watch.

"Got somewhere to be?"

"Yeah, I do, as a matter of fact. I have to make a run downtown to pick up a few new CDs. Then I have a meeting with a very important person this afternoon." Trey said.

"A woman, ain't it?"

"No!" he lied, "Penny, I'll call you later tonight," Trey said, as he turned and walked out the front door.

Penny sat at her desk fuming. Trey had her sprung off the black dick and there was nothing she could do about it.

When Trey walked over to his Navigator truck, DJ Sherri Star was pulling up and parking beside his truck. Sherri Star stepped out of her Jaguar with a big smile on her face.

"What's up, Handsome? Leaving so soon?"

"Yeah, I have to go make a run downtown. Then I have somebody to meet up with this afternoon."

"I really enjoyed last night," she said, blushing.

"So did I. Maybe we can hook up again later."

"Sounds good with me. I see your little white girlfriend still trippin'," Sherri Star said.

"What do you mean?" Trey asked, curiously.

"I be catching her staring at me sometimes. I'm sure she has her assumptions about us."

"So what? I'm a single man. Just trying to do me," Trey said, with a smile on his face. "Sherri, I'll text you later."

Sherri Star watched Trey climb into his truck and turn it on. Instantly, the sound of the booming bass blasted out of the fifteen inch woofers. Moments later, Trey was driving out of the parking lot.

When Sherri Star walked into the radio station, she strolled by Penny's desk without speaking to her. She knew that Penny didn't like her; ever since she started working at the station and getting all of Trey's attention, she felt Penny's negative attitude. Sherri Star didn't care if Trey was sleeping around with other women; as long as she got to see him from time to time, she was cool with it.

What Every Woman Wants

As she walked through the small lobby, heading toward the kitchen area, Sherri Star could feel something K the evil eyes of Penny staring at her back. With a big smile on her face, she swished her perfectly round ass down the hall.

"Tammy, what the hell was you thinking about-a married naked one at that! I told you to leave Nathan's cheating ass alone. Now look at you, you done lost a man that you really like a lot, over a man who's married and can't give you nothing but dick!" Robin vented. "Damn, Girl, and y'all two looked so cute together."

"Robin, what can I do to get Hakeem back? I've been calling his phone all morning. He won't answer my calls. I know I fucked up but, Robin, I have to get him back!" Tammy said, wiping the tears from her eyes.

"Tammy, I really don't know what to say. I just met Hakeem, you know him more than anyone. Just give it a few days and see what happens. If he was into you just as much as you are into him, then he's hurting also. If it's meant to be, then things will find a way to workout. I'm sorry, Girl, but you're just as much to blame as Nathan. I told you, a dick can build a castle and it can also bring one down," Robin said, in a serious tone.

"Robin, I'm just so damn tired of this shit! I'm almost thirty years old and all my life I've been searching for the right man to share my life with. It seems like every time I get myself closer to finding the perfect man, I let him slip right through my hands. Hakeem was almost too perfect to believe, and now he's gone! Robin, sometimes I feel like I'm gonna die old, miserable, and alone. I'm my mother's only daughter; and I don't have any children or a husband. What is life, Robin, if we don't have no one to share it with—no one to love me unconditionally?" Tammy cried in anguish. "I'm not gonna give up on Hakeem, Robin, because I know how my heart feels about that man."

"Then don't. Still, what Nathan did was uncalled for."

"Fuck Nathan! I don't never want to see that bastard as long as I live!" Tammy yelled.

Robin sat at her desk contemplating the situation. Then she smiled and said, "Tammy, would you like to get that slimy son of a bitch back?"

"Yeah, it's Wednesday, so what?"

"Okay, what days did we use to get our hair done?" Robin asked.

"On Wednesday, why?"

"Remember who used to be at the hair salon with us every Wednesday, faithfully?" Robin asked, knowing that Tammy knew exactly whom she was talking about.

"Carolyn, Nathan's wife!" Tammy said, excitedly.

"That's right, her appointments were always at one o'clock sharp. Can you get off work early?" Robin asked.

"Yeah, that shouldn't be a problem."

"Good, because we have a date at the hair salon," Robin said, with a mischievous smile.

"Will your boss let you leave early again?"

"I'll just lie and tell her I have a family emergency. Look here, Tammy, I have a few calls to make, but first I'll call Valerie down at the shop to set us up an emergency appointment at one o'clock. Just meet me there. Love you. Bye."

"Love you, too," Tammy said, as they both hung up.

After Robin had made a few calls, she grabbed her Gucci tote bag and went to see her boss, Jennifer.

When she walked out of Jennifer's office, a big smile was on her face. Her lie worked, and now Robin was on her way downtown to meet Tammy at Valerie's hair salon.

Robin climbed into her car and turned it on. After she dropped the top, she slid on her tinted Dolce & Gabanna gold frames, and drove off, letting the music fill her ears and the wind blow through her long black hair. It was time to go get some payback.

~

Downtown Philadelphia...

Charles and Nathan were inside Charles' office, talking about Robin and Tammy.

"I got her hooked, Nathan! It's just a matter of time now, and Robin will be all mine. She's never had a lover like me," Charles bragged.

"Yeah, well that's the same way I thought about Tammy until that crazy lil' bitch pulled her gun out on me!" Nathan said. "You should've seen the guy she's bugging over, he looks like a fucking thug in one of those stupid rap videos. He's probably broke and out of a job!"

"Calm down, my friend. All I'm saying is you shouldn't have walked down the stairs in your boxers," Charles said, as they both busted out in laughter.

"Well, it was fun while it lasted. The sex was good, and my wife never found out. I'll find another one to take Tammy's place."

"You always got me," Charles grinned.

"And D.W.A.M.," Nathan said, with a chuckle.

"By the way, Robin had a guy with her at the condo yesterday, and he looked like a thug, too."

"Yeah, well maybe the two losers are brothers," Nathan laughed.

"The man Robin was with was fine as a box of chocolates. I had to look at him a few times to make sure my eyes weren't deceiving me," Charles said.

"That fine, huh?" Nathan asked.

"Finer than our friend, Julio, that we both enjoyed when we went to Brazil a few months back," Charles grinned.

"Do you think Robin is into this new guy?"

"No. He's probably fucking her and taking her out to the movies, but she's only doing it because I'm hardly ever in town. You should've seen her eyes when I gave her the diamond bracelet; they almost popped out of her head. It's probably worth more than her handsome friend's house and car, combined," Charles said. "I'm not worried about the guy. In order for another man to take Robin away from me, he's gonna need two things. Lots of money, and a big dick to calm her horny ass down," Charles said, as they busted out in laughter again. "I got both!" he added.

North Philly…

Hakeem was sitting on the sofa, watching his beautiful three-year old daughter, Hakeemah, playing with the new doll that he had just bought for her. Keisha walked out from the kitchen and looked at him. She knew something wasn't right with him. All morning long, Hakeem had been acting very moody. Keisha walked over to the sofa and sat down beside him.

"Girl, don't you got somewhere to be at? Ain't Na'Kia and Felicia outside waiting on you?" he said.

"Boy, what's wrong with you?!" she snapped, "Nigga, don't be mad at me cause that high-saddity bitch left your broke ass!"

"Shut up, Keisha! You don't know what the hell you're talking about!"

"Yeah, well I bet one thing; whatever it is, it's got something to do with another man! Because that's the only way a bitch can hurt you! You need to learn that all of us bitches are the same, Hakeem; we all running around chasing after money and dick. It doesn't matter if a woman is rich or poor, we all lust for the same thing." Keisha said.

"You're wrong! There's a lot of good women out there who haven't gone through life fucking every Tom, Dick, and Harry they came across."

"Yeah, well name me five good women who ain't fuck a rack of men before she finally found who she was searching for?" Keisha asked, twisting up her lips.

Hakeem sat and thought for a moment.

"Yeah, that's what I thought! Hakeem, wake up and smell the coffee, Baby—every female ain't nothing but a whore! Some are undercover and the others are over the covers. I know God don't like it, but that's just the way it is."

"You're wrong, Keisha, there are some good women out there in the world, and one day I'll find me one." Hakeem said, seriously.

"Yeah, well it won't be that bitch who played you," Keisha said, as she stood up from the sofa and walked out of the living room.

Center City, Philadelphia
Valerie's Hair Salon...

Inside the spacious hair salon, women were sitting around, waiting for their turn to get in their favorite stylist's chair. Eight stylist chairs were situated right next to each other, and each was occupied. A large screen TV was playing "The Young and the Restless". Most of the women inside were watching the TV, while the others were sitting back, reading one of the many magazines that the shop had laid out on the small wooden tables.

When Robin and Tammy walked in, they were quickly greeted by their friend, Valerie. Valerie was a tall, beautiful brown-skinned woman who owned the shop.

"What's up girls? I got both of y'all in," she said, showing her beautiful smile.

"Thanks, Val," Robin said, as she watched Valerie walk over to greet another customer.

Robin and Tammy stood there scanning through the shop. When they spotted Nathan's wife, Carolyn, she was sitting all alone, reading Ebony magazine. Both women walked over and sat down in the two empty chairs beside her. They had only known her from seeing pictures. Nathan had shown Tammy a picture of her and his two children before, and Charles had shown Robin a few pictures that had Nathan and Carolyn in them. So even though both women had known who Carolyn was, she didn't have the slightest clue of who they were.

Carolyn was a very attractive 42-year-old woman. She had a gorgeous dark-skinned complexion and short, curly black hair. Robin and Tammy were both eyeing her down. Though an older woman, Carolyn was dressed in the latest fashions: Manolo Blahnik heels, DKNY jeans, and a white Vera Wang silk blouse. On her left hand was a 4-carat platinum ring that lit up like a white Christmas tree. Even a blind man could see that the woman was swimming in piles of money. All because of her super-rich husband, of course.

"So tell me the rest, Girl," Tammy said.

"Girl, Charles had me calling on God so much last night that I thought I was in Church, I couldn't believe it! He was a total animal," Robin said, making sure Carolyn could hear her.

Carolyn smiled, acting like she wasn't paying the two women any attention.

"How was your night with his best friend?"

"Girl, Nathan's tall, dark body had me crying out in pure bliss. I ain't never been sexed like that before!" Tammy answered.

"Do you think a man that fine is really single? I mean, he's rich, successful, and handsome, it's kind of hard to believe." Robin insinuated.

"I don't know that's what he keeps telling me. Who cares?" Tammy said.

Carolyn kept her eyes on the pages of Ebony, but was listening to every single word. Before it was her turn to get her hair done, she had heard more than enough about her husband, Nathan. She had always felt in her heart that Nathan was cheating on her, but now this had confirmed it. Carolyn now knew that all the weekly business trips with Charles were an excuse to meet up with other women. It was painful to finally find out about her husband's adulterous ways. She was definitely going to bring this news to his attention. However, Carolyn wasn't exactly the perfect housewife. She had her own secret love life that no one had known about. Lately, Nathan wasn't the only spouse creeping around. Carolyn had recently met a handsome young man of her own. After getting her hair done, she was headed straight to the hotel to meet up with him. Their private suite had already been paid for with her cheating husband's own money.

After Robin and Tammy had gotten their hair done, they walked out of the salon cracking up.

"What's up, Girl, what do you want to do now?" Robin asked.

"I'm driving by Hakeem's, maybe I can get him to talk to me," Tammy said, walking over to her Lexus.

"Alright then, I'll call you later on. Will the girls be over at your house later tonight?" Robin asked.

"Yeah, I talked to Anissa, they'll be there at seven."

"Okay, cool, I'm bring the Coronas." Robin said.

"And I'll have the weed," Tammy replied, as she smiled and got in her car.

A Short Time Later…

Tammy pulled up in front of Hakeem's cousin's house, and quickly got out of the car. She then walked up to the front door, pressed the doorbell, and knocked. When no one had answered, she took out her cell phone and dialed Hakeem's cell phone number. Once again, the voice mail picked up and answered. After a long sigh, she closed her cell phone, walked back over to her car, and got inside. She waited fifteen minutes before she finally decided to pull off.

When Tammy had driven off, Hakeem moved away from the bedroom curtains and sat back down on the bed. He sat there, lost in thought. Tammy had left over eight messages on his voice mail. He wondered why she was so desperately trying to find him. What could she possibly want with me after what I found out, he thought. He knew that Tammy didn't need him, and she could easily get herself another boy-toy to have sex with. She was beautiful and successful, so why keep chasing after me, he thought. Hakeem had established some deep feelings for Tammy. He had enjoyed being in her company. He also knew that Tammy had cared for him, but he never knew how much. After catching Tammy with another man, Hakeem now believed that he was nothing but Tammy's young sex toy. But the way she was calling and driving around searching for him made him think that there had to be something more.

~

Robin had called Kevin on his cell phone. When she had reached him, he asked her to drive over to his house. Twenty minutes later, Robin was pulling up in front and parking her car.

When Kevin let her inside the house, they hugged and kissed. Kevin was still dressed in his work clothes. His mother had just left the house, right before Robin had pulled up. They missed each other by a few minutes. Mrs. Silvia had gotten a ride with one of her girlfriends to go to the supermarket.

Kevin told Robin everything about his first day at work, and she could hear the excitement in his voice. He talked about everything, even all the women who had been lusting over him and watching his every move.

"It was funny to see lawyers, secretaries, and paralegals all lusting over the new janitor," he told her, as them both had a big laugh.

"Don't you worry, Beautiful, I'm focus," he told her.

Robin followed Kevin upstairs into his bedroom. Since she had been in there a few times already, it was no big deal.

"Do you want to catch a quick bite to eat? I still have a few hours before I have to meet up with my girlfriends over at Tammy's house."

"No problem, but first, let me go take a quick shower," Kevin said, as he grabbed his washcloth and towel from off the dresser.
Robin watched as Kevin walked over to the door and paused.

"You can pick out the clothes you want me to wear, and the cologne you'd like to smell me in," he said, with a smile.

When he turned and walked out of the bedroom, Robin walked over to the small closet and picked out what she wanted Kevin to put on. She picked out a nice brown cashmere sweater, a pair of blue Rocawear jeans, and his brown suede Timberland boots. Then she opened a dresser drawer and took out a new pair of Calvin Klein sport briefs, and matching T-shirt and white socks. The men's cologne that she chose was her favorite, Georgio Armani.

For about fifteen minutes, Robin had sat on the edge of Kevin's bed waiting for him to come out of the bathroom. Since the small bathroom was right next to his bedroom, she could hear the water from the shower running, and Kevin singing the melody to a song.

Robin heard the singing and the shower water stop at the same time. She had wondered what song Kevin had been singing.

When the doorknob turned, Kevin was standing there with nothing on. He was bare-ass naked, holding his work clothes in one of his hands.

Robin sat on the edge of the bed, speechless, checking out every muscle and tattoo on Kevin's well-tuned naked body. As she stared at Kevin's dick, she just grinned and shook her head. Kevin's dick was much bigger than Charles', and it wasn't even hard. She looked at his broad shoulders, muscular chest, six-pack abs, thick thighs, and perfect round ass, and almost fainted. Oh my God, she thought, feeling her thong becoming wet.

Kevin nonchalantly walked over to where his clothes were laid out on the bed, and picked up the Calvin Klein underwear. Robin was still in a state of shock as she watched Kevin start dressing himself.

"Are you okay?" he asked, seeing the look on her face.

"Yeah... I'm... fine," she muttered.

Kevin's well-toned physique was like it had been delivered straight from God. Every single muscle stood out, and the beautifully designed tattoos that covered his arms and chest only made him look even more desirable. Not only did Kevin have one of the most beautiful faces she had ever seen, but he also possessed the best man's body that her eyes had ever come across. All the years he had done in prison had helped him strengthen his mind, body, and soul.

Robin stood up and walked over to Kevin. She looked him straight in the eyes and said,

"Why are you doing this to me, Kevin?" Her eyes were serious.

Kevin grabbed Robin's trembling hands and said softly,

"When the time is right, Robin, I'm gonna show you why. Now come on, let's go, I'm starving" he said, walking her out of the bedroom.

What Every Woman Wants

Downtown Philadelphia
The Marriott Hotel...
I'm coming again, Baby! Right there! Yes! Oh, yes!" Carolyn shouted out, as her handsome young lover had her pinned down to the bed, and was aggressively fucking her from behind.

Every time he stroked up against her sweaty round ass, the large headboard slammed hard against the wall. Carolyn had her arms and legs spread out on the bed, receiving the best fucking of her life. Her young, handsome, secret lover had made her come more times in the last two hours than her husband, Nathan, had in the last four months.

Both of their naked bodies were covered in dripping sweat. When he had finally come again, he slumped down on her shaking body. He could feel her body trembling beneath his. Today was the third time that they had sex. He was positive that Carolyn would somehow find a way to meet up with him again, whenever he asked her.

Carolyn rolled over in bed and stared into her handsome young lover's sweaty face. Her body was still shivering from the after effects of the wonderful orgasm she had just had.

"Trey, that felt so good! I really, really needed that," Carolyn said, staring deep into his eyes.

"Carolyn, I told you that I'm here for you, baby. What your husband won't do for you, I gladly will," Trey said, as they both smiled at each other.

"Do you have to go back to the radio station?"

"No, Baby, what about you?" he asked.

"I still got about two hours before I should be going back home."
"Then let's stop wasting time," he said, as they began passionately kissing.

Chapter 20

Later That Night...

Robin and Kevin had drove over to the T.G.I. Friday's restaurant on City line Avenue. While they were there they enjoyed a delicious fish dinner along with good conversation before leaving the restaurant. The whole time they were sitting at their small private table in the back, Robin couldn't get Kevin's amazing body from out of her wandering mind. When they left the restaurant, Robin dropped Kevin off back at home. They kissed and said goodbye.

~

On her way over to Tammy's house, Robin stopped by a grocery store and picked up two six-packs of Corona's. Kevin had her mind lost inside his sexual world, and he still had yet to touch her. Robin's women's intuition had already told her that Kevin was going to be a great lover; she couldn't wait to feel his thick love-stick deep inside of her yearning tunnel of love. Just the thought of Kevin being inside of her had given Robin chills that had no explanation. What Robin was now feeling for Kevin was much more that just sex. Now it was feeling more like a need K a need for Kevin's love, affection, strength, and protection. Her lust for Kevin was quickly turning into the deepest love she had ever felt for a man. Hell she had not even felt this way for any woman for that matter.

Inside his bedroom, Kevin was lying across his bed, staring up at the ceiling with a big smile on his face. He knew exactly what he was doing to Robin; bringing her along nice and slowly, giving her just enough, but not too much. It was the same sexual tactics that women had used on men for centuries. Kevin purposely made sure that Robin saw his naked body, but did no touching. He knew that the image of his body would stay inside of her head for a while. Whenever she masturbated, it would only be him that she envisioned. Kevin knew that Robin was a woman who had always been in total control, and it wouldn't be that easy for her to simply give it all up. He knew that in order for two people to reach that ultimate level of love, they would first have to overcome a few obstacles. When true love emerges; the devil would always find a way to interfere.

~

Tammy, Robin, Anissa, Tanya, and Dawn all sat around the living room, sipping on Corona's and smoking rolled up sticks of marijuana.

Anissa, Tanya, and Dawn were Robin and Tammy's three girlfriends from college. All three of them were beautiful, educated, and married to wealthy, successful men. At least once a month, the women would all choose a place to have one of their womanly gatherings. Even though Anissa had lived in New Jersey and Tanya and Dawn both lived in Delaware, they always found a way to be there. Even after twelve long years, the D.L.M. crew was still in effect. Robin and Tammy were the only two women who were still childless and single.

"So, you think this Kevin guy is finally the one?" Dawn asked.
"I'm positive he's the one," Robin said, passing the weed over to Tanya.

"That's what you said about your millionaire friend Charles, until you found out that his dick was the size of my pinky finger," Anissa said, as everyone busted out in laughter.

"So what does this guy, Kevin, do for a living, and what college did he go to?" Dawn asked.

"He's a lawyer and he graduated from Harvard," Robin lied. Tammy almost threw up her beer. When she looked over at Robin, she just smiled and shook her head.

"Damn, girl, you done finally hit the jackpot!" Anissa said, excitedly.

"Do you have a picture of him?" Dawn asked.

"Yeah, by the way, I do," Robin said, reaching down into her Prada bag and taking out a color photo of her and Kevin. Robin passed the picture over to Dawn.

"Whoa! When did Harvard start having men like him?" Dawn asked, rhetorically, "He's gorgeous, Robin!"

Tanya and Anissa quickly ran over to look at the picture.

"He is fine!" Anissa said, lusting over the picture.

"Girl, calm your ass down before I go tell your husband," Tanya said, playfully shoving her shoulder. "Robin, this man is a sight for sore eyes. How was the sex?" Tanya asked curiously.

"Just thinking about it makes my body tremble," Robin said.

Once again, Tammy gave Robin a look that said, Girl, you're just too much.

"Is it big?" Anissa asked, as everyone inside the room suddenly got quiet.

Robin looked around at all of her girlfriends waiting faces. Then she put both hands together and slowly started separating them. When she finally stopped moving her hands, they were at least twelve inches apart.

"Oh my God, girl, how can you take all of that?" Dawn asked. "Yeah, cause I can't even imagine half of that inside of me," Tanya said, as they all started laughing again.

After a long sigh, Robin said, "It took some time getting used to it, but now I can handle every single inch," she said with a grin. Tammy just sat back inside her chair, smiling and shaking her head. For the next half hour, she listened as Robin told lie after lie about her and Kevin's amazing sex life. The three women were so into her fabricated stories that they were all ready to rush back home and fuck the shit out of their rich black husbands.

When they all walked out of Tammy's house and got back into their expensive automobiles, they were all high, and horny as hell. "Girl, why you lie like that?" Tammy asked.

"The same reason you lied about Hakeem," Robin replied.

"Well, his dick is big and he is very handsome," Tammy said.

"I'm not talking about that part, I'm talking about the part where you told everyone that Hakeem was a silent partner at a new casino that was being built out in Vegas," Robin said, as they busted out in laughter.

"It was the first thing that came to my mind," Tammy replied. "Girl, what the hell has happened to us? We can't even tell our closest girlfriends the truth about the men in our lives."

"Your life, Robin, I lost mine. Remember?" Tammy said, in a sad tone. Both women sat down on the sofa.

"You know that sooner or later, they're gonna find out the truth about everything," Tammy said, passing Robin the last rolled up joint.

"So what? I couldn't tell them that Kevin's a janitor who just got released from federal prison. They would've laughed me right up out of there," Robin said, blowing smoke through her nose.

"Me, too, if I would've told 'em the truth about Hakeem," Tammy said, taking the joint from Robin's hand.

"So you still couldn't get in contact with Hakeem, huh?"

"No, I think he's avoiding me. At least that's what I feel he's doing," Tammy said, upset.

"Well, just don't stop until you find out the whole truth about how he feels."

"I'm not. Tomorrow is Thursday, my day off, I'm gonna look for him until I find him. If I'm gonna lose Hakeem, then I'm going down fighting," Tammy said.

"You go, Girl!"

"Robin, would you ever run after a man?"

"Hell no! It's just some things I won't do! Then again, I've never been seriously in love, so who knows."

"Well, I think I'm in love with Hakeem and I'm telling you, Robin, it's not a good feeling when you're in love with a man who's not around anymore," Tammy said, in a serious tone.

Before Robin could reply, her cell phone started vibrating on her hip. After listening to her voice mail, she hung up and said, "I have to get ready to go. That was Charles, he's waiting at my condo with a new gift for me."

Tammy just shook her head.

"Lucky you."

~

Lower Marion, Pennsylvania
Suburbs of Philadelphia...

When Nathan had gotten in bed, Carolyn had her back toward him, pretending to be asleep. She had decided not to say anything to him about the upsetting news she had overheard at the hair salon. Even before hearing about her husband's adulterous ways, she had long suspected it.

Nathan was handsome, wealthy, and very successful, so it was obvious that women constantly threw themselves at him. Twenty-two years earlier, she was one of those women. Even now, Carolyn loved her husband more than anything. Nathan had provided her with a life she had never dreamed of. Expensive cars, a house, clothes, and all the money she could handle. She had enough for both her and their two children. She lacked nothing but Nathan's affection. He rarely ever made love to her. Most of the time, he claimed be too tired from working all day with Charles at their successful real estate company. But Carolyn had always felt in her heart that there was more to it, and now she knew the real truth about her cheating husband. The two women inside the hair salon had confirmed it.

Two weeks ago, when Carolyn had met Trey at an Amaco gas station, she was pumping gas into her new Mercedes Benz, Trey insisted on doing it for her. She smiled and gave him the pump and stood back watching him. As she watched the handsome young man pumping her gas, lust filled her eyes. Carolyn knew that she was old enough to be the young man's mother, but his gorgeous face and tall, slim body was appealing to the eyes. Especially to the eyes of an older woman who was now at her sexual peak, and wasn't getting sex from her husband. She took Trey's number and watching him get into his big black truck and drive off, Carolyn thought about the throwing his number away, but for some strange reason, she changed her mind. Lots of men had always approached her, giving her their phone numbers, but Trey's was the only number she had ever kept. After the first time they had sex, Carolyn was glad that she had kept it. Trey had fucked her so good that Carolyn couldn't wait to see him again. Now, not a day went by that she didn't yearn for his sex.

As Carolyn lay there beside her sleeping, adulterous husband, she knew that she was no better than him. If her husband would give her the attention that he once did, she wouldn't hesitate to get rid of her handsome young sex toy. But Carolyn knew that would never happen. Nathan would never change, so why should I, she thought.

~

After taking a nice warm shower, Tammy threw on a large white T-shirt and got in bed. Lying back on the sheets, she reached over and picked up the telephone. After dialing Hakeem's cell phone number, she waited. When the voice mail answered, Tammy decided to leave another message.

"Hakeem, I know you got all my calls. Will you please call me back? Please! I really want to tell you something that's been on my mind a lot. Baby, I'm sorry that I hurt you, please just call me back, Hakeem. I'm not giving up on us. So please, just call me," Tammy said, before hanging up the phone.

Inside Robin's bedroom, Charles saw her staring up at the ceiling and asked, "What are you thinking about?"

"Nothing," she lied.

"Do you like your new gift?" Charles said, referring to the new diamond stud earrings he bought her.

"Yes, they're beautiful, just like all the gifts you buy me. I put them inside the drawer with the rest of my jewelry. Thank you, Charles."

"Anything for you Beautiful; I really wish I didn't have to go to L.A.; but me and Nathan have to be there. I'm sorry that I have to miss your birthday."

"When will you be back in Philly?"

"I'm not sure, maybe a week or two. Don't worry, I'll call you." Charles smiled, and coiled over on top of Robin's body as she closed her eyes.

She lay there, lost in thought, imagining that it was Kevin's body making love to her instead of Charles.

Chapter 21

Thursday Morning...

As soon as Tammy had got out of bed, she brushed her teeth, washed her face, and quickly got dressed. Moments later, she was rushing out the front door. Driving around in her Lexus, Tammy's first stop was Hakeem's cousin's house. His cousin had told her that Hakeem had just left, and he was probably on his way to 42nd Street K the neighborhood where he had grown up.

Tammy got back into her car and headed toward 42nd Street.

Twenty minutes later, she was driving around the poor dilapidated neighborhood searching for him. Tammy drove up and down 41st, 42nd, and 43rd Street. When she didn't see him, she drove by Spiros Pizza Shop on 40th and Girard Avenue. Nothing. Tammy then headed over to Lex Pizza shop, located on Lancaster Avenue. Still nothing, but Tammy was desperate to find him.

When Tammy had gone to sleep the night before, she had had a bad dream about him. In her dream, Hakeem was in a lot of trouble, and her presence had somehow saved him. Plus, Tammy had missed him more than she had missed any other man before. Her mind, body, and soul were all yearning for him.

After an hour of driving around with no luck, Tammy disappointingly headed back home. Then, in the silence of her car, a tear fell down from the corner of her left eye.

~

When Kevin had walked out of the men's bathroom, after dumping out the trash cans and mopping the floor, two attractive black women were standing nearby, watching him very closely.

Since being hired, Kevin had become the talk of the law office. Almost every woman who worked on the floor was plotting and scheming on ways to get him. "The fine new janitor" was constantly being talked about _ and lusted over. Both black and white women were attracted to him. But Kevin had paid them no mind at all. All he was focused on was doing his job and being the best janitor he could be. Plus, Kevin knew that most women were nothing but trouble. In his opinion they were all little Delilah's waiting to bring down Samson. The sad part about it, it was that Kevin felt that ninety percent of the women he worked with would risk their job just to have sex with him—even if they were married or not.

As he walked down the hall carrying his mop and water bucket, he could feel the scanning eyes from lusting females watching him from behind. Even for a man straight out of prison, it felt uncomfortable. What do women want? He thought. Is it all about sex? Does love even exist anymore? The questions filled his head. As he walked into another men's bathroom, he stopped and looked into the large wall mirror. With a smile on his face, Kevin paused. I wonder if there are more female dogs in the world than there are male, he thought.

~

Inside Robin's condominium, the two maids were cleaning up. Maria was inside the living room vacuuming the carpet. They had already washed the dishes and did all the laundry. Carla looked at her older aunt and walked down the hall toward the master bedroom. She made sure that she kept her ears on the running carpet cleaner. As soon as Carla entered the bedroom, she ran straight over to the dresser. She opened the middle drawer and moved a few pieces of Robin's underwear out of the way.

Staring down at the pile of shining jewelry instantly brought a smile to her face. There were gold rings, diamond earrings, bracelets, watches, chains, and a few other expensive items all stashed inside the drawer. Carla had been stealing from Robin since her first day working there. Robin wasn't her only victim;

she had been stealing from most of the tenants that lived in the building. Carla looked and decided on what piece of jewelry she would take this time.

After she chose her piece, she slipped it into her pocket. Then she put the underwear back over all the jewelry and closed the drawer. With a big smile on her face, she calmly walked out of the bedroom and back into the living room where her aunt Maria was still vacuuming.

~

West Philadelphia
41st and Brown Street...

Hakeem, Black, and Noonie were all standing around inside the living room of a small brick row house. Hakeem had been desperate for money, so he decided to come to Black and Noonie for another small loan.

A week earlier, he had borrowed some money and used it to pay for his daughter's monthly day care bill. Black and Noonie were the neighborhood loan sharks; besides all the many other things the duo was into.

"What's up with that other money, Hakeem?" Black asked, as he peeled off three hundred-dollar bills and passed them to Hakeem.
"Don't worry, Black, I'll have it in a few days."

"That's what you said two days ago," Noonie said, eyeing him down.

"Look, I told y'all that after I pay my tickets and get my car out of the impound lot, I'll sell it and pay y'all back every penny I borrowed," Hakeem said.

"And interest!" Black snapped.

"Yeah, and the interest, too," Hakeem said.

"Hakeem, you a homeboy and all that, but remember, business is business. Don't have us chasing after our money." Noonie said, in a serious tone.

"Haven't I always paid y'all the money I borrowed?"

153

"Yeah, that's when you had a job." Black replied.

"Listen here, fellas, y'all money is in safe hands."

"For your sake, we hope so," Noonie said. Black and Noonie stood there watching Hakeem put the money into his pocket, then turn and walk out the front door.

"If he don't have all our money soon, we're gonna make an example out of pretty boy," Black said.

"Fine with me. I don't like them pretty niggas anyway," Noonie said, as they both started laughing.

~

"Come in and make it fast!" Robin said, as she sat at her desk typing into her computer. The door opened and Trey walked inside, carrying a white shopping bag.

"Trey, please, not now!"

"Robin, calm down, I just wanted to come by and drop off the birthday present I got you," he said, with a smile.

Robin's expression quickly changed.

"Oh, you remembered!"

"How can I forget? I hear you talking about turning 31 all the time," Trey said, walking over to the desk and passing Robin the bag.

Robin smiled and dug into the bag, pulling out a beautiful yellow and white Dina-Bar-El dress.

"Trey, thank you so much," she said, standing up from her chair and walking around the desk to give him a hug.

"How do you know about Dina-Bar-El dresses?" she asked curiously.

"An older friend of mine put me up on it." Trey answered.

"Older, huh? You found some horny older woman to take my place?" Robin asked, playfully frowning up her face.

"Can't nobody take your place, Robin."

"Better not, cutie. So why you ain't wait till my birthday to give me my gift?" she asked.

"Cause tomorrow I'ma be real busy. And I'm sure you are too, birthday girl."

"Yeah, I have a dinner date reservation down at Bookbinder's, with my older brother and a few friends," Robin said, walking back over to her seat and sitting down.

"Enjoy yourself, Beautiful, I'll see you soon."

"Alright Trey, thanks for the gift," Robin said, watching as Trey walked out of the office and shut the door.

Robin still has tons of work to still do, Robin faced her computer and went back to typing.

~

Tammy was sitting on the sofa listening to Mary J. Blige's classic album, "My Life". No other female singer had touched her soul like the ghetto-diva Mary J. Blige. When she heard her musical ring tone, she quickly answered her cell phone.

"Hello!"

"Hey, what's up, Tammy? It's me, Chuck. I was wondering _ "

"Listen Chuck, I don't think we should see each other anymore. I have someone in my life now," she said, cutting him off. Click! Tammy hung up on him, then sat down her phone and finished listening to her music. Chuck was the fourth different man to call her, and Tammy told all them the same thing. From now on there was only one man she wanted to be bothered with; Hakeem.

~

Later That Afternoon...

After Robin had gotten off work, she got inside her car and headed over to Kevin's house. She waited downstairs in the living room, talking to Mrs. Silvia, Kevin was upstairs in his bedroom, getting dressed. Robin couldn't help but think about the day before, when she watched Kevin walk into his bedroom totally naked.

"Me and my brother will come by and pick you and Kevin up around six," Robin said.

"Okay, that's fine, we'll both be ready. I'm really looking forward to getting out of the house. And being with you on your birthday makes it so much better," Mrs. Silvia said.

"You're gonna like Billy, he's really nice."

"If he's anything like you, Robin, then I'm sure I will."

"Plus, I told him that you are very pretty," Robin grinned.

"Oh Robin, why did you do that? I'm gonna feel so embarrassed now."

"Well you are, and I think my brother will be surprised when he sees you."

"You didn't tell me that you were playing matchmaker."

"Well to be honest, Mrs. Silvia, I wasn't, but then yesterday it dawned on me that you're just a few years older than my brother and both of y'all are single." Robin said.

"Well just don't expect too much from it, I haven't thought about a man in years."

"I'm not. My brother's very picky, but who knows?"

Kevin walked down the stairs, before leaving, Robin gave Mrs. Silvia a warm hug and then she and Kevin left. After they got inside Robin's car, she drove off down the street.

Robin was taking Kevin to a live poetry show down on South Street. Working at the radio station came with its share of perks. She was able to get her hands on two free tickets.

Los Angeles, California...

Inside the Beverly Hills Hotel, Charles, Nathan, and an attractive blond haired white woman were lying on king-sized bed in a large elegant suite. They had just finished another round of wild sex. Man on man. Man on woman. And everything else that three adventurous people could think of. Just like Charles and Nathan, the woman was also a member of the secret society of D.W.A.M.

"I can't wait for the large D.W.A.M. gathering tonight," Charles said, excitedly.

"Me either," the woman said.

"Maybe there will be a few new recruits there," Nathan hoped. "Spencer and Thomas told me that they had both invited a few new people, but they weren't sure if they would show up," Charles said.

"It's too bad they're the only two members in D.W.A.M. who can give out guest invitations," the woman said.

"Well, don't forget, that's how we all became official members, by being invited as a guest first," Charles replied.

"Maybe there will be a few more attractive women?" Nathan said.

"Or a few more men," Charles responded, with a smile.

"Or a few more fine black men," the woman joined in, with big grin on her face.

"Did you talk to your wife, Nathan? She called twice," Charles asked.

"Yeah, since the kids are over at their grandparents for the weekend, I told her to go and enjoy herself. I'm sure she's tired of being stuck in the house," Nathan said, running his hand through the white woman's long blond hair.

"Let her get out and blow some of that money, huh?" Charles said.

"Yeah, she needs a little excitement in her dull life. Since I'm never around to give it to her, maybe getting out of the house will bring her some." Nathan laughed.

"Just remember fellas, after L.A., next is our big anniversary in Miami," the woman interrupted.

"How could we ever forget," Charles said, with a big grin on his face, "We've been waiting all year!"

~

That Night...

After the poetry show had ended, Robin and Kevin walked up and down South Street, talking and holding hands. When they got back inside the car, they drove over to Robin's condo. Together, they sat on the sofa talking, while listening to some smooth jazz music. Afterward, they walked out onto the balcony and started passionately kissing.

"Follow me," Kevin said, grabbing Robin's hand and walking her towards the master bedroom.

As soon as they walked inside, Kevin turned to her and said "Get undressed and lay across your bed.

Robin didn't ask any questions. In less than two minutes, she was completely naked and lying across her bed.

"Where's your body lotion, I'm sure you have some around here," Kevin said, smiling.

Robin looked over to the dresser and noticed that the maids had put away all of her lotions and perfumes.

"Check in the drawers, the maids usually put up everything when they come to clean the apartment," she said.

Robin lay there watching as Kevin went through a few of the drawers.

"Bingo," he said, finding what he was looking for.

When he turned around, Kevin was holding a bottle of peach and apricot body lotion.

"Mmm, one of my favorites!" Robin spoke softly as Kevin walked back over and sat down beside her.

"Now, I just want you to relax," he said. Then he started pouring the lotion all over Robin's back, ass, arms, and legs. When Kevin dug his strong hands into Robin's back, chills instantly entered her trembling body. Like a trained massage therapist, Kevin was maneuvering his hands all over Robin's naked body. He turned her around on her back and gave the same attention to her breast, neck, face, stomach, and inner thighs.

Robin lay there lost in a sensual zone. Kevin started performing his massage magic on her feet and toes, Robin had to hold back

158

from screaming. The feeling was sending a million chills all throughout her shivering body. An hour later, after Kevin had finally finished, Robin was yearning for his body to enter hers. But, all Kevin did was kiss her cheek, and whisper into her ear, "Okay, Beautiful, it's time to get dressed and take me back home. I have to be at work early in the morning."

After Robin had dropped Kevin back off at his house, she hurried back home and had a quickie with her vibrator. She then picked up the phone and called Tammy, telling her all about the wonderful day she had enjoyed with Kevin.

~

Inside his bedroom, Kevin was lying on his bed, staring up at the ceiling, with a big smile on his face.

"Yeah, she's ready now," he said to himself.

Robin's upcoming birthday was the day that Kevin had been patiently waiting for. He had been purposely preparing her for that special day. Now Kevin felt that Robin was ready. Kevin had studied every inch of Robin. He personally knew every one of her sensitive spots. He knew where she liked and didn't like to be touched; Kevin had memorized it all.

~

Atlantic City, New Jersey...

Locked away inside $700-a-night private suite, Trey had Carolyn's naked body spread out on the king-size bed, giving her long, powerful strokes. So far, she had already climaxed three times. But the night was still young. After Carolyn had gotten off the phone with her husband, Nathan, she rushed over to Trey's apartment, picked him up, and they headed straight to the Taj Mahal Hotel and Casino in Atlantic City. Now, for the next three days and nights, they planned on enjoying each other's lust and affection.

What Every Woman Wants

In the tranquility of their private suite, the only sounds being heard were the intense moans of two very sexual adults. Both caught up in a secret world of blissful, untamed sex. Carolyn loved every single moment of it.

"Oh yes, Trey! Yes! I'm coming again!" she yelled out in ecstasy.

Chapter 22

Friday Afternoon...

Robin had carried all of her birthday gifts over to the car, she put everything on the backseat, and climbed inside. Then she pulled off, headed for home. Her boss had given her a half-day off work since it was her birthday.

Robin pulled her car into the underground garage, and saw Tammy's blue Lexus parked in her visitor's parking space. They got out of their cars and gave each other a hug.

"Hold up, let me get your gift, birthday girl," Tammy said, walking back to her car.

When Tammy walked back over to Robin, she was carrying a white shoe box.

"Here Robin, happy birthday," she said, passing Robin the box. Robin grabbed the box, took off the lid, and her eyes widened with excitement.

"The new Jimmy Choo's, you got them for me!"

Inside the box was a pair of black Jimmy Choo's heels; the latest ones to hit the stores. Tammy knew how bad Robin had wanted them, because Robin was a bigger shoe fanatic than she was. They both had well over a hundred pairs of designer shoes inside their closets. Tammy helped Robin carry all of her gifts over to the elevator. Moments later, they walked into Robin's sweet smelling condo.

"Did you ever get in contact with Hakeem?" Robin asked.

"No, he's still not answering my call. And I've left over 20 voice mail messages on his cell phone. I also drove back over to his cousin's house; nobody answered the door," Tammy said sadly.

They walked over to the sofa and both sat down. Robin looked at Tammy and said, "Tammy, the man was deeply hurt. It's obvious, because he's not calling you back. This only shows that

Hakeem was really feeling you, too. Maybe you need to just wait for him to come to you?"

"I can't, something has been bothering me," Tammy said.

"What?"

"Robin, the other night I had a dream about Hakeem. It wasn't a good one, something was terribly wrong," Tammy said, in a serious tone.

"Do you remember it?"

"No, not really, but I do remember that it was something I did that helped save him."

"Well, Tammy, just keep following your heart, Girl. I really hope that you and Hakeem can kiss and make up. I must admit, out of all the men I've ever seen you with, he's the one who compliments you the best. Y'all seem so perfect for each other."

"Yeah, that's what my heart tells me, but the other night, with Nathan, I just let my lust talk for me. All it did was mess things up between us," Tammy said.

"Anyways, enough about me, what all do you have planned for your birthday?"

"Nothing much Me, Kevin, my brother, and Mrs. Silvia are all going out to dinner."

"That's it? Your birthdays usually be wild and crazy. Remember last year when me, you, and all the girls went down to Miami?" Tammy said, with a smile.

"How can I forget?! When we left the party on South Beach, it was early the next day," Robin said, as they both sat back reminiscing.

"My brother is picking me up in a limo he rented for tonight, and then we're gonna go pick up Kevin and his mother, I'm really looking forward to it, Tammy. Something keeps telling me that today is gonna turn out very special. My insides have been tingling all day," Robin said.

"Girl, your insides are always tingling!"

"I'm serious, Tammy, it's different this time."

"Maybe it's your body still recovering from the massage Kevin gave you last night? You said it was the best you ever had."

"It was, Girl! I'm telling you, the man should be certified," Robin said, with a chuckle.

"Come on, let me show you what I'm wearing tonight," Robin said, as they both stood up and walked toward her bedroom.

~

North Philly...

When Hakeem walked into Keisha's house, she was sitting on the living room sofa, smoking a blunt with two of her neighborhood girlfriends. The TV was on, and so was the radio. Keisha quickly stood up and said,

"Boy, you scared the shit out of me!"

"Where is my daughter, Keisha?"

"She's upstairs sleeping! You think I'd have her around while I'm smoking weed?" Keisha said, with a sassy attitude.

Hakeem disappointingly looked at his child's mother, then turned and walked away. When he walked into Keisha's bedroom, his beautiful daughter, Hakeemah, was sitting up on the bed crying.

"Daddy!" she cried out. Hakeem rushed over to his crying child and picked her up into his protective arms. He kissed her on the lips and wiped away her tears. Twenty minutes later, Hakeemah was sleeping peacefully in his arms. After Hakeem had laid her back down on the bed, he put the cover over her and tiptoed out of the bedroom. After walking back downstairs, he rushed into the living room and snatched Keisha up from the sofa. With his grip tight around her arm, he walked her back into the kitchen.

"Boy, what is your damn problem?!" Keisha snapped.

Hakeem looked into her red eyes and said,

"While you and your nappy-head-ass girlfriends were down here smoking weed, watching TV, and talking shit, our daughter was upstairs in your bedroom crying! What the fuck is wrong with

163

you? Will you ever grow-the-fuck-up?! Keisha, is everything to you a damn game? Can't you see where your life is headed, Keisha?" he vented.

"Maybe if you were here with me, my life would be much better!" Keisha said, as the tears welled up in her eyes.

"Me, you, and our daughter; everything would probably be perfect."

"You fucked that up! If you wanted to be with me as bad as you always claimed, then you wouldn't had done all the shit you done to me! I will never give you my all again! Never!"

"Fuck you, Hakeem! Nigga, I can't stand you! Sometimes I wish I never met your broke ass!"

Hakeem stared deep into Keisha's eyes and said,

"Bitch, you're disgusting!"

Keisha stood there with a shocked expression on her face. It was the first time that Hakeem had ever called her out of her name. In fact, it was the first time that Hakeem had ever called any woman out of their name. His whole life, he had always had a high respect for women, but Keisha had always found a way to get under his skin; especially when it came to situations involving their daughter. Keisha saw the seriousness in Hakeem's eyes.

After calling her a bitch, she didn't know what he would do next. Hakeem reached out and grabbed Keisha's shirt collar. For the first time ever, she saw a deep anger appear in Hakeem's eyes.

"I don't care what you say or think about me, but if you don't start treating our child with more respect, I swear to God I'll do something real bad to you!" he said, filled with anger.

"The next time I come over here, there better not be no TV and radio on. I better not see your trifling-ass girlfriends sitting around smoking fucking weed! Do you hear me? DO YOU?!"

"Yeah, Hakeem, I hear you!" Keisha said, as the tears rolled down her face. Hakeem released her collar, pushed her to the side and walked away.

Inside the kitchen, Keisha stood there, crying; knowing that Hakeem had meant every word he said.

What Every Woman Wants

Later Than Evening…

Robin and Tammy stepped off the elevator and into the underground garage. A white stretch-limousine was parked over by their cars. Robin was looking as glamorous as ever. She was dressed in a beautiful black Badgley Mischka dress, and a new pair of Manolo Blahnik heels. Around her neck was the two-carat diamond necklace that Charles had bought her. Her long silky black hair was tied in a ponytail, hanging down her back. And the sweet scent of Vera Wang perfume hovered around her entire body.

After Tammy walked over to the waiting limo, they hugged before Robin climbed inside. Tammy stood there watching the limo slowly pulling off through the garage. Then she got inside her car and started up the engine. Moments later, she was driving out of the underground garage, headed back to Hakeem's cousin's house. If he still wasn't home, she would drive around 42nd Street next. One thing was for sure, Tammy was going to search for Hakeem until she found him. And she didn't care how long it would take her.

Inside the limousine, Robin and Billy sat back talking while the chauffeur drove toward West Philly.

"Here you go, baby sis," Bill said, passing Robin a small white box.

When Robin opened the box, she smiled and reached out to give her brother a big hug.

"Thanks Billy, it's beautiful!" she said. Inside the small box was a diamond-studded Cartier watch.

Robin took it out of the box and put it around her wrist. Billy sat back in his dark brown tailor made suit, watching his spoiled younger sister smile from ear to ear.

Thirty minutes later, the limousine pulled up in front of the small row house. Standing outside their home, all dressed up, was Kevin and his mother.

Kevin had on the blue Salvatore Farragamo suit and matching loafers that Robin had bought him. He looked like one of the male models that posed on the pages of GQ Magazine. Mrs. Silvia was looking just as good. She was wearing a lovely black and red floral dress, and a pair of red heels. Her beautiful caramel complexion bore the imprint of her black and Indian heritage: gleaming skin, arched eyebrows, and long black hair. At 54 years old, Mrs. Silvia was looking as if she was 15 years younger. For an older woman, her natural beauty was still undeniable.

Kevin and his mother stepped into the limo and closed the door, the limo slowly pulled off down the dark street. When Billy saw Kevin's mother, he couldn't believe his eyes. She is beautiful, he thought.

"Mrs. Silvia, this is my older brother, Billy," Robin said, introducing the two.

They both smiled at each other. It was obvious that there was some attraction between them. While Mrs. Silvia tried to look away, Billy couldn't keep his eyes from off of her.

"Billy, why don't you sit over here and talk to Mrs. Silvia," Robin suggested.

"Sure," Billy said, switching seats with Kevin.

Now Robin and Kevin were seated next to each other. Billy was next to Kevin's beautiful mother. Mrs. Silvia looked into Billy's beaming face and smiled. They actually looked good together.She didn't expect Robin's older brother to be as handsome as he was; Billy was an attractive man, and very tall. She secretly liked them tall. Ever since she was a young woman, she had preferred taller men. What a strange coincidence, she thought.

~

A Half-Hour Later…

When the limousine pulled up in front of the famous Bookbinder's Restaurant, they all got out and walked into the crowded establishment. Since their table was already reserved, they were escorted to it without a problem. While in the limo, Billy and Mrs. Silvia had struck up a nice conversation, and they seemed to get along pretty well. They were smiling and laughing like two teenage kids out on their first date. Kevin couldn't remember the last time he saw his mother smile so much.

Both couples were seated next to each other at a private table. They all ordered the best steak dinner on the menu, and Billy ordered a bottle of Moet & Chandon champagne. Kevin had been whispering in Robin's ear all night, making her face hurt from blushing so much. For her birthday, he and his mother had given Robin two beautiful birthday cards. Robin loved them both.

Inside the famous restaurant, they sat back talking, laughing, eating, drinking, and celebrating Robin's 31st birthday. Under the dinner table, Robin had her hands feeling on Kevin's hard dick. When Kevin didn't protest to what she was doing, Robin knew that tonight would be the night she had been desperately waiting for. Kevin leaned over and whispered something into her ear. Whatever it was that he said had Robin's body shivering in her chair.

~

After leaving Hakeem's cousin's house, Tammy drove all around the 42nd Street area, looking for Hakeem. She drove up and down Mantua Ave., Belmont Ave., Westminster Ave., Wyalusing Ave., Pennsgrove St., Otter St., Brown St., Brooklyn St., 41st St., and 43rd St. Then she drove her car up and down Lancaster Ave., until she got tired and sadly drove back home.

When Tammy walked into her house, she called Hakeem's cell phone three times. Each time, she had left an emergency message on his voice mail. Tammy turned on her stereo system and slid in another one of Mary J. Blige's classic CDs. Then she walked over to the sofa and sat down. When her cell phone started ringing, she quickly picked it up and answered. "Hello?"

"What's up, Tammy? It's me, Eugene," a man said.

"Who?"

"Eugene. Remember, I met you down at the bank you work at?" he said.

"A tall, brown-skinned guy?"

"Yeah, that's me."

"Short, curly black hair?"

"Yeah, Baby."

"Pretty straight white teeth, and hazel eyes?"

"Yeah, that's me," he said, with a chuckle.

"Eugene?"

"Yeah, what's up, Baby?"

"Can you please not ever call back here again? I'm having some serious man problems and you can't fix them!" Click! Tammy hung up the phone.

As the soulful voice of Mary J. flowed out of the speakers, Tammy sat back, in deep thought. Thinking about Hakeem, and being alone on a Friday night.

~

After everyone had enjoyed a delicious steak dinner, champagne, and good conversation, Robin, Kevin, Billy, and Mrs. Silvia all happily walked out of the restaurant and got back into the waiting limousine.

"Billy, how about me and Kevin get dropped off at my place, and you make sure Mrs. Silvia gets back home safe?" Robin suggested.

"Sounds fine with me," Billy said, with his arm now around Mrs. Silvia's shoulders. Kevin had noticed it, but he didn't say a word. He knew that his mother was out enjoying herself, and her happiness was all that mattered to him. Just to see her smiling was a gift in itself.

The limousine pulled into the underground parking garage and parked by the elevator, Robin and Kevin said their goodbyes and got out, both smiling from ear to ear. When the limo pulled off, they rushed over to the empty elevator. Robin quickly pressed the button to her floor. Without any hesitation, they started passionately kissing.

What Every Woman Wants

Chapter 23

Robin and Kevin entered the condo, and locked in a long, passionate kiss. Then Kevin walked her out onto the balcony. The night was calm and tranquil. A full moon and some bright stars filled up the dark sky. Outside on the balcony, Kevin slowly began to undress her.

After Robin was totally naked, Kevin started undressing himself. A soft wind brushed up against their naked bodies. Kevin kissed all around Robin's sensitive neck and shoulders,. While the whole time, he had his middle finger playing inside of her wet, warm pussy. As Kevin kissed on her arms and stomach, Robin's light moans escaped into the air. Kevin continued to play inside her wetness. Robin closed, her eyes feeling Kevin's pleasing finger inside her. His mouth gently sucking on her breast. Then, in one smooth motion, he turned Robin around, and slid his rock hard dick into the deepness of her paradise. She moaned out in pleasure, feeling every inch of him pushing deeper inside her.

Kevin stood there delivering slow, intense strokes. Each time he entered her, he gripped her hips tightly, making sure she felt every incoming thrust. Robin wanted to say something, but Kevin's lovemaking skills were so good that she was unable to let a single word escape from her mouth. Tears of bliss started falling from the corners of her eyes as she moaned, groaned, and cried, all at the same time.

Robin was completely turned on. She had already climaxed twice, and Kevin was still rock hard. Her cries of passion continued to escape her mouth, into the darkness of the sky. Kevin's powerful lovemaking had sent tingling sensations all throughout her body. Streams of sweat began to roll down both of their foreheads.

"Whose pussy is this?" he yelled out.

"Yours, Kevin! Yours, Kevin! It's all yours, Daddy!" Robin screamed out in ecstasy.

Kevin could feel Robin coming once again, so he slid out his dick and turned her shivering body around. He noticed that her eyes were filled with tears of passion. Kevin lifted Robin's naked body up into his muscular arms, then slowly brought her back down on his dick. She wrapped both arms around his strong shoulders and held on as he carried her back into the condo. They headed straight back to the master's bedroom.

When Kevin laid Robin back on the bed, her entire body was shivering. While his dick was still deep inside her, Kevin lifted both of Robin's legs onto his broad shoulders. She moaned out loudly. As Kevin started giving her long, thunderous strokes, Robin dug her nails deep into his back.

"Whose pussy is this?"

"Kevin's pussy! All Kevin's pussy!" Robin cried out.

Her breathing became more intense. Robin was now totally lost in a world of Kevin's powerful lovemaking skills. Kevin was introducing Robin to highest sexual peaks that her body had ever experienced. She had no control over her body, as it was now being taken over by pure bliss.

Kevin continued to stroke away, sucking all around her neck, ears, shoulders, and face. He was like a wild untamed animal. When Kevin had finally exploded inside of her, Robin came again at the same time. Kevin was so turned on that his dick was still rock hard. He continued to grind and thrust his body into hers.

"Kevin, I'm coming again! Oh, Kevin! I'm coming!" Robin screamed.

Kevin pushed even harder, going as deep as he could go, making Robin's body tremble uncontrollably. The powerful orgasms that Kevin was giving her body were like none she had ever felt before. Robin had never been fucked like this in her entire life. Her body was climaxing every few minutes. Until tonight, she had never known that was possible.

What Every Woman Wants

"Kevin! Kevin! Kevin! Kevin! Oh my God! Kevin! Oh, ahh! Kevin!" Robin yelled out.

She had just experienced her most powerful orgasm ever. For the first time in Robin's life, it felt like the earth was moving beneath her.

~

Early Saturday Morning...

After Kevin had made passionate love to Robin all through the night, they finally managed to get a few hours of rest. Both of their bodies were sexually drained. Robin had climaxed so many times that she stopped counting after the tenth one. All night long, Kevin had her body trembling and hypnotized under his sexual spell.

When Kevin woke up early the next morning, he rolled over on top of Robin and made love to her once again. Before breakfast, he made love to Robin three more times The escapade started out, out on the balcony, under the bright beaming sun and white clouds. It continued on inside the living room; and then back in the master bedroom. After Kevin had wiped down her sweaty body with a wash cloth, he laid Robin down on her back, and spread open her legs. With his warm mouth, he began to make love to her sensitive clitoris. Robin moaned out in ecstasy as Kevin slid his middle finger into her love cave and curled it up on her G-spot. Then he reached under the pillow, with his free hand, and grabbed Robin's small black vibrator. Kevin turned it on and then gently slid it beneath the small of Robin's back. When he removed his hand, he started massaging the soft area right below her naval. Now, all at once, Robin was being stimulated by four different feelings going at the same time. The vibrator under her back, one hand massaging her lower stomach, a finger on his other hand rubbing around her G-spot, and his wet, warm tongue slithering around her clitoris. The quadruple combination of all four sensations, had Robin at the highest peak of sexual satisfaction that she had ever felt. As she laid there, crying and moaning out in satisfaction, the G-spot orgasm began sweeping through her body like a powerful hurricane. The feeling was indescribable. Once again, the earth seemed to be moving beneath her.

Kevin wasn't able to buy Robin all the expensive jewelry, designer clothes, and other nice gifts that she had gotten for her birthday. What he did give her was the best birthday present she had ever received in all 31 years of her life.

~

A Few Hours Later...

When Hakeem showed up around his 42nd Street neighborhood, a friend of his told him that Black and Noonie were looking for him. He told Hakeem that they both seemed very pissed off about something. Hakeem had run his loan-shark bill up to $800. Still, he had no intention of running out on the two men and not paying his street tab. It's just that lately he had been down on his luck. Most of the money he had given to Keisha, to help her out with their daughter, Hakeemah.

All night long, he had thought about calling Tammy back to hear what she wanted to tell him, but he never did. Over and over, he would listen to her crying voice mail messages. Hakeem didn't know what to believe. He had caught her with another man - a married one, at that. How many more were there, he wondered. He remembered being over at her house, when her telephone and cell phone would both be constantly ringing. She had never answered either phone in his presence. Hakeem was almost sure that most of the late-hour callers were men who were in search of late night booty calls. Any man who called a woman's house after eleven o'clock had just one thing on his mind—sex. Once he called, it was up to the woman to accept or refuse.

After Hakeem had heard the news that Black and Noonie were looking for him, a bit of fear and nervousness entered his body.

What Every Woman Wants

One on one, he could take any one of them; but Black and Noonie were two thugs who didn't play fair. Now, Hakeem wished that he had never borrowed the money from them in the first place. It was too late. As he walked down 43rd Street, Hakeem knew that sooner or later, their paths would cross.

~

Tammy was sitting on the sofa, sipping on a hot cup of tea, and listening to her music. Michell'e's "Something in My Heart" was playing out of the speakers. The song made her think about Hakeem. Tammy had called him three more times on his cell phone, but he never answered. Three days had passed since she had last seen or heard from him. As she sat there in deep thought, the ringing phone snapped her out of her thoughts.

"Hello," she said, picking up the phone.

"The earth moved!" Robin said, into the phone.

"What?"

"Tammy, me and Kevin finally made love last night, and I'm telling you, Girl, the damn earth moved!" Robin said, excitedly.

"No way!" Tammy screamed.

"Yes way! Tammy, I can't explain what that man did to me _ all last night, and early this morning! I'm telling you this, what Kevin did to my body was the most amazing sexual experience I ever had in my life," Robin said, in a serious tone.

"Damn, Girl, so your body was telling you something when you said you felt a tingle in it."

"I told you, Tammy! But that's nothing. This morning, he ate my pussy in a way that simply blew my mind! I can't even explain what he did. I had the strangest feeling running all over my body! The man puts T.J. to shame!"

"Hell no!" Tammy said, shockingly.

"Girl, are you listening? Kevin is the only man to ever stimulate me mentally, physically, and emotionally."

"Did you tell him you love him?"

174

"No. But only because I had no control of my own mouth!" Robin said, as they both started laughing.

Robin's face was vibrant and alive. Just the thought of Kevin's warm tongue had her pussy trembling.

"Where is Kevin now?"

"He's inside my bedroom, getting dressed. We're about to go out and get something to eat. Plus, the maids will be here soon to clean up the mess we made."

"So what's next?"

"Tammy, I don't know. I'm more confused right now than I've ever been. If Charles weren't in my life, things would be so much easier. The man treats me so good," Robin said, seriously.

"But Charles will never be able to do the things that Kevin did, or make you feel the way Kevin makes you feel," Tammy said.

"What do you think I should do?" Robin asked, honestly.

"Leave it all up to God. He's the only one who knows which man you should be with. The truth about them both will soon emerge and you'll have your answer, so just be patient and open-minded about everything, and enjoy your moment."

"Did you ever get in touch with Hakeem?"

"No, he still hasn't returned any of my calls. Later, I'll get dressed and go out looking for him. He can't keep running forever."

"Well, if I see him, I'll definitely tell him that you're looking for him," Robin said, as she watched Kevin walk into the living room. When Kevin walked behind Robin and started kissing the small of her neck, Robin said, "Tammy, I have to go, I'm going to call you later. Love you. Bye!"

Tammy hung up the phone and sat back on the leather sofa. She was happy that Robin had finally found a good man. She had never seen Robin happier. Tammy could also tell that Robin was falling deeply in love with Kevin. Tammy knew because she had felt those same feelings for Hakeem.

As Tammy sat there in a daze, a few thoughts had come to her mind. She had been so caught up in her own selfish needs that she had forgotten all about Hakeem's needs. His current situation was far worse than hers. Not only was Hakeem living in a room at his cousin's house, but he was also short on money, and jobless with no car. Tammy quickly stood up from the sofa. She knew exactly what to do. Why didn't I think of this before, she thought to herself. It was time to get dressed, because today, she was determined to find her man.

What Every Woman Wants

Chapter 24

Later That Evening...

Mrs. Silvia walked off the porch and got into the brand new silver Cadillac Escalade truck.

"Hey, Beautiful, are you all set?" Billy asked.

"Yes, I'm ready," she answered, strapping the seatbelt across her chest.

Billy put the truck in drive and slowly pulled off down the street. They were going out to dinner and a movie.

"Where's Kevin?" he asked.

"He's still out with Robin. He never came home last night. But he did call me early this morning, and he told me that he wouldn't be in tonight either," Mrs. Silvia said, with a grin.

Billy looked over at Mrs. Silvia and just shook his head.

"What is it?" she asked, blushing.

"You are so beautiful. I can't believe that you've been hiding that pretty face of yours for so many years."

"Well, I didn't have anyone to show it off for," she teased.

"Well, now you do," Billy said, as he stopped the truck at a red light.

"You seem so sure."

"Is that a bad thing?" he asked.

"No. In fact, I love a confident man."

"I'm gonna have to call my sister and thank her."

"For what?"

"For introducing me to a very beautiful, God-fearing woman," Billy said, as he pulled off after the light changed to green.

"Make sure you thank her for me, too," Mrs. Silvia said, with a smile.

What Every Woman Wants

The night before, after the limousine had pulled up in front of Mrs. Silvia's house, she and Billy had ended up talking until the late hours of the night. They were so into their conversation that Billy had paid the limo driver an extra hundred dollars just to sit around and wait. Billy and Mrs. Silvia had talked about everything from being single and middle aged, to their favorite colors. In fact, they had more in common than they had both originally thought. Billy told her that she was one of the most attractive women he had ever laid eyes on. He told Mrs. Silvia that she had reminded him of an older version of the actress, Halle Berry. Mrs. Silvia told Billy that she thought he was very handsome when she first saw him. When Bill had asked to see her again, she said, "*I would like that.*" Then they stepped out of the limousine and walked over to the front door. Before Mrs. Silvia walked into the house, Billy gave her a warm hug and gentle kiss on the cheek, then he walked back over to the limousine. When Mrs. Silvia walked into her quiet, empty house, she had a wonderful feeling about Billy. As they headed toward Center City, Billy reached over and grabbed Mrs. Silvia's hand.

~

Hakeem was walking down the street with a male friend, when Black and Noonie turned the corner and ran straight into him. They had been looking for him all day long, but somehow they kept missing him.

Both men had an angry look on their faces. When Hakeem's friend saw the two men's facial expressions, he said, in a scared voice, "Hakeem...I'ma... see you...tomorrow." Then he turned around and ran off down the street.

"What's up fellas?" Hakeem asked, nonchalantly.

"We need to talk. Come on, let's go for a lil' walk," Black told him.

After a long sigh, Hakeem started walking up the street, with Black and Noonie on each side.

~

"He's not here, Tammy. I told 'em that you came by a few times. I thought he would've called you by now."

"Alright Rob, but when he gets in the house, can you please tell your cousin to call me? It's very important," Tammy said.

"Yeah, no problem. Did you drive down 42nd Street? That's where he hangs out at."

"Yeah, I drove all around that neighborhood, looking for him," Tammy said, sounding disappointed.

"Well, just keep calling his cell phone, he'll answer it sooner or later."

"Just tell him to call me," Tammy said, as she turned and walked over to a blue Nissan Maxima.

Moments later, Tammy pulled off down the street, headed back toward her townhouse. When she stopped the car at the red light, she sat there, lost in thought. After the light had changed to green, Tammy made a sudden U-turn. Something deep inside her soul was telling her to drive back down 42nd Street one last time.

~

When Robin and Kevin entered the condo, they attacked each other like two wild savages. They had spent all day together, driving around site-seeing, and doing a little clothes shopping. Now they were back where they had both been yearning to be- in each other's loving arms.

After Kevin had carried Robin into the bedroom, he took his precious time undressing her. Once she was totally naked, Kevin stood there in front of her, slowly undressing himself. Robin stared at Kevin's hard, muscular body and couldn't help but smile. Kevin had the total package, and Robin couldn't wait to have him feeling up her insides once again.

~

Tammy drove down 43rd Street and then turned on 42nd. Her eyes were watching everyone who was walking up and down the sidewalks. It was dark out, and only a few people were still hanging out on the street. When she turned her car on Pennsgrove Street, she saw two faces that she instantly recognized. It was the two troublemakers, Black and Noonie. Tammy saw the two thugs standing behind a parked car. She could tell that something was going on, the expressions on their faces told her. Plus, her intuition was telling her that something wasn't right.

Tammy quickly pulled over and parked the car. Then she reached inside her Coach bag and took out her loaded .380 pistol.

On the opposite side of the car, Black and Noonie had Hakeem down on the ground, stomping him. Hakeem's face was bruised and beaten. His mouth and nose were both bleeding.

"Ahh!" Hakeem grunted, after Black kicked him hard in the back.

"Motherfucker, you better get us our money!" Noonie yelled.

Once again, both men started punching and kicking Hakeem. He tried his best to protect himself from all the incoming kicks and blows. They had beaten Hakeem for almost five minutes, enjoying every minute of it.

"Get the fuck away from him!" a voice shouted from behind.

When Black and Noonie turned around, they both stepped away from Hakeem's beaten down body. Tammy was standing there, aiming her .380 pistol at both of them. When Hakeem managed to look up and see who the person was that rescued,. A relieved smile came to his beaten face. He knew that the two thugs would've beaten him to death if no one had saved him. Strange as it seemed, out of all the people who could have saved him, it was the one person he never would have imagined K Tammy.

"Hey, Pretty, don't get yourself involved in this. This nigga owe us money!" Black said.

Tammy was moving closer to Hakeem's side, but she never took the gun off the two thugs.

"We just want our money!" Noonie snapped.

"How much does he owe y'all?" Tammy said, helping Hakeem to his feet.

Beaten and bruised, Hakeem put his arm around her shoulder.

"Eight hundred!" Black said.

He thought about rushing straight at her, but seeing the seriousness in the woman's eyes had told him that she wouldn't hesitate to shoot. They stood there just a few feet away from each other. The tension could be felt in the air.

"Baby, reach inside my left pocket," Tammy told Hakeem.

Hakeem reached down into her jacket pocket and pulled out a small stack of money. It had a thousand-dollar wrapper around it. Tammy had withdrawn the money from the bank earlier in the day. She was planning on giving it to Hakeem with a few other surprises; Tammy had been driving around all day, buying things that Hakeem could use.

"Take out two-hundred," she said.

Hakeem took out two of the brand new hundred-dollar bills.

"Okay, toss the rest of it to them," she said.

Hakeem tossed the money over to Noonie. He caught it in mid-air.

"That's all y'all money! Now I hope everything is over with," Tammy said to the two men.

Both men looked at the small, pretty woman and just shook their heads.

"Yeah, everything is squashed!" Black said, as he and Noonie disappointingly turned and walked away.

Black and Noonie turned the corner,, Noonie paused and said, "Black, why you ain't pull out and shoot that crazy-ass bitch?!" Black looked deep into his friend's eyes and said, "Noonie, couldn't you see Homeboy?"

"See what?"

"That woman was in love with that nigga. She wouldn't have hesitated to pull the trigger to save Hakeem's life. It's two things you never play with. Those two things are the white man's taxes, and a black woman's love," Black said, in a serious tone.

~

After Tammy had helped Hakeem get into the car, she ran around the other side and quickly got in. She then started up the car and sped off down the street.

"I'm taking you to the hospital," she said.

"No, I'll be alright, just take me back to my cousin's house," Hakeem said, using his hand to wipe the blood from his nose and mouth.

"No, you're going to our house!" Tammy said, reaching into her right pocket and taking out a small key chain with three new keys on it.

She handed the keys to Hakeem. He was shocked.

"You're moving in with me, Hakeem. Those are the keys to my townhouse, my car, and your car," Tammy said, as she made a right turn down Market Street.

"My car?"

"Yes, the one I'm driving right now. I bought it for you earlier today," Tammy replied.

"Tammy, it's not all that simple, first we need to talk," he said.

"And we will as soon as we get back home. Hakeem, I'm not letting you go anywhere!" Tammy said, pulling the car to the side of the road. Tammy looked over at Hakeem's beaten and bruised face. At that moment, tears started falling from her eyes.

"I love you, Hakeem! I really love you! I made a terrible mistake, but please don't hold it against me forever! I don't want to lose you, Hakeem. I know you have feelings for me, too, so don't keep running away from me. I'm here for you, baby, and if you want me, I'm here for life!" Tammy cried out.

Hakeem listened, then he just turned and looked straight ahead.

"Alright, then take us back to our house. But there are some things you still need to know," he said, seriously.

"Whatever you want baby," Tammy said, as a big smile came to her face.

Without saying another word, Tammy drove down the street.

What Every Woman Wants

Chapter 25

Outside, On The Balcony...

Robin looked out into the dark sky, staring at all the bright stars that seemed a lot closer than they really were. She could feel her third orgasm moving throughout her trembling naked body. Kevin had made wild, passionate love to Robin in every room of the condo. Then he picked her up into his arms and carried her back out onto the balcony. It had become his favorite place to make love to her. There was something truly exotic about making love to Robin outside on the balcony, surrounded by the stars, the moon, and the darkness of night.

As the calm wind brushed up against their naked bodies, Kevin had his hands gripped on Robin's hips, He stood behind her, delivering slow, intense strokes, while lightly biting all around her neck. Every time Kevin had entered her, Robin could feel the thickness and length of his dick feeling up her walls.

"Yes, Daddy! God, yes! Oh! Kevin!" she shouted out into the wind.

Kevin was turning Robin's ass out! She was no match for his stamina and aggressive sexual energy. With Kevin, all Robin could do was submit and surrender, while enjoying the most amazing sex her body had ever felt.

~

An Hour Later...

Hakeem had changed out of his bloody clothes, he went into the bathroom and took a long, hot shower. He walked back into the bedroom, Tammy was sitting on the bed, holding some new clothes that she had bought him. She handed him the clothes and watched him as he dressed.

184

What Every Woman Wants

After Hakeem had gotten dressed, he walked over and sat down besides her. They stared deep into each other's eyes.

"Baby, I'm sorry that I hurt you," Tammy said, as her eyes welled up with tears.

Hakeem grabbed her trembling hands and said,

"Look here, Tammy, you hurt me but I do forgive you. I hope we never have to go through anything like-"

"We won't!" she said, cutting him off.

"Tammy, first you need to understand that I'm not one of those tight-suit, Wall Street guys that you have always been with. I don't have no college degree, or CEO position at some Fortune 500 company. I'm a 24-year-old black man from the ghetto, Tammy! The real ghetto! I grew up around poverty, the homeless, rape, drugs, and any other fucked up situation that you can name."

"Hakeem, I know this…"

"Hold up, Tammy, because you don't know!" Hakeem said,

"This is not some gangster rap video, Tammy, this is my life! The real life of a black man raised in the ghetto. Most of my friends are in prison or the grave! My own father is locked up in prison, and my mother's lost out on the streets somewhere, strung out on crack! This is my life, Tammy; the only life I've ever known. Still, with all that has been placed up against me, I never gave up. I tried to work, and I do everything in my power to take care of my child. Every time I've been faced with another obstacle, I didn't run away, I ran into it! Tammy, all I've ever wanted was to just get away. Because even though this is the only life I've ever known, I hate it! And all I've ever wanted was a good woman who would be there for me, and would love me unconditionally. After we met, Tammy, I really thought that you were that woman."

"I am that woman," Tammy mumbled, through falling tears.

Hakeem looked at her and said, "I know now. What you did tonight has told me so much. More than your mouth could ever do," he said, as they hugged each other and began passionately kissing.

"Hakeem, I had a dream a few nights ago. In my dream, you were in some trouble. I wasn't gonna stop looking for you until I found you. I'm glad I had my gun with me," Tammy said.

"Where did you get that thing?"

"I had it for years. I'm licensed to carry. Remember, I work at a bank," Tammy grinned, "plus, I would never drive down into that wild-ass neighborhood without having my gun on me."

"Smart girl," Hakeem said.

"Hakeem, I want you to know that I'm going to do everything I can to help you. Just know that I'm here for you, no matter what. And you no longer have to worry about any other men in my life, I got rid of them all," Tammy said.

"Tammy, I want you to know that I would never hurt you or take advantage of you in any way. All I need from you is your 100% love, and together, we can become something very special."

"You got it! I've never been more serious about anything in all my life," Tammy responded, in serious tone.

"Tammy, can I just ask you one question?"

"Anything."

"Why didn't you give up and stop trying to find me?"

"Because my heart wouldn't let me give up! In my life, Hakeem, I've made so many mistakes; mostly with men. I've been used so many times, and I've also used others. Out of all the men I know, you're the only one I feel truly comfortable with. And my lust almost cost me to lose you. I can't tell you what other women out there wants, but I can tell you what Tammy Camill Washington want. She desires a good man who will love me on all levels. You don't have to be the richest or most successful man out there. That was the main source of all my problems. I was always chasing after handsome, wealthy men, and getting lost in my own selfish greed. What you give me, Hakeem, I can't even put a price on. Your honesty, and genuine love is worth more to me than all the money in the world."

What Every Woman Wants

West Philadelphia…

Billy's silver Cadillac truck was parked in front of Mrs. Silvia's small row house. They had just returned from dinner and a movie. While inside the theater, Billy had kept his arm around her shoulders the whole time, Mrs. Silvia felt so safe being in his company. Mrs. Silvia was a woman who had a lot of respect for herself. She had lived long enough to know that the more respect a woman had for herself, the more respect a man would give her. Billy was the perfect gentleman. He would open doors, pull out chairs, and always look into her eyes when he talked to her. A man who looked straight into a woman's eyes when he talked had nothing to hide, she thought, Her mother had told her that many years ago. The words had always turned out to be true.

"Did you enjoy yourself tonight?" Billy asked.

"Yes, tonight was a lot of fun," she answered, "and you?"

"Silvia, just being in your company and seeing that lovely smile is a blessing," Billy replied. Billy reached and turned on the radio. The deck was tuned to W.D.A.S. FM, Philadelphia's classic soul and R&B station. A song by the Isley Brothers was playing. "Remember the good old days?" Billy said, as he moved his head to the soulful melody.

"How can I ever forget?" Silvia smiled. She was one of the Isley Brothers' biggest fans. She loved all the groups from the late 60s and 70s.

"You know the O-Jays, Stylistics, and the Delfonics will be having a show soon," Billy said. The Isley Brothers' song faded off a song by The Temptations came on right after it. Billy reached over and grabbed Silvia's hand.

"Did I tell you how beautiful you are?"

"Fifteen times, but who's counting?" Silvia said, jokingly.

"Well, how about I make it sixteen? Silvia, you are so beautiful," Billy said.

"Thank you, Billy," she blushed, "So are you."

What Every Woman Wants

~

Atlantic City, New Jersey…

Trey lay back in the chair, enjoying Carolyn's pleasing oral performance. He had just finished doing her, and now she was returning the wonderful favor. Carolyn patiently took her time, letting her warm mouth make passionate love to Trey's rock hard dick. She watched Trey the whole time she performed, and it only turned her on more to see the satisfied look she put on his face. When she felt her handsome young stud's body jerk, Carolyn knew that he was now on the verge of coming. She gently placed one of her hands around his testicles and started slowly massaging them. The whole time, she never stopped stroking his dick with her mouth. When Trey's body jerked again, an explosion of his thick love juices entered into her mouth. Carolyn began moving her head faster, making sure she swallowed every single drop of his cream. When she stood up from her knees, Trey's drained body slumped down in the chair. Carolyn just stood there, looking at her young stud with a big smile on her face.

For the last few days, they had been fucking non-stop. Trey looked at Carolyn and grinned. She was a beautiful 42-year-old woman at the height of her sexual peak. Now that her husband had finally let her out of the house, she was taking it all out on Trey. This beautiful, innocent looking housewife had turned out to be an undercover nymphomaniac. Carolyn could fuck all night long and still want more early the next morning.

Carolyn grabbed Trey's hand and helped him stand from the chair. They walked over to the bed and sat down. Carolyn climbed on to the bed and sat behind Trey. Then she wrapped her legs and arms around his naked body and started kissing his neck. Her soft breast was pressed up against his back. She put her mouth to his ear and whispered,

"Baby, get it back up, I want you to fuck me again."

Trey turned his head to the side and said, "One moment, Baby, just let me rest up."

"Okay, Handsome. Remember, I told you that I've been locked up inside my house for years, and I have so much built up inside me that needs to be released," she said, seriously.

"Don't worry, Beautiful, I'm going to make sure you release it all," he replied.

Carolyn laid her head on his shoulder and smiled; then she closed both of her eyes. Trey had turned out to be a wonderful lover. Nathan was the last thing on her mind. Ten minutes later, both of their moans were escaping from their mouths, and once again filling up the private suite.

~

After a satisfying round of blissful lovemaking, Tammy lay cuddled in Hakeem's strong arms. She lay there listening to the snores coming from his mouth. The familiar sound was like music to her ears.

The tears started falling down from her eyes, but this time they were the tears of joy and happiness. Her persistence had paid off, and now she had her man. Tammy knew that Hakeem was her true soul mate, because being wrapped inside his arms felt like the safest place in the world. This is what she had always been searching for. The feeling was priceless. Now that Hakeem was back in her life, she would do whatever needed to be done to keep him there. He was worth it. She could easily see herself marrying Hakeem and giving him a bunch of beautiful babies.

This was the first time Tammy had felt that way about any man. Now there were no more secrets between them; everything had been laid out on the table. They had cried and laughed together, and through it all, both found what they had always been searching for. A placed called love.

~

Sunday…

What Every Woman Wants

Sunday wasn't just a day for the Lord, it was also a day for love, sex, and lust. Kevin, Robin, Billy and Silvia had all went to church together. After church services had ended, Robin and Kevin climbed back into her car then rushed back to Robin's condo. Since Robin's birthday, they had been making love non-stop to each other. While Kevin was spending his time with Robin, Mrs. Silvia invited Billy over to the house, where she cooked him a delicious home cooked meal. After they ate, they sat back on the living room sofa, enjoying each other's company. They talked, laughed, and watched a movie on HBO. Before Billy left, he promised to drive back and come see her the next day. Mrs. Silvia couldn't wait.

~

Atlantic City...
Carolyn and Trey both stepped out of the jacuzzi and dried each other off with large towels. Since coming to the hotel, neither one of them had left their private suite. Inside the luxurious suite, they had everything they needed: condoms, champagne, fresh fruit, music, cable TV, and the large king-size bed. After they both climbed back on the bed, Trey laid his naked body back, and let Carolyn place a silk scarf around his eyes. Then she climbed on top of Trey's hard body and positioned herself for a pleasurable ride.

~

When Hakeem and Tammy returned home from dropping off some money at Keisha's house and seeing his daughter, they both got undressed and went into the shower together. Under the warm, sprinkling water, Tammy and Hakeem enjoyed a wet love session.

Los Angeles, California...

Inside a private room at a downtown hotel, T.J. was putting back on her clothes. A few feet away, an older white man was laying across the bed with a big smile on his face.

"You sure you don't want to be my special invited guest tonight?" he asked.

"No Spencer I told you, I'm a very private woman," T.J. Said, sliding her black dress back on.

"I'll see you in Miami next week right?" she said, stepping into her heels.

"Definitely! We can go out to dinner again. My wife will be out of town," he grinned.

T.J. reached down to the floor and picked up the open condom packs and bottle of champagne. Then she walked over by the door and dropped everything into a small round trash can.

Spencer Lloyd was one of T.J.'s super-rich white tricks. She had met the judge on one of her flights. That was almost a year ago. T.J. was originally from Atlanta, Georgia, but the gorgeous airline attendant had lovers all over the country; men and women.

Spencer reached for his white robe and put it on, then he got off the bed and walked over to the chair in the corner of the room. T.J. Stood there watching Spencer pick up his folded jacket and reach into one of the pockets. Spencer took out a small white envelope, then turned around and walked up to T.J.

"Here beautiful, I threw a bonus in there for you," he said with a smile.

T.J. opened the envelope; a neat stack of hundred dollars bills were inside. She smiled and said,

"I'll see you in Miami, Spencer. I have to be back to the airport in an hour."

"Can I just taste it one more time?" he begged.

"Spencer, you _ "

"Please! I promise I won't take long!" he said, cutting her off.

After a long sigh, T.J. said,

"Alright, hurry up."

Spencer fell to his knees and quickly lifted up her dress. After sliding down T.J.'s thong, he licked his lips and dove his tongue into her wet pink paradise.

What Every Woman Wants

Chapter 26

Monday Evening...

Robin stood in front of her dresser with one of the drawers pulled out. She had been standing there for a few minutes, crying. Her mind was clouded with disturbing thoughts, and her heart had never hurt more. A few pieces of her finest jewelry had been stolen. Robin knew that the last person who had been inside her bedroom was Kevin. She thought about the two maids, but the maids hadn't worked since Saturday morning, and she was almost positive that all of her jewelry was there the last time the two maids had worked.

Robin thought about the night when Kevin had opened a few drawers, looking for the body lotion to give her a massage. Besides Tammy, Kevin was the only other person who knew where she kept her jewelry. She couldn't believe that Kevin had stolen from her. All this time, he had been using me, she thought. She remembered what T.J. had told her, "*A man like Kevin can only turn out to be one of two things; either he is the perfect man for you, or a handsome, scheming manipulator that's playing you, like a flute.*" The more Robin stood there thinking about it, the more she thought that she had been played.

Kevin was an ex-felon who had been manipulating and taking advantage of all her love, she thought. Even Tammy had told her, "*The truth about Kevin would soon emerge and you'll have all your answers.*" Robin walked over to the bed and disappointingly sat down. The tears fell down her face like a runaway stream. She was hurt beyond words. All this time, she had actually thought Kevin was the one K her long-lost soul mate. Robin was so caught up in Kevin's spell that she was ready to tell all her other male friends, including Charles, that she could no longer see them anymore. But now, Robin knew exactly what she was going to do. This had only made her realize that Charles was the man she should be with.

Robin reached over and picked up the phone. After dialing a number, she waited.

"Hello, my love, what is it?" Charles answered.

"Charles where are you?" Robin said, wiping her tears away.

"I'm just getting off the plane now. I'm on my way to the office with Nathan. I have a few things to take care of."

"Charles, I think I'm ready!" she said.

"Ready for what, my love?" he asked curiously.

"I'm... I... I'm ready to be your wife!" Robin said, in a low voice.

Charles couldn't believe his ears. He stepped into the waiting limo with a shocked look on his face.

"Are you sure, Robin?"

"I'm positive, and I want to get married soon. We can have a big fancy wedding later."

"Robin, I'm gonna run past the office with Nathan, and then I'll drive over to your condo," Charles said, excitingly.

"Can you be here at eight o'clock? I have a few quick runs to make."

"Eight o'clock, I'll be there. I love you, Sweetie."

"I love you, too, Charles. Bye," Robin said, before she hung up. With her head staring down to the floor, Robin was in deep pain. The tears continued to fall from her eyes.

"Why, Kevin?! Why?!" She screamed out.

Robin knew that Charles could never satisfy her in the ways that Kevin did, but she no longer cared. She knew that Charles loved her and would never do anything to hurt her. Besides, he was rich and successful, and wouldn't hesitate to give her the world on a silver platter. Hopefully the sex would get better with time, she thought. After wiping her tears away, Robin grabbed her Dolce & Gabbana jacket and rushed out the bedroom.

Inside The Limousine...

"She's ready to get married!" Charles said, as he looked over at Nathan.

"That was Robin?" he asked.

"Yes, and she wants to be my wife. I can't believe it! I knew she would come to her senses one of these days, but I never imagined it being this soon," Charles said, excitingly.

"Congratulations Charles, soon you'll be married with the wife of your dreams. Robin will be perfect for you, just like Carolyn is perfect for me," Nathan said.

"I need to go by my house and get the diamond ring I bought her. I've been waiting to give it to her for a very long time."

"Just remember, Charles, we're going to Miami in a few days," Nathan said, picking up his cell phone.

"Don't worry, I'll never miss the annual D.W.A.M. Anniversary gathering. Everyone will be there," he said.

Charles sat back with an excited look on his face. Everything in his luxurious life was going well for him. His company was successful; he had his lover Nathan, and all the members of the D.W.A.M. society. Now the woman he had been patiently waiting for was going to finally be his wife.

"Hello honey, how was your weekend in Atlantic City?" Nathan said, into the cell phone.

"Wonderful! Just wonderful!" Carolyn replied.

"Well, I'm glad you were able to get out and enjoy yourself," Nathan said, as he looked over at Charles and winked his eye.

~

"Are you sure, Robin?" Tammy said, looking into her girlfriend's crying eyes.

"Yes, Tammy! Kevin's been using me to steal all my jewelry. He's the only one who could've taken it."

"What about the maids?"

"They haven't worked since Saturday. I looked into my jewelry drawer the last time they came to work. It was quick, but I'm almost positive that everything was still there. Plus, Maria has been my maid for a while now, she's never stolen anything from me."

"I just can't believe it! Why would Kevin do something so petty?" Tammy said, confusingly.

"Because he is a lowlife ex-con! And a fucking manipulator! He's been using me all this time to help him get back on his feet. He never cared about me, Tammy! How could I be so damn foolish? So damn stupid to sleep with that man without a condom and give him my heart!" Robin vented.

"You slept with Kevin without a condom?" Tammy said, shockingly.

"Yes! On the first night we had sex! And every other time too! Kevin's the only man I've ever made love to without using protection. I let him get close enough to hurt me!" Robin cried out. "Tammy, why? Why do this shit keep happening to me?" Tammy leaned over and gave Robin a sisterly hug.

"Everything will be alright, Robin."

"It's not, Tammy," she sobbed. "It's not because I love Kevin _ and I...I already called Charles and told him that I was ready to be his wife."

"What?!" Tammy sat up and said.

"I called Charles before I drove over here, and I told him that I was ready to be his wife. I don't care how I feel about Kevin right now. I'm sure in time it will all fade away."

"Robin, don't you think you're rushing through this thing? You just can't stop loving someone like that. Not true love."

"Kevin's a damn thief! A liar! A manipulator! I'm not gonna spend the rest of my life searching for love when I have a man who I know loves me! I'm 31 years old and I'm tired of being single and childless," Robin fumed.

"But you don't love Charles, Robin," Tammy said, looking into her eyes.

"Maybe one day, I will," she mumbled.

"And what if you never do?"

"Then it will just have to be a decision I have to live with. One thing for sure is, I will never be with Kevin, because now I hate him just as much as I love him!" Robin said, as she stood up from the sofa.

Tammy stood up and gave Robin another long hug. Then they walked over to the front door.

"Robin, I'm sorry," she said, as her own tears began falling

"I'll be okay. I should have known better anyway."

"Where are you going to, now?" Tammy asked.

"I'm going to see Kevin, then I'm meeting Charles later tonight," Robin said, as she opened the door.

Tammy watched Robin sadly walk out the door and head toward her car. After Robin got into her car, she waved goodbye. Then she pulled off down the street, unable to stop her eyes from crying. Then Tammy walked over to the sofa and sat back down with a confusing look on her face. She still couldn't believe that Kevin had been stealing Robin's jewelry. He just didn't seem like the stealing type, she thought. Tammy could feel all of Robin's pain. Just a few days earlier, she had been dealing with her own love problems. But now her situation with Hakeem was fixed and everything was going smoothly. Tammy sat there and closed her eyes, then she said a prayer for her friend. *"God, please help her with this problem. Help Robin like you helped me. Amen."* At that very moment, Hakeem walked into the house and closed the front door. When he saw Tammy sitting on the sofa, crying, he rushed over to her side.

"What's wrong?" he asked.

Without saying a word, Tammy reached out and gave him a hug. With her head resting on his chest, she just cried in his arms.

~

Robin had called. Kevin on his cell phone and asked him to be outside when she got there. She didn't want to go inside the house and have Mrs. Silvia hear their conversation. Mrs. Silvia and her brother, Billy, had become very close, and she didn't want to be the one who messed things up for them. She felt it was best to keep them both out of it.

Since they had met, Billy and Mrs. Silvia had been with each other almost every day. And Robin was happy for both of them. When she pulled in front of the house, Kevin was standing outside, talking to Black and Noonie.

"I'll see ya'll later, but like I said, I'm cool," Kevin told them. Both men turned and walked away. Then Kevin smiled and walked over to Robin's car.

When he looked into Robin's face, he saw that she was crying. He quickly opened the door and got inside.

"Robin, what's wrong?" he said, in a sincere tone.

Robin looked over at Kevin and said, "You! Why did you do it, Kevin? Why? I would've given you anything! Anything!" she cried out.

"Robin, what are you talking about, Sweetie?" Kevin asked, confusingly.

"Please, Kevin, stop playing me like a fool! I'm no longer under your spell! Just tell me why you did it! Why, Kevin?"

"Robin, will you stop talking in riddles and tell me what the hell you're talking about?!" Kevin said, with a serious look now in his eyes.

"Save it, Kevin! You can't fool me any longer! You didn't think I would find out? Or you just thought that your dick was so good that I wouldn't care? You can keep the jewelry you stole, I'll get more!"

"Stole!" Kevin said, shockingly.

"Yes, Kevin! My diamond earrings, and my diamond bracelet! The ones you stole from out of my dresser drawer, you thief!" Robin shouted out.

Kevin sat there with a shocked look on his face. He couldn't believe what he was hearing.

"Don't try to deny it, Kevin, you're the only one who knew where I hid my jewelry! I should have known all this time that you were up to something! But I let you fool me. Then I let you fuck me! Now I'm the only one who's been getting screwed. I don't know what I was thinking about by letting you come into my life. You're a petty, broke-ass ex-felon!" Robin vented.

Kevin looked deeply into her eyes. Robin's hurtful words had pierced his heart, but what had hurt him even more was that she actually believed that he had stolen from her. The one thing that he had never been was a thief. For Robin to believe this was like a smack in the face.

"So you think I stole your jewelry, huh?" he asked calmly.

"No, Kevin, I know you stole my jewelry! You lucky I didn't call the cops on your sorry ass!" she said angrily.

Kevin just sat there, shaking his head in total disbelief.

"Robin."

"What? What do you want now? My money? Credit cards? What?" she snapped.

"Do you love me?" he said, calmly.

"No!" she lied.

"Did you ever love me?"

"No! I just wanted to fuck you! Since that's been done, you can now stay the fuck out of my life!" After a sigh, Robin continued, "So please don't ever call me again, I'm getting married. And I don't think my husband, Charles, would like that."

Robin looked into Kevin's face and saw a tear falling from the corner of his left eye. She didn't expect this at all. Damn, he's good, she thought.

"Save it! No one's a better actor than me. Now get the fuck out of my car and stay the fuck away from me."

Kevin opened the door and sadly got out of the car. After he shut the door, he turned and walked away.

"Kevin!" Robin called out. Kevin paused and turned around. "I hope it was all worth it!" she said, before putting her car in drive and pulling off down the street.

What Every Woman Wants

A few blocks away, Robin pulled her car over to the side of the road and busted out in tears. She had loved Kevin more than any other man she had ever known. Now, just like that, it was all over. The thought of never seeing him again was killing her inside. Her eyes were red from crying so much, and her heart felt like it had been broken in a thousand pieces. She looked at her watch and saw that the time was 6:53. She knew that Charles would be at her condo at eight o'clock, sharp. After a long sigh, Robin wiped her eyes and drove off down the street. She had about an hour to get back home and get herself ready for her future husband.

When Kevin walked into the house, his mother was sitting on the sofa, talking on the phone with Billy. Since meeting Billy, Kevin could see a new excitement in his mother's life. She and Billy would talk on the phone for hours, like two love-sick teenagers. Kevin walked up the stairs and straight to his bedroom. He entered and shut the door, then he walked over to the closet and took out a large black suitcase. After Kevin laid the empty suitcase on his bed, he unzipped it. Then he walked around the bedroom, snatching up everything that Robin had bought him: jackets, shirts, pants, shoes, pictures, and everything else she paid for, was placed inside the suitcase. Now, everything that had reminded him of Robin was inside the suitcase. The first chance Kevin had got, he was going to drop the suitcase off at her condo. After he closed the suitcase, Kevin sat it on the floor beside the bed. Then he kicked off his Nikes and laid back on his bed. Robin's penetrating words were still screaming inside his head, and heart.

Once again, he had been hurt by another woman, and he still couldn't believe that it was all over. The sad part was that someone else was the culprit behind the stolen jewelry. Still, Kevin knew that he would never call Robin again, or go chasing after her. She had called him a liar to his face. Even worse, Robin told him that she never loved him and was now about to marry another man.

In the quietness of his bedroom, Kevin stared up at the ceiling, more confused than he had ever been in all his life.

Robin had taken a quick shower and got dressed. As soon as she walked into the living room, the doorbell rang. She looked at her watch and saw that the time was 7:59. She knew that it was Charles. Like always, he was right on time.

After she walked over to the intercom and buzzed Charles into the building, Robin went over to the sofa and sat down. Her mind drifted back to Kevin. Was that a real tear, she wondered. The soft tap on the door snapped her from her thoughts.

"Come in, Charles."

The door slowly opened and Charles stepped inside. He shut the door and walked over and sat down beside her. Robin was doing her best to hide all the hurt and pain she was feeling, but Charles was beaming, looking like a man who had just won a million-dollar lottery. They hugged and kissed.

Robin was dressed in a white Vera Wang silk chiffon night gown. The only thing she was wearing under it was a Victoria's Secret thong. The first thing that Charles had noticed was her nipples sticking out from under the nightgown.

"So tell me beautiful, what made you change your mind so soon?"

"I just felt that it was the time. My birthday influenced my decision a lot. I'm 31 years old now, and I can't stay young and single forever," Robin said.

"Well, you said that you would like to get married soon. What did you have in mind?"

"This weekend, me and you can go somewhere and just get it over with."

"Well, Wednesday, Thursday, and Friday, I have to be at an important engagement down in Miami. But how about on Saturday morning when I get back? You and I can catch flight out to Vegas.

I know a place out there that will marry us on the spot. All we'll need is the proper identification," Charles said, as he reached over and grabbed Robin's hands.

"Okay, that will be perfect. That will give me a few days to get things in order."

Charles looked into Robin's face, then he got down on his knees. He reached into his suit pocket and pulled out a small white velvet box. When he opened the box, a Harry Winston personally crafted three-carat diamond and platinum engagement ring was lying inside.

"I wanted to do this the proper way. So Robin Davis, will you be my wife?" he asked.

"Yes, Charles! Yes, I would love to be your wife!" Robin said, as the tears begin rolling down from her eyes.

After Charles took the ring out of the box, he slid it on her finger. Then they hugged and had a long passionate kiss. The ring was one of the most beautiful rings that Robin had ever seen, but it wasn't because of the ring that she was sitting there crying. Her tears were from heartache and loss. Robin knew that once she and Charles got married, Kevin would become a thing of the past. Even though she was very upset and disappointed with Kevin, the thought of him not being a part of her life anymore was crushing her soul. Still, Kevin had manipulated and deceived her, and for those two reasons alone she had decided, to marry Charles.

"I love you, Robin."

"I love you too, Charles," Robin said.

Charles stood up from his knees and grabbed her hand.

"What's wrong? I've never seen you cry before," he said.

"I'm just happy to have someone in my life, someone who truly loves me and who will never hurt me," Robin said.

"I will never hurt you, Robin, and I will always put you first. I can't wait until you become my wife and the mother of my children"

"Well, after Saturday, you no longer will have to use protection. We can start on our family immediately," she replied.

"And I can't wait! Come on, let's take this back into the bedroom," Charles said, as they walked toward the master bedroom.

As the tears continued to fall down from her eyes, Robin couldn't get Kevin out of her mind. His spell still had some control over her, but she had decided to marry Charles. She wasn't changing her mind.

~

Inside Their Beautiful Home...

Nathan was sitting at the kitchen table, across from his wife, Carolyn. Since coming into the house, he noticed her vibrant attitude. She was smiling and beaming with a lot of energy. It had been years since he had last seen her like this.

"So, you must have really enjoyed yourself in Atlantic City," he said.

"Yes, I had a wonderful time. It felt good get out of this house; especially with you and the kids gone."

"Well, I'm happy for you, but I have some bad news," he said, putting his fork down on his plate.

"What is it, Honey?" Carolyn asked, nervously, hoping that he didn't somehow find out about her and Trey.

"Me and Charles have to make a important trip down to Miami on Wednesday. We'll be there until Friday, so I won't be back home until Saturday morning."

Carolyn sighed with relief. Nathan didn't have a clue about her sneaking around having sex with a man young enough to be her son. He never called her cell phone once while she was in Atlantic City, even thought she had called him twice to let him know that she was doing fine. The last thing on Nathan's mind was that his wife was out cheating on him.

"I'll be fine." Carolyn said, with a smile.

"But I like seeing you this way, you seem so full of life. How about you start getting out a little more, at least when I'm not around," Nathan said.

"You sure, honey?" Carolyn asked, beaming with excitement.

"I'm positive. You seem 20 years younger. I see that getting out does you good."

"It does, believe me it does wonders."

"Well, find something to do for the three days, I'll be gone this week," Nathan said, as he picked up his fork.

"I surely will," Carolyn said, feeling herself getting excited. Just the thought of being with Trey again had a smile on her face and wetness between her legs.

~

"I can't believe it!" Hakeem said, as he and Tammy were inside the bedroom, both getting undressed.

"Why would Kevin steal from Robin? That girl loves him, and I honestly thought he had some strong feelings for her, as well," he said.

"I've never known Kevin to be a thief!" he added.

"I feel so sorry for Robin, she thought that Kevin was her savior, her true soul mate. Kevin really hurt her," Tammy said, lying her naked body on top of the bed.

Hakeem just shook his head in total disbelief. When he climbed on top of the bed, they just cuddled in each other's arms.

"You don't think Robin made a mistake and misplaced her jewels?"

"No, Robin's no fool. She wouldn't have blamed Kevin if she wasn't positive that he had stolen her jewelry. Now Robin's so upset that she and Charles are gonna get married," Tammy said, in a sad tone.

"That's the rich guy you told me about, right?"

"Yeah, he owns a very successful real estate company. He and his partner Nathan travel all around the country buying up property and then selling it."

"Do Robin love this guy?" Hakeem asked, curiously.

"No, not in that way she don't."

"Then why would she marry him? Won't nothing good come out of it."

"Robin thinks that she will one day change her mind about how she feels about Charles. He loves her, and the man gives Robin the world."

"That's not enough. In order for their relationship to work, she has to feel the same exact love that he feels for her. You can't run away from love and think money will change it," Hakeem said, running his hands through Tammy's hair.

"Robin is very stubborn _ and spoiled. She's gonna do whatever she wants and can't nobody stop her. Once she makes up her mind, it's set. She'll marry Charles just to get Kevin from out of her system." Hakeem just continued to shake his head.

"She seems desperate for love," he said.

"I think that deep down inside, every woman is," Tammy said, seriously.

Hakeem rolled over on top of Tammy's naked body. He looked into her eyes and said,

"Well, you no longer have to be."

"Promise?"

"I promise," he said, before they started kissing each other.

~

Tuesday Afternoon
Inside Her Office At The Radio Station...

Robin had just hung up the phone with Tammy, She told her all about her and Charles' plan to fly out to Vegas on Saturday to go get married. Tammy was not enthused about the idea, but she congratulated her anyway. She knew that Robin's mind was now made up and there was no changing it, so she decided to just leave it alone.

After Robin had finished some paperwork, she had a quick meeting with Jennifer and all the DJs at the radio station. When the meeting was over, she went back into her office and called her brother Billy.

"Hello," he answered.

"Hey Billy, it's me," she said.

"Lil' sis, I been meaning to call you. What the hell is going on?" he said upset.

"What are you talking about?" Robin said as she got comfortable in her chair.

"Kevin called me early this morning and said he was quitting the job."

"What? Kevin quit?!" she said, shockingly.

"Yeah, I asked him why and he didn't say. All he said was that he could no longer work here anymore, and he was deeply sorry for wasting my time. What's going on Robin?" Billy said, demanding an answer.

After Robin had told Billy everything that had happened, he couldn't believe it.

"Are you sure?" he said.

"I'm positive, Billy!" Robin cried into the phone.

"It just doesn't make any sense. Why would Kevin stoop so low and steal from you?"

"I don't know why, Billy. I told you about those two thugs I've seen him with. He probably sold my jewelry to them!"

"Now let's not jump to any conclusions you--"

"Billy, I'm not jumping to anything! Kevin played me and used my love. I hate that bastard!" Robin said, wiping the tears from her face.

"Billy, there's something else I need to tell you."

"What is it?"

"Me and Charles are going to Vegas on Saturday to get married," she muttered softly.

"Robin are you sure that's what you want to do? I like Charles, always did, but you and I both know that you don't love the man."
"Maybe one day I will. Sometimes things just take a little time. Charles loves me, Billy, and right now that's all that matters to me."

"Do you think that running away from your problems will solve anything?" he asked.

"Billy, I'm not changing my mind! Charles is leaving to go to Miami for a few days. When he returns back to Philly, we're leaving for Vegas to get married! The only thing I'm running from is lies, deceit, and manipulation!" she vented.

"You sure it's not love?" Billy calmly said.

Robin got very silent. She knew that was the real reason why she was running away from Kevin. She was still very deeply in love with him.

"Robin do you love Kevin?" Billy asked, waiting for an honest answer.

"Billy, please don't..."

"Answer my question, Robin," he said, cutting her off.

"Yes, Billy! Yes! Is that what you wanted to hear?" she shouted into the phone.

"Then do me a favor, Robin," he said, in a low voice.

"What, Billy?!" she said, as the tears fell fast from her eyes.

"I want you to really find you some time and pray on this. Can you please do that for me, lil' sis?" Billy said, in a concerned tone.
"Billy, what good would it do?"

"Robin, I promise you, if you're sincere about it, God will fix everything."

"Everything is too broken to be fixed, Billy," Robin said softly.
"Just pray and let God decide if everything is broken or not. Please do this before you marry Charles."

"I will, Billy."

"You promise me?"

"I promise you, Billy. Bye," Robin said, hanging up the phone.

After Robin left the office, headed for lunch, she walked out of the radio station and climbed inside of her car. With her eyes filled with tears, she drove out of the parking lot. Robin stopped by a nearby Kentucky Fried Chicken restaurant and ordered a two-piece chicken meal,. Then she sat alone at a back table. When she looked out the window, she noticed that the bus stop where she had met Kevin at was right across the street. She thought about the first time they met; the day she had pulled over and offered him a ride home.

Robin stood up from the table and walked out of the restaurant. When she got back into her car, she just sat there. 'Why would Kevin quit his job?' she wondered. It was something she couldn't quite understand. She knew he was excited about working and making his own money," Was that just a part of his plan to manipulate me also," she thought to herself.

When Robin looked over to her left, she saw Trey's big black Navigator truck parked in the far end of the K.F.C. parking lot. Her woman's intuition had already told her what was going on inside K Trey's truck was nothing but a motel room on 28-inch rims. She had been a visitor there many times. Trey had told her one too many times that she was only person he ever had sex with inside his truck. But Robin knew he was lying through his pearly white teeth.

Robin started up her car and drove towards the Navigator. She parked a short distance away, then got out of her car. She walked over to Trey's truck, curious to see who was inside. When Robin approached the truck, the first thing she noticed was the rap music coming from out the speakers. She had also heard some loud moaning from the backseat. Robin walked along the side of the truck and looked inside.

"Damn!" she said to herself.

Trey had Penny's long white legs up on his shoulders, fucking her brains out, and Robin stood there watching with a shocked look on her face. She had always felt that something was going on between the two. Robin watched as the skinny white secretary yelled, moaned, and begged for more.

After seeing enough of Jungle Fever Part Two, Robin walked back over to her car and got inside.

"Niggas ain't shit!" she said, before starting up her car and driving away.

When Robin had gotten back to the radio station, she went into her office and finished up all her paperwork. She and Tammy had talked again, and she also had a nice long conversation with Charles. He was coming back over to her condo later that night. Still, the thoughts of Kevin had never left her mind. She knew it would take some time before Kevin was completely out of her system. She had read once in a magazine that no pain lasts forever. Neither do lies.

At 3:57, Robin grabbed her brown Louis Vuitton tote bag and strolled out of her office. When she walked passed Penny's desk, she couldn't help but notice her bright beaming smile. Robin waved goodbye before she left.

She noticed a black Power 99 FM van was parked next to her car, and Trey was standing outside, talking to the man that was sitting behind the wheel. When Trey spotted Robin walking towards her car, he told the guy that he would see him later, and rushed over to Robin.

"What's up, Beautiful, when can I see you again?" he said, as he watched Robin get into her car ignoring him.

"Oh, you ain't talking today?"

Robin looked in Trey's face and said,

"Yes, I'm talking today, Trey. Didn't you have enough pussy today? Yeah, I saw you and your white snow bunny inside your truck earlier this afternoon. I knew something was going on with y'all. It's cool. Anyway, I'm getting married soon, so please don't ever call me again. We had fun while it lasted, and now it's over. Bye." Robin said, as she started her car and sped off, leaving Trey standing there with a stupid look on his face.

~

Forty minutes later, Robin pulled up and parked her car in front of Tammy's townhouse. Tammy walked out the front door, carrying her black Prada bag. When she got inside of the car, Robin pulled off down the street. They were headed to the Cherry Hill Shopping Mall, over in New Jersey. Robin told Tammy about her emotional conversation with Billy, and also seeing Trey and Penny having sex inside his truck. They talked and laughed the whole ride to the mall, but not once did either of them mention a word about Kevin. Even though both of them had wanted to.

When they left the mall, it was dark outside, and lightly drizzling. They headed back toward the Benjamin Franklin Bridge, that connected Camden, New Jersey to downtown Philadelphia, they listened to a new song by Jill Scott, playing on the radio. Jill Scott was the queen of soul music, and everyone in Philadelphia loved her. Robin had known the talented songstress personally; her job at the radio station had introduced her to a lot of celebrities.

"It's supposed to rain for the next few days. At least that's what the TV weather woman reported," Tammy said.

When Robin didn't respond, Tammy looked over and saw that Robin was somewhere deep in thought, even though she was still very conscious of her driving.

"Robin, did you hear me?"

Robin snapped out of her daze.

"Huh?"

"I said that it's supposed to rain for the rest of the week."

"Yeah, I know. I watched the Fox afternoon news today at work."

"What time is Charles coming by to see you?" Tammy said, changing the subject.

"Around ten o'clock. He's staying until early tomorrow morning. Then he and Nathan are catching a flight to Miami for some important business meeting they have to be at." Robin said, as she drove her car across the large blue bridge.

"The hell with Nathan! I can't stand his cheating ass!" Tammy joked.

Robin looked over at Tammy and smiled.

"So how are thing going on with you and Hakeem?" Robin said, entering downtown Philadelphia.

"Things couldn't be any better. Hakeem is the perfect man for me, and I'm never losing him again," Tammy answered, in a serious voice.

"Well, at least one of us found true love." Robin said, turning her car down Market Street.

For the rest of the ride, the two women sat in total silence. Only the sound of dripping rain, bouncing off the windshield, could be heard. After Robin had dropped Tammy off at her townhouse, she headed straight home. The rain was now falling harder, and people everywhere were rushing to get out of it. When Robin walked into her condo, the first thing she noticed was the vacuumed carpet and the sweet scent of burning candles. The two maids had come by and cleaned up the entire place. Robin rushed into her bedroom and opened the drawer that had all her jewelry inside. Everything was still there; all except the diamond stud earrings, and the platinum and diamond bracelet that she had accused Kevin of stealing from her. Robin walked over and sat down on the edge of her large oval-shaped bed, then once again the tears started falling from her eyes.

"Why, Kevin? Why?" She shouted out.

Suddenly Robin got down on her knees and placed her hands in the praying position. Then she closed her eyes and said, *"Dear God, can you please show me the right way, and bring into my heart some needed relief. Please take away this pain that I'm going through, and please fix my broken heart and send me the right man to share my life with. Please... Please... Please...Please...bring me my soul mate. Amen."*

In the quietness of her bedroom, she looked over at the window and watched the rain tapping against the window pane.

~

Kevin was lying on his bed, staring up at the ceiling, when the soft tap on his bedroom door snapped him from his thoughts.

"Come in, Mom," he said.

The door slowly opened and Mrs. Silvia peeped in, then walked inside. She was wearing a beautiful new dress. Billy had bought the dress and a new pair of matching shoes for her. Mrs. Silvia walked over and sat down on the side of the bed.

When she looked into Kevin's face, she instantly knew that something was wrong.

"Baby, are you okay?" she asked.

"Yes, Mom, I'm fine," she said.

"You sure, it seems like I haven't heard from her in a few days. Is everything okay?" Mrs. Silvia asked, curiously.

"Yes, Mom, everything is fine." he lied. Kevin hated lying to his mother, but he didn't want to tell her the truth and end up spoiling her mood. Eventually, I would tell her the whole truth, just not today, he thought.

"Okay, well I just wanted to tell you that Billy's on his way over to get me. We're going out to dinner again," she smiled.

"Be safe, it's starting to rain pretty bad outside."

"Oh, we'll be fine," she said.

"Have fun Mom, I'll wait up for you to come in," he said.

"Are you having fun, Mom?"

"Yes Baby, the most fun I've had in many years. Meeting Billy was truly a blessing," she said, with excitement in her voice.

"I'm really happy for you."

"I know you are, Kevin, I'll see you later tonight." she said, standing up and walking over to the door.

What Every Woman Wants

After his mother had left the room and shut the door, Kevin placed his hands behind his head and stared back up at the ceiling.

~

Robin was sitting on the sofa, enjoying the soulful voices of Rachelle Ferrell and Will Downing coming from the two speakers. A song by Chante Moore and Kenny Latimore had just ended.

Inside the tranquility of the living room, she stared out at the outside balcony, just watching as the rain drops bounced hard against the sliding glass door. Robin was dressed in a large white D.K.N.Y. T-shirt, and she wasn't wearing anything under it. Sitting on the glass coffee table, a few feet away, was a tall glass of red wine and a rolled-up joint that she got from Tammy. Robin took the joint out of the ashtray and put it to her lips, then she inhaled the marijuana fumes into her mouth and released the smoke through her nose. She glanced up at the wall clock and saw that the time was 9:12 p.m. She still had a lot of time to get rid of the marijuana scent before Charles came over. Charles hated the smelled of it, but that didn't stop her from smoking it anyway. It helped her with her acting whenever she had sex with him. The marijuana had always made it easier for Robin to concentrate on other things, and other people.

Robin stood up from the sofa and walked over to the sliding door that led out to the outside balcony. She stood there, staring out at the dark sky and the hard falling rain. She couldn't help but think about the times when she and Kevin were out on the balcony, making passionate love. As the rain continued to fall, so did her tears, and at that very moment, Robin never felt more alone in her entire life.

Two Days Later, Thursday Evening
Miami, Florida...
Inside a large, elegant restaurant on South Beach, T.J. and Spencer Lloyd were sitting at a back table, talking and enjoying their meals.

"So Spencer, did you enjoy yourself last night?" T.J. asked.

"Yes, I really enjoyed myself. I'm still waiting for you to accept my offer and come to one of the D.W.A.M gatherings. I'm telling you, T.J., you'll really enjoy yourself."

"Maybe one day, Spencer, but right now, I'm happy with the friends I got."

"I told you before that it's strictly confidential; no one will ever know anything about you. Plus, all of our members are highly successful individuals, so privacy and confidentiality is a must." Spencer said.

"So why do you always invite me?" T.J. asked.

"Because I'm one of the only people that can offer guest invitations to non-members. If you like it, you can join. So far, everyone who's ever been invited has joined our D.W.A.M. secret society."

T.J. smiled and sipped on her glass of champagne.

"Okay, Spencer, tell me more about this D.W.A.M. organization," she said.

"Well, there are just 35 official members. As you know, we are all bi-sexual and very rich. Once a week, we meet up in different cities around the country to celebrate. Usually, we'll stay in a city for two or three days. I can't make all the D.W.A.M. gatherings because of my job as a federal judge, but we have some members that never miss a reunion," Spencer laughed.

"So when do y'all meet up again?" T.J. asked, curiously.

"Tonight at ten 'o'clock at the Bentley Hotel on Ocean Drive."

"Wasn't you there last night?"

"Yes, and I'll be there tonight and tomorrow night also," Spencer replied. "This week is our yearly anniversary, everyone will be in Miami for the reunion."

While they sat there talking, two well-dressed black men approached their table.

"Charles, Nathan, good to see y'all." Spencer said, as he reached and shook both men's hands.

"This is my good friend, T.J., she's airline--"

"Stewardess. I remember seeing her face a few times," Charles said, cutting him off.

"That's correct, T.J. is the person that I told y'all about," Spencer said.

T.J. sat in her chair, staring hard at both men. She couldn't place where else she had seen the two men's faces before. While the three men were talking, T.J. was sitting there, thinking real hard. Then it came to her. *Oh shit*, she thought. They were the same two men that she had seen in the pictures Robin showed her. Charles was Robin's super-rich lover. She had seen the two men many times on different flights that flew back and forth across the country. T.J. sat there in total disbelief. Robin's super-rich lover was gay! And he was a member of a secret society of bisexual men and woman who called themselves D.W.A.M.

T.J. had to control her inner anger. She really cared about Robin; they were more than just secret lovers, they were also good friends. T.J. knew that Robin had feelings for Charles, but the super-rich guy that Robin would sometime talk about was nothing but a undercover homosexual living a big lie. T.J. stood up and excused herself from the table.

"Do you think you can get her to come out tonight?" Charles asked.

"I'm trying my best." Spencer said.

"Well, keep trying, I would love to hit that," Nathan said, as he playfully pushed Spencer's shoulder.

"Me, too!" Charles added.

"Cross y'all fingers, maybe I'll get her to come out tonight," Spencer said, with a grin.

~

Philadelphia, Pennsylvania
The Holiday Inn Hotel, City Line Avenue...

When Trey walked into the bedroom of the private suite, Carolyn was lying on top of the bed with nothing on. While Trey stood a few feet away from the bed, getting undressed, Carolyn had her right index finger moving around inside her mouth, and her left hand playing inside her pussy.

The day before, they had secretly met inside the same suite, where they enjoyed wild, untamed sex all night long. Carolyn couldn't get enough of her young handsome stud, and Trey made sure she never would.

"What's that?" Trey said, pointing to a white shopping bag on top of the dresser.

"I went shopping today, and picked you up a few things that I thought you would like," Carolyn said, with a smile.

Trey grinned and walked over to the bed. When he climbed on top of Carolyn's beautiful black body, she looked into his young handsome face and said, "I want you to fuck me real good tonight, baby." Then she reached under the pillow and pulled out a lubricated condom.

After Carolyn slid the condom on his dick, Trey turned her around on her stomach. He kissed up and down her back, ass and legs. He could feel her trembling beneath him. Then Trey crawled behind her and spread apart her legs. Carolyn was wet with anticipation. Then, in one smooth motion, Trey slid his hard dick deep into her tunnel of love. She moaned out in pleasure, as he stroked her with every muscle in his 20-year-old body. While Trey stroked Carolyn from behind, he started smacking her hard on the ass. Just the way she had liked it.

What Every Woman Wants

Miami…

When T.J. returned back to the table, Spencer was sitting there all alone. She sat back down at her seat and said,

"Were those two gentlemen members of the D.W.A.M. society?"

"If you come as my guest tonight, you'll find out," he said.

"Come on, Spencer, are they or not?" she asked curiously.

Before T.J. decided to call Robin she wanted to first make sure that Robin's friend, Charles, was an official member of D.W.A.M. "Yes, they are, but you must keep that between us," he said, in a low whisper.

"How long have they been members?"

"Oh, them two have been loyal members for a few years. Charles and Nathan never miss a gathering. Plus, they are very deeply involved with each other as well. They've been lovers since college," Spencer told her.

"Is that right," T.J. asked.

"So, did you change your mind about coming tonight?"

"On one condition," T.J. said.

"Name it."

"That I can bring a girlfriend. She would love it," T.J. said.

"Can you trust her? There are a lot of very important members in D.W.A.M. Like I said, it's a very private organization of some of the most successful people from around the country. Where does this person live?"

"In Atlanta," T.J. lied.

"What does she do?"

"She's the owner of a large chain of beauty salons all throughout the south," T.J. lied again, "So she'll have just as much to lose as all the rest of the members. And she's very beautiful also."

Spencer sat there contemplating on what he should do.

"You sure you can trust her?" he asked again.

"Yes."

"Alright, you can bring her tonight," Spencer said, reaching into his pocket and taken out a black pen. He grabbed the napkin on the invited guest off the table and asked, "What's the name you want me to list?"

"Lavern and Shirley," T.J. said, with a grin."

"Okay, your names will be on the list for tonight. We'll be inside the large private downstairs ballroom. It starts at ten at night and ends at ten in the morning," he said.

"Perfect, we'll both be there. Tomorrow morning I have to be on a flight to Chicago, so tonight I want to really enjoy myself," T.J. said.

~

Philadelphia, Pennsylvania
Inside Her Condominium…

Robin and Tammy were sitting around, talking and enjoying the music from the radio. Outside, the rain was still falling down hard from the sky.

"Will this rain ever go away?" Robin said.

"I told you that it's supposed to rain all weekend. The weatherman said we won't be seeing sunny skies until probably Sunday," Tammy replied.

"Damn!" Robin said, shaking her head, "I hate when it rains."
When Robin heard her musical ring tone going off, she grabbed her cell phone from the coffee table. When she saw the name that was showing on the caller I.D. screen, she quickly answered,

"T.J., what's up?" Robin listened on while T.J. ran everything down to her. T.J. told her everything that she had learned.

When Tammy saw Robin's serious expression, she stood up from the sofa and walked over and turned off the music. Then she walked back over and sat down.

"T.J., are you sure!" Robin said, as the tears started falling from her eyes. Robin sat there, shaking her head in total disbelief. She couldn't believe what T.J. was telling her.

"I can't believe this shit!" Robin yelled out.

Tammy sat there with a frightened look on her face. She knew that the news couldn't be good.

"And you're absolutely positive it's Charles and Nathan?" Robin asked.

"One hundred percent!" T.J. answered.

"Okay, tell me where to meet you, I'm catching a plane down there," Robin said, tearfully.

Tammy ran and grabbed a pencil and pad. When she came back into the living room, she passed them both to Robin. Robin wrote down the address to the Bentley Hotel in Miami, Florida. T.J. told her that she would meet her at the Miami airport.

"T.J., I'm on my way, bye!" Robin said, pressing the 'end' button on her cell phone.

"What's wrong?" Tammy asked, looking at Robin's disappointed expression.

"I'm, going to Miami!" Robin stood up and said.

"Miami? For what?" Tammy asked, following Robin back into her bedroom.

"T.J. just found out the real reason why Charles and Nathan travel around the country so damn much!" Robin said, grabbing her Gucci purse off the dresser.

"What do you mean, the real reason?" Tammy asked, confusingly.

Robin stopped what she was doing and looked into Tammy's eyes.

"Charles and Nathan are gay lovers!" Robin said, in a serious tone.

"What?"

"Yes, Tammy, they are two fagots! T.J. just found out that they both belong to some secret bi-sexual organization called D.W.A.M.!" Robin said, as she turned and walked out the bedroom. Tammy followed Robin into the living room.

"Robin are you sure about this?"

A disgusted look was on Robin's face.

"Yes, Tammy, T.J. has been invited to one of their orgy parties tonight. She met Charles and Nathan at dinner earlier, while she was eating with Spencer Lloyd."

"Who's that?"

"The man who started D.W.A.M.!" Robin said, as they both walked out the door, and over to the open elevator.

"I'm going to Miami with you! I'll call Hakeem and tell him I have something important to do," Tammy said, taking out her cell phone.

Tammy called Hakeem and told him she would be out for a while with Robin. When she closed her cell phone, she said,

"Everything is cool!"

As the tears rolled down from Robin eyes, she and Tammy climbed inside of her car. Robin drove out of the underground car garage and into the pouring rain. As they headed toward the Philadelphia International Airport, both women sat in complete silence.

~

An Hour Later...

Kevin was sitting inside the living room, watching television. The knock at the front door startled him. Who would be outside in this kind of weather, he wondered. Kevin stood up and walked to the door. When he looked out the small peephole, he smiled and shook his head. Then Kevin opened the door and let Hakeem in from the rain.

"Man what are you doing outside in weather like this?" he said, closing the door.

"I was driving through the neighborhood and I decided to come pay you a visit," Hakeem said, taking off his wet jacket.

"Where's Mrs. Silvia?" Hakeem asked.

"She's out with a new friend," Kevin said, "Why, what's up?"

"Nothing much, I just came by to talk to you."

"Where's Tammy?"

"She's out somewhere with Robin. You know how those two are when they get together."

"Yeah, I remember," Kevin said, as both men sat down on the sofa.

"Kevin, I heard about you and Robin, and I'm really sorry, man. I thought y'all two were made for each other."

"Me too, until she accused me of something I didn't do." Kevin said, disappointed.

"Kevin, I know you didn't steal her jewelry. I told Tammy that you've never been known to be a thief. A hustler, but never a thief," Hakeem said, as they both laughed. "What do you think happened?"

"Hakeem, I don't know, but what I do know is I ain't the one who stole her stuff. I really didn't appreciate Robin blaming me for it! Besides accusing me of stealing her jewels, she drove over here and said a lot of hurtful words to me."

"So it's definitely over between y'all?"

"As far as I'm concerned, it is. I have to get my life in order, Hakeem. I just came home from prison. I ain't do all that time to come home and let a woman destroy everything I worked so hard for; especially a woman who's more confused than I am."

"Is there anyway y'all can ever reconcile?"

"Yeah, if she found out the truth, drove over here in the pouring rain, and cried her poor, little heart out to me. Then, just maybe, I would forgive her for what she did to me," Kevin said, "We both know that will never happen."

"Do you know she's getting married?"

"I heard. She told me herself that she was marrying the rich dude, Charles."

"Yeah, they're leaving for Vegas on Saturday morning. That's what I found out from Tammy," Hakeem said.

"Well, I wish her the best. She's a sweet girl when she wants to be."

"Did you love her, Kev?" Hakeem asked curiously.

"I still have very strong feelings for her, but unlike Robin's and so many other confused women out there, my feelings can't just change over night, I actually thought she was my true soul mate," Kevin said.

"Only God knows how many times in prison I asked to get out and meet my future wife and soul mate," Kevin said.

"Well, you never know, you still might meet your true soul mate one day. The women all love you, Kev," Hakeem said, playfully pushing his arm.

"Yeah, but it's just never the right woman. Most of the women look at me like a piece of meat, with nothing but sex on their minds. It's not like it was years ago. Now we gotta worry about AIDS, herpes, and crazy baby mommas," Kevin said, as they both laughed.

"Right now, Hakeem, I have to fix my broken life. A woman will just have to wait," Kevin said.

What Every Woman Wants

Chapter 30

Over 10,000 Feet In The Air…

Sitting in their seats on the plane, Robin and Tammy both had bemused looks on their faces. They were fortunate to catch a flight that was headed straight for Miami. Robin had purchased two round trip tickets. As Robin sat by the window, looking out at the dark sky, T.J's words were still ringing loud inside her ears. If everything that T.J. said was true about Charles and Nathan, then Robin knew she would never forgive him. To Robin, an undercover homosexual man was worse than a thief; because he only cared about himself and not the women he slept around with without using protection. Robin felt relieve that she never had sex with Charles without making him use a condom. She had heard to many stories about undercover brothers, men who ran around sleeping with other men on the down low. Just the thought of it made her feel sick in the stomach. Robin and Tammy were both very anxious to find out the whole truth. Tammy was also relieved that she had never slept with Nathan without making him, use protection. Most times Nathan was the one who had brought it up. That was because he had a wife at home, and he didn't want to give her anything she couldn't get rid of. Tammy looked over at Robin's crying face and said, "Don't worry this is all a part of God's way of showing you the truth. Maybe it's just all a big mistake."
"Tammy, I don't know what to believe anymore. What is wrong with my life!" Robin cried.
"Robin, we don't know anything yet, so don't start blaming yourself."
"But T.J. wouldn't lie to me about something so serious!"
Tammy grabbed Robin's trembling hand and didn't say another word. Then both women sat back on their seats in total silence, each lost inside her own world of fear and confusion.

What Every Woman Wants

~

After Hakeem had left out and headed home, Kevin turned off the TV and walked upstairs to his quiet bedroom. He took off all his clothes and climbed in bed. The window was cracked just a little, letting a cool rainy breeze blow into his bedroom. The breeze felt good. The fall was Kevin's best time of the year. It wasn't too hot or cold, but somewhere in the middle.

Kevin reached under his pillow and pulled out a picture. The picture was one that he and Robin had taken when they were out at the shopping mall. Out of all the pictures they had taken, this was the only one he had kept for himself. After looking at the picture, Kevin placed it back under his pillow.

~

Mount Erie, Philadelphia…

Inside Billy's beautifully decorated two-story home, he and Silva was cuddled up on the sofa, talking. The large flat-screen TV was on, but neither of them paid it any attention at all. From the moment she had entered Billy's house, Silvia had been very impressed by the way it was well furnished and decorated. The large house had four bedrooms and three bathrooms, with wall-to-wall carpet laid all throughout it. It was Billy's own private castle.

"Billy you have a very beautiful home, I'm very impressed," Silvia said, as she looked around the plush living room.

"Thank you, Silvia, there's nothing better than living one hundred percent comfortable," Billy said, with a smile.

"Would you like to see the bedroom?" he asked.

Silvia slowly sat up on the sofa and removed Billy's arm from around her shoulder. Then she grabbed both of Billy's hands and stared straight into his eyes.

"Billy, first of all I want you to know that I've been really enjoying the time we've been spending together; Lord knows how much I truly needed it. But you need to know something about me."

"And what's that?" Billy asked, confused.

"That there are certain things that I don't rush into. I've learned that most people who rush only hurt themselves in the end. Billy, right now this dating game thing is all new to me. Still, I'm a woman with very high morals. Lately we have been having so much fun together, I don't want sex to spoil it. I feel that quick sex will do just that. We still have so much more to learn about each other, I've only told you about half of the skeletons inside my closet," Silvia said, jokingly.

"Don't worry, when you decide to tell me about all the rest, I'll still want you," Billy replied.

"Well, that will take some time. Right now, my poor old heart is all I have left. Having sex with you will only confuse it. Do you understand?" Silvia asked in a serious tone.

"Yes beautiful, I do understand." Silvia smiled and placed Billy's arm back around her shoulders. After they cuddled back into the sofa, Silvia leaned over and kissed Billy softly on the lips.

"What was that for?"

"For understanding," Silvia said, as she laid her head down on his chest. "Remember, Billy, patience is a virtue," she said softly. Inside the tranquility of the living room, Billy and Silvia sat there in silence, enjoying each other's company.

~

Miami, Florida
Later That Night...
Robin and Tammy rushed through the crowded airport terminal and straight out the front entrance. T.J. spotted them instantly.

"Over here!" she shouted out the window of the rented car she was driving.

They ran over to the gray Ford Taurus and got inside. The last time Robin and Tammy had been in Miami, they had partied at

Club Opium on Collins Avenue, but this time, the mood was a lot different.

T.J. quickly pulled off and maneuvered the car through the late night Miami traffic. Once they were inside the car, T.J. told them everything that she had found out. They both listen in complete disbelief, but Robin still had to see it to believe it. Charles is a homosexual? She sat there thinking to herself. This was something she definitely had to see with her own eyes.

Nervousness filled her entire body, and her heart felt like it was pounding hard inside her chest. Charles and Nathan had never shown any signs of being gay, she thought.

T.J. turned the car on Ocean Drive, headed for the Bentley Hotel, that was just a few blocks away. She looked at her watch and saw that the time was 11:38pm. When T.J. pulled the car up in front of the hotel, she found an empty space to park.

"Tammy, I'm not going in, I'll let you go in instead. I'll be out here waiting for y'all. Just remember, y'all two are Lavern and Shirley. Those are the two names on the invited guest list. Walk through the lobby, straight back to the private ballroom," T.J. told them.

"Thanks, T.J., this won't take long," Robin said, as she and Tammy got out of the car and shut the doors.

T.J. sat inside the car, watching both women rush towards the hotel's entrance. When they had walked inside, she reclined back in the seat, and patiently waited.

~

Robin and Tammy walked through the crowded lobby, searching for the way to the private ballroom. People inside the lobby were coming and going. They stood by an elevator, looking completely lost. Then, a tall, slim white man, dressed in a gray suit, approached them and said, "Excuse me, but are you two ladies looking for something in particular?"

"Yes we are," Robin said, showing a fake smile on her face.

"I'm one of the assistant hotel managers, maybe I can be of some assistance," he said.

"We're invited to a party in the private ballroom," Robin said.

"Well the hotel has a few—"

"The D.W.A.M. party!" Robin said, cutting the man off.

"Oh! Why didn't you just say so? Follow me," the man said, as he turned and walked in the opposite direction.

Robin and Tammy were right on his heels. They walked back through the lobby, then down a long narrow hallway. At the end of the hallway was a black door with the word, "Private," written on it in bold silver letters.

"This is it," he said, before he turned and calmly walked away.

Robin and Tammy stood there with nervous expressions.

"Come on, let's find out if this is true or not," Robin said, reaching for the doorknob and walking inside.

They walked into a small room, and an older white man was sitting behind a desk. He looked up at the two unfamiliar faces and said, "Can I help y'all?"

Robin approached the man and said, "Yes, we were invited to the private D.W.A.M. party, our names are Lavern and Shirley."

The man grabbed a white piece of paper with a list of names on it. Both women stood there waiting as he scanned up and down the paper. Two closed doors were inside the small room, and people's voices could be heard coming from behind the doors.

"Oh, there y'all go. Lavern and Shirley. Y'all were both invited by Mr. Spencer," the man said, with a smile.

"Okay, use the door on the right to go in and change out of your clothes, he said.

"Hell no!" Robin said, as she ignored the old white man and rushed

over to the other door.

"Hey, y'all can't go in there with any clothes on!"

"Yeah, well, try to stop us!" Robin said, as she opened the door and her and Tammy walked inside. They both stood there with shocked looks on their faces. The ballroom was large and spacious, and everyone inside was completely naked. Men and woman of all races, sizes, and colors, were walking and talking, drinking glasses of champagne, and having sex on small blue floor mats. Robin and Tammy couldn't believe their own eyes. They had just entered a secret world of human sex freaks.

Robin walked throughout the large ballroom, scanning through the crowd of onlookers. Tammy was right behind her. There were men having sex with other men, women with other women, and threesomes going on everywhere. A few people sat around on the mats, masturbating alone.

"Hey, y'all are not supposed to be in here!" a man said.

They paid the short naked man no mind at all.

"This is a private party!" an older white lady shouted.

"Shut up, bitch!" Tammy said, making the woman stop dead in her tracks.

Robin and Tammy both spotted Charles and Nathan. They couldn't believe their own eyes. In the far end of the ballroom, both men were indulged in a sex act that neither of them had ever seen before.

"Oh my God!" Robin screamed out.

On a large blue mat, Charles and Nathan were down on all fours, facing each other. They were locked in a passionate kiss, while two naked white men were standing behind them, fucking them in their asses!

"Charles! Charles, what the hell is going on?!" Robin yelled, as she ran over and pushed the naked man from off of him.

They were all now surrounded by a large crowd of naked onlookers.

"Someone call security!" a man yelled.

Charles and Nathan both stood up on the mat. Both were nervous, scared, and embarrassed. Charles looked into Robin's crying eyes and walked over to her.

"Robin _ "

SMACK! Robin smacked Charles with everything she had.

"You fucking fagot! Get away from me!" She yelled out, angrily.

"Please, just let me explain, Robin," Charles said, in a desperate tone.

"Explain what?! How you can take more dick than me, you damn fagot! You're pathetic Charles! Both of y'all are!"

Nathan stood there in silence. Standing a few feet away from him was Tammy. She had her arms folded across her chest, just shaking her head in total disappointment.

"Please, Robin! Please, can we fix this?!" Charles begged.

"Fix what?! You're a homosexual cheater! We can't fix shit! You like men! All this time, you have been lying to me! How could you do this to me, you gay-ass bastard!

"Robin, let's just go somewhere and talk," Charles said, reaching for her arm.

"Motherfucker, you better not touch me!" she said, in an angry tone.

Charles backed away from her.

Robin stared deep into his crying eyes and said, "I'm warning you, motherfucker. From this moment on, you better stay as far away from me as possible. If you don't, I will expose you, Nathan, and this entire freaky-ass organization!"

"Please, Robin!"

"Shut up, you punk! Like I said, if you ever call me or come anywhere near me, you'll regret it! Everyone in this room will regret it!"

Robin said, looking around at all the stunned faces.

"Come on, Tammy, let's get away from these freaks!" Robin said. She and Tammy turned around and walked through the naked crowd.

Charles fell down to his knees in tears. He knew he had just lost the only woman he ever loved.

Nathan walked over to him and said, "Charles, everything will be alright."

"No, Nathan, I lost her, and we both know it!" he cried.

Then Spencer approached both men with an angry look on his face.

"We need to all talk!" he said.

~

When Robin and Tammy walked out of the hotel, they rushed back over to T.J.'s rental car and got inside. T. J. quickly started up the car and drove off down the dark street. T. J. looked at both women's expressions and knew that they found out the truth. Robin sat in the front passenger seat in total silence. Streams of tears fell from her eyes. The pain that she was feeling was indescribable. The man that she was about to marry and spend the rest of her life with was an undercover homosexual. She had been having sex with him for over a year. And even though she had always made him wear a condom, just the thought of Charles being gay had made her feel filthy and nasty. Charles and Nathan? Who would ever believe that the two rich business partners were also secret gay lovers, Robin thought. If it wasn't for T.J. finding out, she would have never discovered the truth about Charles.

As T.J. continued to drive back towards the Miami International Airport, no one in the car said a word. Everyone was lost in their own thoughts. When T.J. pulled the car in front of the main entrance, she double-parked. After Robin and Tammy had said their thank yous and goodbyes, they got out of the car and walked inside the crowded airport.

When they got back to Philadelphia, it was almost six hours later. Due to a few plane delays, they had to sit around waiting to catch a plane back to Philly. Tammy had called Hakeem and explained everything to him. He was just happy to hear her voice; knowing that Tammy was safe was all that mattered to him.

~

Inside her condominium, Robin and Tammy sat on the sofa.

"Tammy, why is God punishing me like this? First. I loose Kevin, and now I find out the Charles is gay!"

"Robin, God wanted to show you the truth. He loves you and that's why Charles is no longer a part of your life," Tammy said, trying her best to console her friend.

"Look at my life, Tammy! Everything is fucked up! The man I was falling in love with is a thief, and the man I've been sleeping with for over a year is a damn fagot! I'm the only one from D.L.M. who don't have nobody! Am I cursed?" she yelled, angrily.

"No Robin, stop it! There's nothing wrong with you, so stop blaming yourself!" Tammy said.

Robin stood up from the sofa and walked over to the glass balcony door. She stared out at the gray sky and the hard falling rain. When she looked over at the wall clock, she saw that the time was 7:13am. The plane ride back to Philly had them both fatigued. Tammy stood up from the sofa and walked over to her side. They both stood there staring out at the rain. Tammy put her arm around Robin's shoulder and said, "Don't worry, everything will be alright. God will bring you your true soul mate, just keep praying." "Tammy, I don't think so anymore. I even got down on my knees and prayed. Look what happened," Robin said, in a soft voice.

They stood there in total silence as the rain drops bounced off the glass. Suddenly, a knock on the front door startled them both. Robin stood there wondering who could it be. She wiped the tears from her face, then she and Tammy walked over to the door. Robin nervously looked out the small peephole. When she saw the building manager standing there, she quickly opened the door.

Chapter 31

The American Airlines flight was leaving Miami and headed for the Windy City of Chicago. T.J. walked up and down the aisle of the first class section, making sure all the passengers were being well taken care of.

When she reached the front of the aisle, she noticed a short Asian man staring at her. She had seen the man on many of the flights that departed and arrived in Chicago. The short Asian man was dressed in a dark black suit with his laptop computer laying across his lap. He smiled at T.J., she smiled and winked back. T.J. had already known that the man was a wealthy businessman, who spent a lot of his time traveling back and forth from Miami to Chicago. Plus, she had seen his face once in Forbes Magazine. The article in the Forbes Magazine was showcasing America's top thousand wealthiest people. The smiling Asian man, who was still staring at her, was number 847 on Forbes exclusive list.

T.J. straighten up her stewardess uniform and walked over to the man.

"Is everything okay, Sir?" she asked, pleasantly.

"Yes, everything is fine," he smiled.

"Back to Chicago, huh?"

"Yeah, I have a few important meetings to attend," he said, as he closed his laptop computer.

"One day I would really like to take out some time and enjoy the city," T.J. said.

"Well, maybe I could show you around town."

"Really? I would like that," T.J. said, with a smile.

The man reached into his jacket pocket and took out a small yellow business card.

"My name is Peter Chang. When you're ready to see the town, please call me," he said, passing the card to T.J.

T.J. quickly slid the card into her jacket pocket.

"Well, Peter, I have a two day layover in Chicago, maybe you'll be hearing from me very soon," she said.

"The sooner, the better."

T.J. smiled and turned around. When she switched back over to her post she turned and saw that Peter was still staring. She winked and he winked back. Another rich trick, she thought. T.J. couldn't wait to wrap her thick black legs around Mr. Peter Chang. One thing she knew for sure was that #847 on the Forbes list was going to be spending a whole lot of that money; just like all of the other wealthy lovers she had around the country.

~

"Mr. Wesley, what's the problem?" Robin said looking at him carrying a large black suitcase.

"I'm very sorry to disturb you, Ms. Davis, but I had some very important news to bring to you," he said.

"First, this is a suitcase that was dropped off at the front desk late last night. A young man said that all the items inside had belong to you." Mr. Wesley said, passing Robin the suitcase.

Robin grabbed the suitcase and sat it down by the side of the door. She knew it was all the stuff she had bought for Kevin, and now she was even more confused. First, Kevin had quit his job, and now he was returning all the stuff she bought him. 'What is he up to?' she wondered.

"Thank you, Mr. Wesley," she said.

"Oh, that's not all, Ms. Davis, there's more," Mr. Wesley said, reaching into his jacket pocket. When Robin saw what he had pulled from out of his pocket, her eyes almost popped out of her head.

Inside Mr. Wesley hand was her stolen jewelry. Tammy stood there with a shocked look on her face as well.

"He returned my jewelry!" Robin said, shockingly.

"He?"

"The man who dropped off the suitcase?" Robin said, as Mr. Wesley handed her the diamond stud earrings and the diamond and platinum bracelet.

"No, the jewelry is not from the same young man who dropped off the suitcase," Mr. Wesley replied.

"Then who dropped off my jewelry?" Robin asked, confused.

"No one! That's why I'm here, Ms. Davis. Your jewelry along with, and a lot of the other tenant's as well, had been stolen by one of the new maids," he said.

"What? Are you serious?!" Robin yelled.

Tammy stood there looking dumbfounded.

"The maid stole my jewelry?!"

"Yes, one of the maid was caught yesterday, stealing out of an apartment on the 18th floor."

"Was it Maria?" Robin asked, curiously.

"No, it was her niece, Carla Ortiz," he said.

Robin couldn't believe what she was hearing; neither could Tammy.

"Kevin didn't steal my jewelry!" she said, as her eyes started to well up with tears.

"No, Ms. Davis, the police got a signed confession from Ms. Ortiz. She's in police custody as we speak. All the stolen jewelry was discovered inside her employee locker, she told me and the police officer everything, she even told which of the jewels belong to each tenant that she had stolen it from."

Robin fell down to her knees in tears. She had accused Kevin of something he didn't do.

"Are you okay Ms. Davis?" Mr. Wesley asked, concerned.

"Yes I'm fine, can you please leave now," she mumbled.

When Mr. Wesley had turned and walked away, Robin slammed the door behind him. Tammy got down on her knees beside her.

"He didn't steal from me, Tammy!" she said, as her voice trembled in pain, "Kevin was telling me the truth! His tears were real!" she cried.

Tammy reached out and grabbed Robin's shoulders. Then Robin looked into Tammy's face and she saw her smiling.

"Didn't you hear me, Tammy? Kevin told the truth!"

"Yes, Robin I heard you," she said. "Robin, don't you see?" she said, looking at the tears falling down from Robin's eyes.

"See what?"

"That God just delivered your prayers!" Tammy said, excitedly.

"Huh?"

"Robin, Kevin is your true soul mate! All the smoke is clear now, your prayers have been answered!"

"But Kevin would never take me back! I accused him of something he didn't do," Robin said, wiping the tears from her face.

"Robin, do you remember the things I did to win Hakeem back?"

"Yeah," she grinned.

"Well, everything I did was well worth it, and now I got the man of my dream. I'm now the happiest I've ever been in my life. Hakeem is my soul mate, just like Kevin's is yours!" Tammy said, in a serious tone.

"But Tammy, I--"

"No buts, Robin! You said it yourself, you got down on your knees and prayed to God to bring you your true soul mate!" Tammy said, cutting her off.

"Do you love Kevin or not?"

"Yes I love Kevin, more than I have loved any man in my life."

"Then go tell him!"

"It's raining outside! And I have to go to work."

"The hell with the rain! And you can call out for a sick day!" Tammy snapped.

"Your soul mate comes first, Robin. You can't keep playing with love or love will play you!"

They both stood up from the floor. Tammy tearfully grabbed her hands and said, in a soft tone, "I don't care if you have to beg or cry, Robin, go get your man."

"Will you come with me?"

"Don't I always got your back?" Tammy said, with a grin.

After they gave each other a hug, they grabbed their jackets, keys, and cell phones, and rushed out the door.

Robin raced the Mercedes through the early morning traffic. The hard rain had slowed down to a light drizzle. When she called the number to Kevin's cell phone, it just kept ringing. He never answered it.

Nervousness filled up her entire body. Robin had never run after a man before, it was always the other way around. This had been the strangest week of her life. She had blamed Kevin for something he didn't do, she found out about Trey and Penny, she had flown down to Miami to catch Charles in a homosexual act; now she was on her way to go see Kevin again.

Robin called Kevin's house number and that phone kept ringing as well. Tammy looked over at Robin and smiled. She had never seen Robin so nervous before. She could only imagine what Robin was thinking.

When they pulled up in front of Kevin's house, Robin pressed on the horn. Then she found an empty parking space across the street from Kevin's house. She continued to press down on the loud horn. The drizzling rain was still falling down from the gray sky. Tammy sat there, watching Robin press on the horn again. She did it over and over.

When Kevin heard the loud horn sound coming from outside, he walked over to the living room window to see who it was. He couldn't believe his shocked eyes. Parked right across the street from his house was Robin's gold Mercedes Benz. 'What is it now?' he wondered. The loud horn kept beeping. Kevin was dressed in a white tank-top, blue denim jeans, and a pair of Timberland boots. After a long sigh, he walked over to the front door and opened it up.

When Robin saw Kevin walk out the door, she quickly got out of the car. Then, once again, the morning rains started coming down hard. Robin walked a few steps, then she stopped dead in her Prada sneakers. She just looked at Kevin and completely froze. This is that vision I had, she thought to herself. Kevin was standing on the dry porch looking at Robin as she just stood there in the middle of the street. Her drenched body was shivering, while the rain was smacking against her crying face.

Tammy rolled down the window and shouted,

"Robin, get the hell out the rain!"

Robin stood there without saying a word. Her crying eyes were focused on Kevin the whole time. When the loud sound of thunder roared from the sky, she still didn't budge.

"Kevin!" she yelled out,

"Kevin, I love you! I love you, Kevin!"

Kevin stood on the porch, watching her in total disbelief. He still couldn't believe his eyes.

"I'm sorry, Kevin! Please forgive me!" Robin cried out. Some more thunder exploded from the sky, and the rain was still coming down hard.

Tammy sat there in tears. She knew that only the power of unconditional love could make Robin do what she was doing K a power that Robin had no control of.

"Kevin, I love you! I really love you!" she shouted.

"Robin, please, get out the rain!" Kevin yelled.

"No, Kevin! No! I'm not afraid no more! I'm not afraid of love! This is love, Kevin! Kevin, I want to spend the rest of my life with you!" she yelled, as the raindrops streamed down from her forehead.

"Kevin, you're my soul mate! I asked God for you! God brought you into my life, Kevin!"

Kevin stood on the porch smiling and just shaking his head. His eyes welled up and, once again, a lonely tear fell down from the corner of his left eye. Kevin slowly walked off the dry porch and into the pouring rain. More thunder exploded from the gray sky. Robin didn't move; she just stood there watching as Kevin walked towards her.

When Kevin approached her, he stared deep into her crying eyes. Her eyes told the truth. His eyes did the same.

"Kevin, I love you," she mumbled.

"Robin, I love you too," Kevin said, as he reached out and then pulled her into his strong arms.

Right there, in the middle of the street, they started passionately kissing. As the loud thunder continued to roar from the gray sky, the hard rain poured over their two yearning bodies.

And finally, after all the years of searching, Robin had finally gotten her D.L.M. - a Decent Loving Man...

WHAT EVERY WOMAN WANTS!

A Message from Jimmy DaSaint

This book is dedicated to all the l onely, depressed women out there that yearn for unconditional love. It is also dedicated to the strong women who stand by their man, no matter the obstacl es that the devil puts in their path.

From being in prison for almost a decade, I've learned that most women run away from their man, husband, or lover as soon as he is sent to prison. They search for any excuse to leave him,so they can continue on with their life with someone else. A smart woman knows that for most men, prison is life's collegea wakeup call, a chance for a man to educate, discipline, and more importantly learn to love himself and others. A time for a man to exercise, read, wr ite, study, cry, find God, and focus on his true meaning of life. But the weak women that run from them will be the ones who hurt in the end. Because what you give to the world, the world will return back to you. You cannot run from love and expect love to find you! It's the universal law of karma' what goes around, comes around.

For all the strong women out there th at stand by their man's side, I consider y'all the true queens of God's Earth. Please, don t let your so-called friends and ha ting family members distract you. Never let someone else turn you away from love; especially someone who has no love of their own, because th ey want you to be miserable- just like them. Follow your own heart and soul, and listen to your intuition and God's voice within. Be the true friend, soldier, rock, wi fe, and lover that your man needs to overcome the darkest time of his life. Be the queen that God has always wanted you to be.

The prison system is designed to br eak and destroy even the strongest relationships. Why do you think they send prisoners so far away from their family and loved ones? Don't become a vi ctim. Don't be afraid to love your man. The prison system is the devil in disguise, and only love can destroy this powerful beas t. Don't let the year s blind you, instead learn from it. Try and see through all the confusion. See love!!!

I think every woman should experience a real man coming home from prison. The love will be like none you have ever known; mentally, spiritually, and definitely sexually. So to all the women out there holding their man down, please don t stop. Never give up. Never quit! It really gets greater later. And to all the lonely women out there who can't find true love and are tired of all the lies, cheaters, and down- low in-the-closet bisexuals, get you a prison pen pal and learn all about him. Stick with him, and just become a real friend. Believe me, that man will be a friend for life; maybe even more.

Don't get caught up in all the lies ladies. All prisoners are not ruthless killers, rapists, psychos, thugs, or uneducated losers. There are a lot of good men in prison, I m surrounded by many of them. And most are non-violent men that just made a big mistake, or got caught up in the streets by trying to make a better living for himself and his family. So please, don t be afraid to love a prisoner. We are human beings too; yearning to be loved and eager to return the love back!

Jimmy Dasaint

Loyal Fans Are Welcomed To Send Letters and Inquires To:

DaSaint Entertainment, PO Box 97 Bala Cynwyd, PA 19004

DASAINT ENTERTAINMENT ORDER FORM
Ordering Books
Please visit www.dasaintentertainment.com to place online orders.

Or

You can fill out this form and send it to:

DaSaint Entertainment
PO Box 97
Bala Cynwyd, PA 19004

Title	Price	QTY
Black Scarface	$15.00	_____
Black Scarface II	$15.00	_____
Young Rich & Dangerous	$15.00	_____
The UnderWorld	$15.00	_____
A Rose Among Thorns	$15.00	_____
Contract Killer	$15.00	_____
On Everything I Love	$15.00	_____
Money Desires and Regrets	$15.00	_____
What Every Woman Wants	$15.00	_____
Ain't No Sunshine	$14.99	_____

Make Checks or Money Orders out to: DaSaint Entertainment

Name: _____

Address: _____

_____

City: _____ State:_____ Zip:_____

Telephone: _____

Email: _____

Add $3.50 for shipping and handling
$1.50 for each additional book
($4.95 for Expedited Shipping)

Ain't No Sunshine
A Novel By Tiona Brown

Coming Soon
Black Scarface III
The Wrath of Face

CPSIA information can be obtained at www.ICGtesting.com
Printed in the USA
LVOW081644090713

342073LV00019B/873/P